# CAST OF CHARACTERS

**NICHOLAS "NICK OR NICKY" MATHENY.** Now in his 60s, he came to America as a child immigrant but created Seaboard Petroleum, one of the largest oil companies in the world. He is in the hospital with a brain injury and afflicted with amnesia.

**HERO MATHENY.** A former assistant at Seaboard, she is now his much younger second wife. It was more an arrangement than a marriage but there is a kind of love there.

**ROBIN MATHENY.** His son by his deceased first wife. The acorn fell quite some distance from the tree.

**CHARLEY VAN NORMAN.** Hero's father, he spent time in prison for financial shenanigans.

**EMIL KUTTNER.** A Jewish refugee, he has developed a cheap synthetic gasoline that could win the war for the Allies and bankrupt most oil companies.

**ELSA KUTTNER.** His daughter.

**OLIVER GRANT.** Emil's assistant but he doesn't know the formula.

**STUART HANSON.** Matheny's confidential secretary.

**JIMMY DUNCAN.** Matheny's test pilot.

**CARMELITA.** A Brazilian night club dancer who may be blackmailing Robin.

**BEULAH.** A plus-size dancer in the same nightclub. She has information for sale.

**DR. HATCH** and **NURSE CHAPIN.** The staff members responsible for Matheny at the sanitarium.

**PROF. WYNDHAM, JUDGE SCOTT** and **PHILLIP COREY.** Fellow patients and roommates. They have their role to play.

# Alarums
# & Excursions
## by Virginia Perdue

**Rue Morgue Press**
**Lyons, Colorado**

*Alarums & Excursions*
First Published in 1944


New Material Copyright © 2013 by The Rue Morgue Press


ISBN: 978-1-60187-079-7



Rue Morgue Press
87 Lone Tree Lane
Lyons CO 80540



PRINTED IN THE UNITED STATES

# Virginia Perdue

Born in Minneapolis in 1899, Virginia Perdue died in Los Angeles, in 1945 one year after the publications of *A larums & Excursions,* her fifth book in as many years. While her first four books were flawed and really quite ordinary, her fifth was a stunning tour de force and one can only wonder what she would have produced had she not died at 46. National Book Award winner Jacques Barzun and his collaborator *(Catalogue of Crime)* thought so highly of the book that they included it in Fifty Classics of Crime Fiction, their list of best mysteries published in the first half of the 20th Century. It's a book that literally starts with a bang as a bullet whistles by our hero's head and ends with one of the most chilling and yet beautiful lines in the history of the genre. What makes the book so remarkable is that it is told from the point of view of a man who wakes up in a sanitarium, his memory mostly gone as the result of a brain injury suffered during an explosion at his plant. His memory gradually returns, bit by bit, and those scenes are augmented with flashbacks. The result is one of the best examples of the unreliable point of view to be found anywhere in the field. The overwhelming atmosphere of impending dread and disaster may remind some readers of Cornell Woolrich. Perdue's other books were *The Case of the Grieving Monkey* (1941), *The Case of the Singing Clock* (1941), *The Case of the Foster Father* (1942) and *He Fell Down Dead* (1943). All were published by the Doubleday Crime Club.

# Alarums
# & Excursions

**PART ONE**

# ALARUMS

*. . . For now they kill me with a living death.*

KING RICHARD III

# 1

The first bullet missed him. It sang over his head and smacked into the bushes that grew in a row along the stout wire fence. He halted, angry and incredulous, but not much frightened. Here in the long valley, with its flying fields and aircraft plants, the dimout was strictly enforced. A wall of darkness stood between him and the man with the gun. If he kept still, if no betraying footsteps crunched on the sandy rubble or set the dry grasses to rustling, he was quite safe.

He waited several minutes, until a plane rose from a near-by air strip. When the engines roared overhead, he began to run. The laboratory was not far away, though he saw it only as a shadow among lesser shadows, an angular black line against the sky.

The second bullet cut right across his path. It smashed into a window. Broken glass pattered down on the brick steps. He ran past the door and around the corner. Here he paused, leaning against the wall, to catch his breath and quiet the heavy pounding of his heart.

Eastward across the valley, dawn was scratching a gray pencil along the rim of the mountains. Somewhere in the darkness a bird stirred and whimpered in its sleep.

He moved on beside the wall. The rough brick raked his fingers. Then he felt the cold smoothness of glass. He stopped at the blacked-out window and called in a low voice, "Emil, are you there?" No answer. "Emil! Are you all right?"

Close by, so close that the noise seemed to come from inside his own head, a siren began to shriek out an alarm. He jumped back from the wall. Something brushed his sleeve. A swift shadow darted past him. He made a grab for it and missed. A faint odor lingered in the still air, the sharp oily smell of raw kerosene. He turned and ran after the fleeing shape. He was gaining. His hands had closed on a fold of woolen cloth when the earth heaved. A great hurricane blast of air jerked him off his feet. A curtain of fire hung before his eyes. Then he was hurled forth, drifting, into an immense gray waste.

For a long while he drifted. Light followed darkness, and darkness light. At intervals sounds came to him: a voice speaking, a footfall, or a whisper of starched linen.

He was aware of discomfort. Unpleasant things were done to him. He felt very cold or much too warm. He was often thirsty.

The light grew stronger. Shadows flickered through it. One of them had form, an outline which he could recognize and label.

"Nurse," he said aloud.

"Yes, Mr. Matheny?"

He heard her move toward the bed. She stepped between him and a painful blaze of light, sheltering, benign, like a mother. He said, "What's the matter with me?"

"You've had an operation."

The word sank into his mind without a ripple. Far below the surface it exploded like a depth charge. A muddy surge of fear came boiling up. He raised himself on one elbow. The nurse's white cap sailed dizzily across his line of vision.

"Lie down, Mr. Matheny. If you want anything, I'll get it for you."

He lay back, panting. "My eyes . . . what did they . . . Am I going blind?"

"Of course not. You'll see all right in a day or two." She patted the pillows, tucked the covers under his chin. "Be quiet now. We don't want that temperature coming up again."

He felt himself slipping over the edge of exhaustion. "What . . . kind of operation?"

"If I tell you, will you stop talking and go to sleep?"

"Yes."

"You had a skull fracture. They had to remove some splinters of bone. That's all."

He was asleep before she finished speaking. When he awoke, the shocking blaze of light was gone and he could see better. He lay in a high, narrow hospital cot. The room was bare, antiseptically clean. Two figures in white stood at the foot of the bed.

One of them said, "You know, he might surprise us. Remarkable old boy. Wonderful constitution. Five hours on the table and he never turned a hair. Arkwright did a swell job, by the way. I never saw a prettier piece of surgery. However, it's too soon to tell. Huh? Why are you making faces?"

"I think the patient's awake, Doctor."

"Oh." The doctor raised his voice. "Are you awake, Mr. Matheny? How do you feel?"

"Not bad." Talking was hard work. His tongue, like his mind, groped over the words. He lifted an unsteady hand to touch the bandages wound in a cocoon about his head.

"Does your head hurt?"

"Itches," he said after a pause.

"I'll bet it does. Your hair's growing out. We had to shave you bald as an egg." The doctor laughed. "I've got to finish my rounds. Be in again tomorrow."

Out of the orderly hospital routine, time was born. Each morning the nurse came and washed his face and turned a crank so that the bed rose under his shoulders. Soon after that his breakfast tray arrived. Next he had a sponge bath, an alcohol rub, a shave. When luncheon was over, he took a nap. After dinner (which occurred long before the sun had set) the doctor's visit made a diversion. Another night would come and go. Sometimes, now, he was lucky enough to sleep without dreaming.

He began to notice things and wonder about them. His room, for instance, seemed rather odd. It had no corners. The walls met in a curve instead of an angle. The furniture was sparse: a bed, two chairs, the adjustable table which held his tray or washbasin. The door into the hall had no knob and there was a peephole in it, a small glass square at the height of a man's eyes.

The windows bothered him. They were in the wall behind his head, on either side of the narrow cot. Late in the day they caught the sun, throwing twin squares of yellow light on the opposite wall. These yellow squares were crisscrossed with violet shadows, thick straight ones running up and down and a finer mesh going both ways.

"Nurse," he said the first time he noticed this phenomenon, "why are the windows barred?"

"We're on the second floor. Sometimes patients get delirious and try to jump out." She popped a thermometer into his mouth. Were all nurses so curt? Were other hospitals like this one? He didn't remember. Still, he couldn't remember much of anything. That was a nuisance, but he'd stopped worrying since the doctor explained matters.

"You're suffering from traumatic amnesia. That is, loss of memory resulting from an injury. It will clear up now that we've removed the cause. Don't get impatient."

The doctor had a blunt, clever face and an air of sureness. You felt that he liked his job and knew what he was doing. If he asked a lot of tomfool questions, you answered them as well as you could, no matter how embarrassing they were. "I have to test your memory," the doctor explained, "so I can check the rate of improvement from day to day. Understand?"

He didn't, but he said, "Yes. All right."

"Do you know who I am?"

"Dr. Hatch."

"And who are you?"

"I'm . . . not sure."

"Are you Nicholas Matheny?"

He picked the name up and put it on, like a shoe which long wear had eased to his foot. The name felt right. That's who he was. Nicholas Matheny. "Yes," he said.

"What do you do for a living? . . . Never mind. Don't try too hard. Just answer if it comes to you. . . . Married?"

"I guess so."

"What's your wife's name?"

"Is she . . . Margaret?"

"You seem doubtful."

Nicholas thought it over. "She's been gone a long time," he said finally.

"Then you're not married."

"I can't remember."

"How old are you, Mr. Matheny?"

"I think I must be old. I don't know."

"Depends on the point of view," said Dr. Hatch with a grin. "According to our records you're sixty-three, but no one would guess it. Know how many teeth you've lost?"

Nicholas explored them with his tongue. "None at all."

"Don't you find that remarkable? I do. I wonder where you got such a constitution. Were you born in this country?"

"America? No, I don't believe I was."

"Good! Of course the early memories usually come back first. You were an immigrant?"

Something stirred in his mind, like a sleepy animal stretching, yawning. He was seven years old. He had been lifted up on his father's shoulder so that he could look out over the heads of the other passengers. Far off, at the very edge of the blue water, he saw those shining fairy towers. (Are the houses really made of gold, Father? . . . Yes, Son, gold is as common as paving bricks are in the old country. You will have diamond buttons to your shirt.)

"Why are you laughing?" asked Dr. Hatch.

"Our coming to America. It wasn't . . . quite what they told us." No gold, no precious stones lying about, only noise, dirt, confusion; one airless room in a tenement, too much work and not enough to eat. But that wasn't the whole story. He said haltingly, "Just the same, he was right, my father. The gold is here. You have to know where to dig." The bright memory pictures were fading. It was as if he walked along a tunnel: plenty of light near the opening, but as he went on the darkness grew.

"You're getting tired." The doctor stood up. "That's enough for tonight."

He was tired, but excited also. The black curtain had lifted for a moment. It would lift again. "My turn now," he said. "What hospital is this?"

"Crestview. Say, you didn't finish your dinner. Can't get strong that way."

Nicholas persisted. "How did I come to be hurt, Doctor?"

"There was an accident. . . . How are your bowels? Okay? Guess you don't need much but rest."

"What kind of accident? Was I hit by an automobile?"

Dr. Hatch looked at him intently. "You're a lot better. Yesterday you wouldn't have had enough strength to insist on anything. All right, I'll tell you. It was some kind of industrial accident. Fire, explosion. That's all I know. . . . Through with your tray? I'll send Miss Chapin in for it. Have a good sleep."

That night the dream came back. He heard the shots and the siren. He leaped upon the fleeing figure; flames rose in front of his eyes and he was hurled to earth. For a time he lay still, floating softly through a gaunt gray waste.

## 2

He woke in a sweat. Moisture trickled down his face and ran into his eyes. He tried to push back the blankets. Nothing happened. He struggled to sit up and found that he couldn't move at all.

His mind grew black with horror. He left off struggling and lay like a trapped animal, panting a little, trembling.

A voice said, "Looks like a chill. Get Dr. Hatch."

He heard quick footsteps on the rubber matting. Someone laid a hand on his damp forehead. A square, clever face bent over him.

"He's not chilled. What's the trouble, Mr. Matheny?"

*"I'm paralyzed!"* Nicholas hadn't meant to shout, but the words ripped from his throat as if they had been jerked out at the end of a cord.

"No, you're not. You're wrapped up in a wet sheet, that's all. We had to give you a pack. You were very disturbed in the night. Don't you remember?"

"No. . . . Except I had a dream."

"That so? I'd like to hear about it. Take him out now, Miss Chapin. He's been in long enough. I'll be back."

Miss Chapin and one of the orderlies took him out of the pack and dressed him in a short hospital gown.

"Do you want to go back to sleep, Mr. Matheny, or would you like some breakfast?"

He felt relaxed, but not at all sleepy. "I'd like breakfast."

She raised the head of the bed, arranged the pillows, and brought him a loaded tray: orange juice and cereal, toast, soft-boiled eggs. The food tasted good. He felt wonderful. His mind was clear, for a change. He was exhilarated as a man who has climbed weary miles up a fogbound trail to come out suddenly upon a sunlit mountaintop.

His room sparkled, and so did Miss Chapin. Funny he hadn't noticed before how good-looking she was. Her round face was rosy with health. Her uniform fitted snugly over a shape that ought not to be wasted on a sick old duffer in a hospital.

"You look pretty peppy," she remarked. "I believe the pack did you good."

"I feel fine. A couple more days, and I'll be going home."

"Here, let me fix those eggs." She avoided his eyes. "Don't you like it here, Mr. Matheny?"

"Of course," he said hastily. "Don't think I haven't appreciated all you've done for me. But . . . I don't know." He looked down at the hand holding the fork. It was large and white, very well tended, not a workingman's hand certainly, and yet it appeared strong, capable. "Maybe I'm not used to lying around doing nothing."

The nurse smiled. She wriggled her shoulders. Made him think of a young pup wagging its tail over the prospect of a walk. "I know what you want. I've just been waiting until you were strong enough." She ran out of the room, her starchy skirt crackling.

He drank his coffee and pushed the tray aside. In a few minutes she came back with a small cardboard box. He took off the cover. Inside he found half a dozen slabs of gray-green stuff that looked like putty.

"Well, that's fine, now. Thanks a lot." He had no idea what the stuff was. Did he eat it, or rub it on? She stood there watching him, wriggling a bit, eager as a puppy. He couldn't disappoint her. He unwrapped one of the slabs. It felt soft, a trifle greasy. He didn't in the least know what to do with it, but his fingers remembered. Without any prompting from Nicholas, they began to mold the stuff into a ball, pushing up a lump here, shoving in a hollow there. First thing he knew, a shape emerged, round young belly, lop-eared head, a comical stub of a tail.

"Oh, the precious!" cried Miss Chapin. "You can almost see his tail wag. Is that supposed to be a cocker pup, Mr. Matheny? Can I have him when you're finished? I just don't see how you do it!"

Neither did Nicholas. He gazed with astonishment, almost with fear, at the thing his hands had made. It was crude, of course. He'd only just started to work, but already the pup lived, had character. It was a clever thing; you couldn't help knowing that.

"Back at work, eh?" said Dr. Hatch over the nurse's shoulder. "You must be feeling better."

"I'm all right," he said, "only scared stiff."

Dr. Hatch sat down and crossed his legs. "Tell me about it."

Nicholas moistened his lips. "I didn't realize I could do this sort of thing until Miss Chapin handed me that box. What else can I do? What sort of man am I? For all I know, I might be anything, from a saint to a murderer." He was actually sweating. The palms of his hands were wet.

Dr. Hatch said, "You can take the tray, Miss Chapin." He waited until the nurse had gone out. "I can give you a few facts. Don't know as they'll help much. You're a businessman. You own one of the big oil companies, Seaboard Petroleum. You have the reputation of being a square shooter and a great philanthropist. I believe you are quite generally liked and respected. Does that help?"

"Yes. Some." He ran his tongue over his lower lip. "Have I got a family?"

"You have a wife. A son by a former marriage. One grandchild."

Nicholas lay back against his pillows. "I don't even know what they look like." He was overcome by a bleak sense of loneliness. "I've lived my life," he said. "I haven't much to look forward to, and nothing to look back on. I'm an old man, but my mind's as empty as a newborn child's."

The doctor contradicted this flatly. "No, it isn't. You're not a bit like a newborn. Your memory has a few blank spots, but you know how to use a knife and fork, how to walk and talk. When we let you get up, you'll be able to dress yourself. You can model things in clay. You remember what words mean and make associations with them. A baby can't do any of those things. A baby is afraid of the dark or a loud noise. You're afraid of blindness, paralysis. Such concepts are based on very precise memories. Do you understand me?"

"Yes, of course."

"Any idea what a complicated mental process you had to go through to understand?"

"No, I guess not."

"Then don't talk to me about being like an infant. You're making satisfactory progress. Right now your mind is a house containing thousands of rooms. You wander in and out of them at will. A few of the doors are locked, though, and that worries you. Are you going to wear yourself out trying to kick the doors in, or just wait quietly until the keys turn up?"

"You're sure they'll turn up someday?"

"Reasonably so."

"How long?"

"I can't even guess at that."

"It'll be embarrassing when I go home," Nicholas fretted. "I'll have to get acquainted with my family and friends all over again, have things explained to me . . . What about my business? Who's running it?"

"I believe your affairs are in competent hands." The doctor looked at him rather strangely. "Don't worry. By the time you're well enough to go home, you'll remember plenty. Now let's hear about that dream you had last night."

"Dream? Oh yes. I'll try, but it doesn't make sense. Funny, I'm almost sure I've dreamed the same thing many times. Even while it's going on, I have a feeling it's all happened before."

"That's a common occurrence," said Dr. Hatch, unimpressed.

Nicholas closed his eyes. "I'm alone, hurrying to get somewhere," he began. "I'm late and Emil is waiting . . ." His eyes flew open. "Who's Emil?"

The doctor shrugged. "Sorry."

"Well, anyhow, I hear a shot. I can even hear the bullet sing past my head. I feel concerned, not just for myself . . ." He closed his eyes again. This part was difficult. "I don't know, but I'm afraid about something more important than my own skin. I start to run. There's a second shot. I run past the door and around the corner." He fell silent. He had a sense of pressure inside his skull, as if an idea were trying to force itself up to the surface.

"What door?"

"Let me think. . . . In the dream, the building seems to be some sort of laboratory, only it's in a field. All around, there's a fence lined with shrubbery. Very thick. No one can look through."

Dr. Hatch took out his pencil and notebook. "That's a typical dream symbol," he said. "Your conscious mind is troubled by the part that's fenced off, hidden from you."

Nicholas felt let down, as if the doctor had failed him. He sighed. The room was quiet. He could hear nothing except his own gentle breathing and the whisper of the pencil moving rapidly across the page. He looked down at his hands. They still held the lump of modeling clay, but its form was changed. While he talked, his fingers had been working. The puppy was gone, transformed into a moth with outspread wings. No, not a moth, a tiny gray-green monoplane! He gazed at it, enthralled. A moving picture, in full color and sound, began to unroll within his head.

He stood at the edge of a long runway, several hundred yards from the gate where the cars were parked. The fierce heat of the August sun fell like a blow on his uncovered head. An east wind swept down from the desert, down the mountain slopes, into the valley. It whipped at the dry grasses and scooped up swirls of dust from underfoot.

Against the rich blue of the California sky the plane looked like a shiny gray bug crawling up a velvet curtain. Nicholas, watching through his binoculars, tried to feel as if it were indeed a bug, not a machine made by imperfect human hands, operated by a creature of flesh and blood and nerves. Just before the take-off he'd shaken hands with the young test pilot, a laughing, black-haired boy straight out of the Song of Solomon. *He cometh leaping upon the mountains, skipping upon the hills . . . like a roe or a young hart.*

The plane turned over on its back in a slow, lazy loop. Nicholas felt his heart turn over too. His eyes began to water smartly. He would never get used to sending children into the jaws of death. He didn't see how the generals stood it.

He was obliged to lower the glasses and get out his handkerchief. "Sun's damned bright," he grumbled.

Emil glanced up at his face. "Do not be afraid, Nick," he said in his careful precise way, which sounded every bit as foreign as broken English. "Jimmy Duncan is a fine pilot."

"Seems to know his job, all right." Nicholas, whose company employed the lad, didn't doubt that he was capable. If anything happened, anything untoward, it wouldn't be the pilot's fault. Of course he couldn't say this to Emil Kuttner, who had invented nicoline, and the assistant . . . What was his name? Oliver something. These scientific fellows were mighty touchy, so sure their stuff would work they'd risk anyone's life on it, even their own.

Oliver turned around and gave him a look that sent his blood pressure up ten degrees. "Nothing to worry about, sir," he said. (Soothing the old man; advising him to calm down.) "All the ground tests went off like clockwork, you know. This is really just a formality."

Nicholas glowered. Maybe the young squirt wouldn't feel so cocky if he were up there risking his neck in loops and power dives, trying out something that had never been tried before. No, that wasn't fair. Oliver had helped with the early experiments which were even more dangerous than this final test flight. Nothing, he reminded himself, was accomplished without some risk. But a man wanted to take his own risks, not have other people do it for him.

He looked out across the flying field toward the squat brick building where Kuttner's experimental work was done. For obvious reasons, it stood at a distance from the hangars, the office, the garages, which were at the far end of the runway. Nicholas glanced back over his shoulder. All around the big square plot of ground a hedge grew inside of a barbed-wire fence to discourage the curious. Just the same, he felt exposed and uneasy.

"Guess I won't wait," he said.

Emil dragged his eyes away from the plane. They were velvet brown, very expressive and definitely non-Aryan, though nothing else betrayed the mixed blood which had cost him home and country and had nearly cost him his life. "But, Nick, it is not yet finished!"

"I've seen enough. You pulled it off, Kuttner." He dropped the glasses into his pocket and thrust out his hand. He hardly knew what to say. You couldn't just offer congratulations, as if the man had got married or fathered a son. This thing was too big, especially when you considered what it would mean to a country at war. "Hanson and I had better start the ball rolling."

Emil shook hands gravely. He said nothing, but young Oliver turned around with a frown. "We'll have to check the instruments, sir, and get Duncan's report on acceleration and——"

His words were blotted out. Abruptly, the far-off steady hum of the motor changed to a roar. The plane shot down out of the dazzling sky. It no longer resembled a crawling bug. It was a missile hurled at the earth with terrific force by an angry sun. The roar increased to a scream which was more than sound. The noise hit you like a blow in the solar plexus. It smashed at every nerve in your body.

Nicholas was shouting against that deep-throated scream. "Pull out! Pull out, you fool! God, he's going to crash."

Emil's fingers dug into his arm. The silvery wings seemed to nip the tree-tops at the end of the field before the plane leveled off and went soaring away into the blue. Nicholas wiped the sweat from his face and wiped his eyes. Once more he saw a shiny gray bug go crawling up the curtain of the sky.

"What's the matter?" asked Dr. Hatch. "Does your head ache?"

Plane and sky faded into the distance. The hospital walls closed around Nicholas. "I'm all right," he murmured.

"Let's hear the rest of the dream."

He smoothed the gray-green wings of the little monoplane with his fore-finger. Was it a dream, or was it a terrible memory struggling up from his subconscious? He didn't know, couldn't tell fact from fancy. "Where was I hurt?" he said. "Was it on Seaboard's flying field?"

"I've no idea." The doctor sounded quite impatient. "What happens next?"

"I'm not sure," said Nicholas thoughtfully. "It's gone. Perhaps it'll come back to me later."


### 3


"Guess what?" said Miss Chapin in her bright nurse's voice. "You're going to have a visitor. Won't that be fun?"

Nicholas wasn't sure. He was a convalescent now. The sterile gauze wound around his head felt more like a bandage and less like a turban. A brushlike stubble was growing up where his hair had been. He was allowed to read. Miss Chapin brought books from the hospital library, though for some unexplained reason she ignored his requests for a newspaper. He wore his own finely made pajamas instead of the coarse hospital gown. When they let him sit up for an hour, he wore a handsome brocade robe.

The two armchairs seemed immovable. Perhaps they were too heavy for his strength. From one of them he could see a sloping red-tiled roof, a hump of brown hillside, and a lot of blue sky. From the other, he looked out upon more red tile, with a waving feathery mass of pepper trees beyond. The first of these excursions from bed to chair was a great adventure, but he found himself unexpectedly dizzy and weak in the legs, so that he was glad to lie down again.

His memory was returning in a way that confused him badly. It came in sudden brilliant glimpses, complete but unrelated, like sequences in a motion picture before it has been cut and edited and spliced together to make a story. Even more bewildering was the vast storehouse of facts in the cellar of his mind, for he never knew they were there until he stubbed his toe on them in the dark. He was both excited and alarmed at the prospect of a visitor, someone, perhaps, who knew all about him, more than he knew himself. He wouldn't enjoy being made to look a fool.

"Who is it?"

Miss Chapin wriggled with pleasure. "Your wife, Mr. Matheny. She's down in the office now, talking to Dr. Hatch. She'll be up in a few minutes."

Nicholas pushed back the rug that lay across his knees. He was panic-stricken. "Miss Chapin . . . I'll go back to bed, Miss Chapin."

"Are you tired already? Don't you feel so well today?"

"I'm all right, but . . ." He struggled to his feet and stood swaying a little, towering over the nurse, although she was not a small woman. He didn't try to explain that his wife's visit would be an ordeal which he preferred to face from the secure eminence of his bed, bulwarked by pillows, armed with the trappings of illness.

Miss Chapin didn't argue. She arranged the pillows, helped him to clamber in between the cool sheets. Working swiftly, she folded the rug and tidied the room so that it should look presentable to a wife's exacting eyes.

Nicholas drew the covers up to his armpits. "Er . . . Miss Chapin," he stammered, "this is awful. I've forgotten her name."

The nurse hesitated. "Let me think. It's out of mythology. Oh yes, Hero." She was just in time. The door opened.

Hero made a casual entrance, talking over her shoulder to Dr. Hatch. ". . . so he tore up the ticket and hopped on his motorcycle, and here I am. Hello, Nicky." She walked over to the bed. "How are you, darling?"

"I'm fine, thank you." He gazed with awe at this sleek and formidable woman who was his wife. She was tall and very slender. Her face was too long for beauty, too high in the cheekbones and firm in the jaw, yet the general effect was one of extraordinary loveliness. Her movements had the liquid charm of running water. Her voice rippled, cool as a mountain stream. She leaned over to kiss his cheek, and the air about him was filled with the scent of pine forests.

"You've improved wonderfully, darling. Last time I was here you didn't recognize me at all."

He didn't know what to say to that, so he kept silent, watching her pull off her driving gloves and throw back her furs. She had a girl's slim body, a girl's clear-eyed freshness, yet he felt certain that she was not young. He wondered what their relations were, exactly? Did they love each other? It seemed improbable. The sight of her stirred in him nothing but curiosity and a startled pride. She was such a lordly creature.

"Why do you stare so, Nicky? Don't you like my hat?"

"Yes, very much." He examined the hat with more attention. It was small, three-cornered, black as soot against her ashen blondeness. "Only it seems to fit your head. Isn't that unusual?"

She laughed, and so did the doctor. "People joke like mad about women's hats, but really it isn't our fault. Blame the designers. If you don't want to look a fright, you go bareheaded, or have something custom made." The smile left her face. "But, Nicky dear, my hats always fit!" Hero stood looking down at him, smoothing her gloves, frowning a little. "I guess you don't remember." She turned away from the bed.

Nicholas cursed himself. Somehow he must have made it plain that he didn't know her from Adam. Maybe the hats were a private joke which he should have understood. Anyhow, it was a damned shame. Hero had been so glad to see him, so happy that he was better. Now the visit would be an ordeal for her too.

Hopelessly embarrassed, he watched her sit down and cross one silken leg over the other. She took a gold-and-ivory cigarette case from her handbag, hesitated, and sent a twisting glance toward the doctor.

Nicholas said, "Go ahead and smoke. I don't mind."

They all seized upon this remark, like shipwrecked people grabbing at a life line. The doctor nodded and smiled. "Sure, that's all right, Mrs. Matheny." The nurse bustled off to fetch an ash tray.

Hero fitted a cigarette into a gold-and-ivory holder. "Rather a dirty trick, though, when Nicky isn't allowed to smoke. By the way, darling, I brought you a box of cigars, among other things, but they made me leave it in the office. Probably you'll get one every other Sunday as a special treat."

"That would be better than nothing." He wanted to help her, but he couldn't for the life of him think of any more to say.

After a tiny pause Hero tried again. "Nicky dear, do you want to tell me about your symptoms and all that?"

"They're not a bit interesting."

"Then you won't mind if I just chatter along? I've been warned not to mention things that would upset you. Since I haven't the remotest idea what they might be, I'll play safe and talk about nothing. Oh, perhaps you'd like to hear about Bunny?"

"That would be nice," he said carefully. He had no notion who Bunny was.

She straightened up in her chair and turned her clear-eyed gaze upon the doctor. "Nicky doesn't remember at all. Why did you tell me——"

"Mrs. Matheny! You gave me your word you wouldn't disturb the patient."

"I'm not disturbed," said Nicholas. "Who is Bunny, anyhow?"

"Our grandson." She smiled faintly. "Or rather yours, Nicky. I'm only a stepgrandmother. In fact I had nothing to do with the great achievement, except hold Joanne's hand. I'd have been glad to lead the singing, but she turned out not to be one of those heroic types who sing the 'Battle Hymn of the Republic' instead of uttering conventional shrieks. Anyhow, she was too full of nembutal to do either."

Miss Chapin returned with a tray of glasses and a small metal bowl for Hero's cigarette. "Time for your orange juice, Mr. Matheny. I thought your wife might like some too." She made a pleasant bustle passing the tray around. "Doctor?"

"Why, yes. Thanks."

When she left, another stiff silence developed.

Hero began again. "Joanne's getting to be quite a Spartan mother, though, determined that her angel—by the way, he *is* an angel—shall not be spoiled by riches. I suppose there are too many dreadful examples always before her eyes. She was much upset by all those toys you ordered from Bullock's for his birthday. Imagine, Doctor, three hundred dollars' worth of stuff for a year-old child! They came the day after Nicky's accident. Joanne was touched, of course, but she packed most of the things away. Brings them out one at a time as a reward when Bunny has been especially angelic."

"Sounds like a pretty sensible young woman," remarked the doctor.

"Oh, she is! Joanne's horribly sensible! I suppose that's why . . ." Hero's eyes flickered. After the smallest imaginable pause she went on ". . . why she tries so hard to bring Bunny up like an ordinary, middle-class child."

Nicholas wondered what she had intended to say. He wondered what sort of person she was, under the sleek lovely surface. The visit was getting him down. It would have been easier if he couldn't remember her at all, but he was aware of a partial recognition. Like meeting your favorite actress at a cocktail party, he thought. You knew every inflection of her voice, every line of face and body, yet the woman herself was a complete stranger. *Who is she that looketh forth as the morning, fair as . . .* What was the rest of it? The verse escaped him.

The doctor was looking at his watch. The time of Hero's visit must be running out, and there were so many things Nicholas wanted to be told. He longed, especially, to ask about his son, but he hated to admit that he didn't even know the boy's name.

"Hero," he said when she came to the end of a bright little yarn concerning Bunny's first attempts at English, "who's looking after the business?"

She set her empty glass down on the floor. When she straightened up her face was flushed. "I am, of course." Some of the rippling smoothness had gone out of her voice. It became brisk, professional. "You should know better than anyone, Nicky, that I'm quite competent."

He believed her. She didn't appear to be the sort of woman who takes an interest in her husband's business, but if she chose to do so, he was convinced she'd make a good job of it.

"Rather a bore, after all these years," she continued with an animation that flatly contradicted her words. "But I had to take over. Stuart isn't worth a darn since his wife died."

"And who," said Nicholas, "is Stuart?"

She looked at him a moment. "My poor darling! . . . Stuart Hanson. He's been your confidential secretary ever since you deprived yourself of my services by marrying me. At least that was his title. Actually he was a sort of combined Henry Wallace, Stephen Early, and Harry Hopkins." She turned to the doctor. "Stuart's a case for you, Dr. Hatch. He had this tubercular wife down in Tucson. Of course he provided for her lavishly, but he hardly ever saw her. Nicky kept him toiling in Los Angeles, and besides, I've sometimes suspected . . . You see, he lived at the house, but he had an apartment in town, also. I rather think he kept a girl there. After all, why not?" She shrugged tolerantly. "But his wife had a hemorrhage and died suddenly, before he could get there. It seemed to prey on his conscience. He's been like a madman ever since. All sorts of complexes and delusions. Such a pity. Stuart was very intelligent before this happened."

Dr. Hatch leaned forward. "What kind of delusions?"

"Oh, you know, Nazi spies lurking behind every bush. That sort of thing."

Nicholas missed a good deal of this conversation. One of those nagging half-memories had begun to prod at him. Stuart Hanson. A round, good-natured face appeared before his eyes. He saw a fat, well-groomed hand holding a yellow telegraph envelope. ("I'm sorry, Nick, but you'll have to go to Washington by yourself. My wife died this afternoon.")

"I remember," he said. "I saw the telegram." He tried to evoke the rest of the picture. Another name sprang into his mind. "What about Emil? Emil Kuttner." There must be some connection, though he couldn't tell what it was.

He saw that Hero knew. She had started to take another cigarette from the gold-and-ivory case. Her hands grew still. Her eyes met his, level and challenging. After a moment she put the cigarette back, snapped the case shut.

"Doctor, I'd like to have a few moments alone with my husband, please. I need to consult him on a business matter. We can't discuss it before anyone, however discreet."

"I'm very sorry. I thought I made it clear——"

"Yes, you did, but this is important."

"We can't make exceptions. Besides, your visit has lasted long enough. We don't want to tire the patient."

Hero rose to her feet, as if her fighting spirit were aroused and she pre-ferred to do battle standing up. "Really, Doctor, this is absurd. Suppose you do have a rule against leaving a visitor alone with a patient? That can't apply to me and Nicky. I'm quite able to take care of myself. Anyhow, you told me he wasn't in the least violent."

Nicholas heaved himself upright. "Hero!" he shouted. They both turned to look at him. "Good God," he said, "you talk as if I were . . . out of my mind." He began to tremble. "What sort of place is this? Hero . . . my God, you haven't——"

She walked swiftly over to the bed. "Nicky! Oh, darling, didn't you know?" Her voice grieved for him. "Didn't anyone tell you?"

Perhaps he should have known. Perhaps he hadn't wanted to understand.

"We had to!" she cried. "Believe me, dear. You're so strong. We had to do it, so you couldn't hurt yourself." She caught up his hand and held it to her cheek. "Or other people."

"Mrs. Matheny, that's enough." The doctor's voice was quiet, but it rang with authority. "Come with me, please."

Hero leaned over. She kissed Nicholas. "You mustn't worry, darling. It's only for a little while, until you get well."

He said nothing. His eyelids felt heavy, as if cruel fingers were pressing down on them.

"Nicky dear," she said, "no one knows you're in a sanitarium. . . . Yes, Doctor, I'm coming." She stepped back from the bedside. "Don't bother to ring for a strait jacket. . . . Nicky, all the public knows is that you're recover-ing from an operation. So you see, there's nothing to worry about."

She took up her handbag and furs and went out of the room, all in one smooth rippling motion, like water slipping down the face of a rock.


# 4


The barber and the masseur had finished with him. Miss Chapin cranked up the head of his bed. Nicholas lay with his eyes closed, inert against the pil-lows, as he had ever since Hero went away the day before.

Miss Chapin said, "I've brought your lunch, Mr. Matheny. It's very nice. Creamed chicken."

He lay still.

After a moment the nurse continued in a sharper tone, "You've been such a good patient. What's the use of spoiling your record by acting like a stubborn child all of a sudden?" He refused to move or speak. "We let you alone last night and this morning," said Miss Chapin, "but you can't get strong without food. Dr. Hatch said if you wouldn't eat your lunch, he'd have to feed you with a stomach tube. That isn't very nice, you know." She waited. "All right, then, I'll call the doctor."

Nicholas heard the door close. He opened his eyes. The first shock had left him stupefied. Now the stupor had worn off. He understood that he was not behaving sensibly. It wasn't Miss Chapin's fault that he'd been railroaded into an asylum. She and Dr. Hatch were trying to help him, but they had to do with crazy people. The patients couldn't be allowed to get out of hand. If you made a row in the night they swaddled you in wet sheets. If you refused to eat, they fed you with a tube. After all, it was their job.

He sat up, pulling the pillows into a wad behind his back. Miss Chapin had left the luncheon tray within reach on the adjustable table. Nicholas swung it around over his lap and plucked the cover from a small casserole. The chicken smelled good. He ate it all and ate his vegetables. With every mouthful his spirits rose. He'd been in tight spots before. The way out was to use your head, keep your feelings under control, map out a campaign.

He turned appraising eyes upon his room. It was clean and quiet. He had a private bath. The food was excellent. He was spared the worst features of life in an institution: the crowding, the regimentation, the lack of privacy. All these comforts must be expensive. They spelled money, another asset and an important one. His liabilities were fewer . . . a cracked head, bars at the window.

Nicholas drank his milk and set down the empty glass. He had something else in his favor, a strong purpose. He'd find a way to get out of the blasted place, and have fun doing it. With something to fight for, he could make a life for himself, by God, even inside the walls of an insane asylum!

Miss Chapin returned with the doctor. She looked at the empty dishes. Her eyebrows went up.

Nicholas grinned. "Never mind the stomach tube, Doc. I got hungry."

The doctor nodded. "I thought you would. May as well take the equipment back, Miss Chapin. I'm glad we didn't need it." He sat down and crossed his legs comfortably. "Curious," he said, "you weren't a bit upset about your operation, but the minute you find you're in a mental hospital——"

"I don't belong here. I'm no lunatic."

Dr. Hatch ignored the interruption. "When people think of a place like this," he said, "it's in terms of strait jackets and padded cells. That's absurd, like believing surgery is still done without anesthesia. Psychiatry has improved a lot in the last fifty years, probably more than any other branch of medicine. There's no reason to fear it, no need to feel shocked or humiliated. You were sent here because we're equipped to handle such cases. Just as some hospitals specialize in orthopedics. Do you see what I mean?"

"No. I should think any decent hospital could take care of a brain operation."

"That's true, as far as it goes. Mr. Matheny, do you remember anything about your accident or what followed?"

"Not a thing."

"I wouldn't expect you to. There is usually complete amnesia for the event. You were found walking along a road, two miles from the scene of the accident. A very interesting example of automatism. You were taken home apparently uninjured except for bruises and a scalp laceration. However, after you regained consciousness, there was a period of confusion which your doctor rightly diagnosed as traumatic delirium. He observed symptoms of increasing intracranial pressure and very wisely arranged to have you sent here."

"What's that?" Nicholas interrupted. "My own doctor . . .?"

"Certainly. Dr. Jerrold, your family physician. Don't you remember him?"

Nicholas pressed both hands to his head. "I thought . . . my wife . . ." he mumbled.

"Naturally she followed Dr. Jerrold's advice. Did you think . . . Oh, I see." He slipped his hand into his pocket and drew forth notebook and pencil. "You and your wife are not on good terms, perhaps?" He leaned forward in his chair. "You feel that she wanted to get you out of the way?"

"I don't know what terms we're on. I can't remember much about her. But she said, 'We had to send you here.' What did she mean by 'we'? Hero is a lot younger . . . beautiful——" Nicholas stopped abruptly. The doctor's eyes were probing, knife-like, at his face. Crazy persons, he thought, often imagined they were victims of some fantastic persecution. He'd better be careful. "If my own doctor arranged it, that's different," he said. "I'm mighty glad to know."

"You have confidence in Dr. Jerrold? You don't suppose he could be one of your enemies?"

"What enemies?" Nicholas laughed. "I tell you, I don't remember Dr. Jerrold, but it's been my experience that most doctors are very decent fellows, honest and conscientious."

"Thanks," said Dr. Hatch dryly. He put away his notebook. "I'm inclined to agree with you. Fortunately, Jerrold is intelligent as well as honest. He didn't upset you with a lot of X rays and examinations. He understood that complete rest was the important thing, so he sent you here where you could get it, and get a proper diagnosis at the same time."

"I don't see the point. Why couldn't I rest at home?"

The doctor hesitated. Finally he said rather primly, "Delirious patients are often hard to handle. They want to get up and go to the office. They fly into rages over nothing." He gave Nicholas a sudden, engaging smile. "You're a husky guy. They couldn't let you go on beating up your nurses."

"Did I do that?" he said, aghast. "Then I really was crazy?"

"Well, yes, just as I would be if I had bone fragments pressing on my brain. Don't worry about it."

"Am I crazy now?" Nicholas demanded.

"Look at it this way: does a man whose broken leg is mending inside a cast have a broken leg or not? All we can say is that he's convalescent. The final outcome depends on his recuperative powers and his doctor's skill. In your case the prognosis is favorable."

"What does that mean?"

"That you should make a complete recovery, given the proper care. I've been talking very freely because we'll get on faster if you cooperate. I know you don't like being here. You won't like the treatment, either, but if you fight, if you worry and get upset and lose your temper, you'll only prolong your illness."

"I see." Nicholas shifted his position uneasily. "What kind of treatment?"

"Rest. It won't be easy. From the little I know about your career, you haven't had any rest since you left the cradle. It's a technique you'll have to learn."

"Do you mean I'll have to lie still and be waited on hand and foot, like a damn baby?"

The doctor laughed. "Not at all. I know you're a scrapper, Mr. Matheny. I want you to fight with us instead of against us."

That sounded better. Nicholas relaxed somewhat.

"First of all, don't allow yourself to worry. That takes will power, but no one can rest and worry at the same time. We'll help. We won't risk any more shocks like the one you had yesterday. We'll try to keep your mind occupied and keep you amused. In a few days I think you can be moved downstairs to the convalescent ward. Later you'll go to one of the cottages."

Nicholas heaved himself into a sitting position. "Look here, how long is this going to take? You sound as if it might go on for weeks."

"Another thing," said Dr. Hatch, "try to put the idea of time right out of your head. In cases of brain trauma, time is an extremely variable factor. Improvement may be rapid during the first month. After that it goes on more slowly." He looked at his watch and jumped up. "I didn't realize I'd been here so long."

Nicholas said, "A month? Do I have to stay here a whole month?"

Dr. Hatch paused near the foot of the bed and looked at him without speaking.

"Good Lord, Doctor, I can't hang around in a hospital forever. I've got work to do. See here——"

"Now, don't get excited. Remember our agreement?"

He was dreadfully excited. His heart hammered in his chest. He made a strong effort to keep his voice down, to act calm and reasonable. "That's all right, but if I'm not to worry, you'll have to give it to me straight. I can stand anything if I know just what to expect."

The doctor tapped his fingers on the footrail. "I don't know. As a rule, I prefer . . . But you're intelligent. I've noticed you don't make trouble when things have been explained to you. All right, then. The minimum rest period is six months. We continue the treatment as long as there is any change, and for at least three months after the patient's condition has become stationary."

"But . . . you can't mean it. That would be almost a year. I thought I'd be going home in a few days." He fell back against his pillows. "A year? I wasn't even hurt much. A little crack on the head!" He needed all of his self-command to keep from shouting.

"We don't know how badly your brain was hurt," said the doctor impatiently. "You still have some neuropsychiatric residuals—the amnesia, for instance. Those may clear up in a month or two, and then we could discharge you as cured. You might get along fine. On the other hand, you might turn up in a few years with epilepsy, or some other sequel. If it were my brain, I'd rather take time for a proper cure than to risk spending the last twenty years of my life in an institution, getting progressively worse until I died. Wouldn't you?"

Nicholas wet his lips with his tongue. "Yes," he said, "yes, I suppose so."

"All right. Make up your mind you're going to be here awhile, then forget about time. That won't be so hard. You won't have any calendars or newspapers to remind you. One day will be pretty much like another. Let them slide by. Your main job is to get well. It's worth working for."

"Yes. Yes, that's true."

"Try to take a nap now." Dr. Hatch turned the crank, lowering the head of the bed. "I'll be in after dinner for your memory tests."

Nicholas lay obediently still, but he couldn't sleep. The afternoon sun had come around to his windows, painting two narrow strips of light on the opposite wall. He lay motionless, watching the yellow strips widen into yellow squares, ribbed from top to bottom with strong violet shadows.

## 5

A man cannot claw his way up from the slums, and achieve wealth and eminence, without an ample supply of will power. He used it now, as one would
a broom, to sweep his mind clear of dismay. He had a job to do. Rest and
worry didn't mix. When his head was quite empty of thought, Joanne walked
into it.

He was in his sitting room at home. Hero called this room "Nick's study"
and had furnished it accordingly with down-cushioned chairs, excellent reading lamps, and towering shelves of books which were only a decoration, for
he never had time to read. He hadn't opened a book in years, except Margaret's
worn Bible and the volumes of Shakespeare he kept on his bedside table in
lieu of a sedative. The stately cadences of Elizabethan poetry soothed his
nerves and gave him a sense of the past standing firm, like a wall at his back.
   He sat at the big mahogany desk in one corner, a sheaf of papers spread out
before him. Someone knocked softly at the hall door. Nicholas gathered up
the papers and thrust them into a folder. "Who is it?"
   "Joanne. Are you busy, darling?"
   He slipped the folder into a desk drawer. "No. Come on in." Actually he
was swamped with work. He was leaving for Washington first thing in the
morning. Interviews had to be arranged with the right people; all the reports
must be in order. He had a hundred things to do, but he always managed to
find time for Joanne.
   She closed the door and came toward him. In her white slacks and pale
green blouse she looked slender, fragile like a young birch tree.
   "Are you working, Nicky? I could come back later."
   "Just sitting here daydreaming," he lied. "Have a chair. How's Bunny?"
   "He's fine." She looked at the top of his desk bare now except for the three
telephones, the bronze inkwell and penholder. Satisfied, she pulled up a chair
and sat down. Her dark eyes met his with a child's candor. "I'd like your
advice, if you don't mind. What does one do with an anonymous letter?"
   "Tear it up and forget it," said Nicholas promptly. He liked the way she
came straight to the point, without fuss or dramatics. In fact, he liked everything about her. She was Robin's third wife. They'd been married four years,
but Nicholas still couldn't look at her without feeling amazed at his luck.
When he paid off Ruby, and later on Anastasia, he hadn't dreamed that his
next daughter-in-law would be at all like Joanne. He had a fierce, bristling
love for his son, but no illusions about his taste in women. He couldn't understand how Robin had chanced to fall in love with a girl so obviously out
of the top drawer. Of course she was beautiful, in a quiet, well-bred way.
Still, she had brains and character too, qualities Robin did not admire. She

had even presented him with an heir, something those other two trollops hadn't bothered to do. Nicholas not only approved of Joanne, he had a deep affection for her.

She moved her chair to avoid a thin blade of sunlight which was beginning to stab through the west windows. "Just pay no attention?" she said. "That's what I thought, but you see, they keep coming."

"I know. We've all had 'em, at one time or another. Too damned many cranks in Los Angeles. We're pretty prominent. I guess you have to expect that sort of thing."

"Oh, I wouldn't have bothered you with crank letters, Nicky. I'm afraid it's much worse. This one sounds like extortion. Blackmail. We can't ignored that, can we?"

He couldn't help smiling. "Must be a psychopathic case. You know, I haven't got many illusions left, but I'd bet my bottom dollar you've never done anything to be ashamed of."

Joanne's straight dark brows drew together. "I don't . . . Oh, darling, how nice of you! But I'm afraid . . . perhaps you'd better read it." She thrust out one slim trousered leg and slipped her hand into the pocket of her slacks. She drew forth a letter, a square envelope in a poisonous shade of blue, slit open neatly at the top.

Nicholas reached across the desk for it. He pulled out a double sheet of matching paper.

Joanne said, "She tried to disguise her handwriting, I think, and she uses the third person, but the blue stationery is rather significant. I've seen it before, a number of times, in Robin's mail."

Nicholas could feel his blood pressure mounting. His ears sang. The crooked writing wavered and danced. He began to swear softly.

She waited a moment, gazing out of the window, giving him time to recover. "Do you suppose it's true?" she said in her quiet, thoughtful way.

"What? About the child? Wouldn't surprise me." He read that passage over again. *You don't seem to mind sharing your husband, but maybe you won't feel so good when your little boy has a young brother. Pardon me, half brother.* He wanted to crush the filthy thing, burn it, stamp on the ashes. Of course he did nothing so foolish. "I don't know. She could be lying. Even if it was true, she'd have a devil of a time proving Robin was responsible."

Joanne kept her eyes fixed on the sunny window. "The other letters," she said, "were quite explicit. Times and places. One of them even had a picture inclosed."

"What kind of picture?"

"I think it was a candid-camera snapshot. I'd . . . rather not describe it, if you don't mind."

Nicholas swore again. He pulled out his handkerchief and wiped his fingers, as if the letter had dirtied them. "My dear," he said in a gentler tone, "how long have you known about this affair?"

"Why, it began, I think, a little while before Bunny came."

"What? You've known all along? More than a year?"

She smiled faintly. "It's difficult to deceive the people you love. Robin was very careful, but one senses that sort of thing. Of course I had no proof until these letters started coming a few weeks ago."

Nicholas marveled at her poise. He couldn't sit still any longer. He got up and paced the room, heartsick, shamed, and so angry that he could have strangled the boy with his own hands. Before Bunny came! That made it inexcusable. Robin's heir had not been produced without difficulty. Indeed, Joanne only just managed to pull it off. She had been months recovering and was still far too thin, although her little bones were so delicate you had to look twice before you realized how fragile she really was.

He tried to get his wits together. She'd come for advice, and all he did was torment her with questions. He swung around facing her, his hands dug into his pockets, his feet planted solidly, as if he were facing a hostile board of directors.

"Look here, Joanne, you've got your proof. If you want to get out, I'll back you up. I'll see that you get the child and a proper settlement. There won't be any scandal. Another thing, I guess you didn't know, but my will leaves everything to Bunny. Hero and Robin share a life interest in the income, but the property itself will be held in trust for you and the boy. Whatever you decide to do, I won't alter my will."

"But, Nicky, really——"

"Wait'll I finish. I worked like hell for my money, and I want to know it'll be used right after I'm gone. I've watched you. I know you'll bring the lad up to be the sort of man I want for my heir. Now, I hope you won't divorce Robin. I'd hate not having you in the family, but just the same, I wouldn't blame you a particle."

"But, darling, I'm not going to divorce Robin. Why, that never entered my head."

Nicholas blinked. "You mean to say you can forgive him for this—this outrageous——"

"No, no. Forgiveness hasn't anything to do with it. You don't 'forgive' Hero because she has a worthless father. You put up with Charley and try to make the best of things."

He walked back to his chair and sat down. Joanne's candor was refreshing, but sometimes it did rather take your breath away.

"That's how I feel about Robin," she continued. "He loves me, you know. If he has qualities I dislike, I simply have to put up with them. It's no use expecting Robin to be faithful. He's like a drug addict. He can't break off the habit."

Nicholas flicked an angry finger at the blue envelope on his desk. "He'll break this off, or I——" He stopped, overcome by a feeling he'd never experienced before: helplessness, inadequacy. After all, what could he do? Robin was thirty-five, a grown man, set in his ways. Nicholas couldn't even crack the bull whip of money. Robin had his own fortune, settled on him when he married Joanne, besides the salary he drew as one of the Seaboard's third vice-presidents. "I'll have a talk with him," Nicholas finished lamely.

His frustration exploded into rage. "Rotten spoilt," he shouted, "that's what ails him. Too much money and not enough work. Damn his lazy, good-for-nothing hide."

Joanne made no comment, except to glance about at the luxurious room. He read the glance accurately. *What else could you expect?* She was right, too. Some of these reformers who wanted to make things soft and easy for everyone (from the cradle to the grave), they ought to take a good look at the children of the rich. Most of them weren't worth the powder to blow 'em up! Character, he thought, was developed only by struggle, hardship, and toil. It was no accident that civilizations flourished in the storm belt.

Joanne leaned forward. "Please don't, Nicky," she said in an earnest voice.

"Eh? Don't what?"

"Say anything to Robin. He hasn't the least idea that I know. If he finds out, he'll feel ashamed of himself, and that will make him hate me a little. We'd have the wretched thing fastened on us for the rest of our lives. He'd never forget it, or let me forget."

"I see your point, but then how can I make him break off with her?"

Joanne's eyes widened. "Didn't you understand, from the letter? He broke it off some time ago. That's why she started blackmailing him."

Nicholas leaned back in his chair. Really she was too much for him, this remarkable daughter-in-law. "I suppose," he said, "you know what you're talking about."

"I think so, Nicky. Haven't you wondered why we stayed on with you and Hero all this time?"

"No. I wish you'd stay for good. You aren't strong enough to reopen the Sherman Oaks place yet.

"That's what Robin says. But I think he wanted to stay because it costs less to live here. She must have been very expensive. I was sure he'd finished with her when he started urging me to go home. Then the blue letters began coming, and he put off the move from week to week. He made different excuses, but I think he just didn't have the money."

Nicholas reached for a cigar, then changed his mind, opened a desk drawer and took out a small lump of modeling clay. He kept the stuff handy, here and at his office, ever since Dr. Jerrold cut him down to two cigars a day. It helped having something to occupy his fingers. He even found an odd satisfaction in his growing skill. For the first time he could understand why those artist fellows would rather starve doing their own work than get out and earn a decent living like sensible folk. There was a lot of pleasure in seeing a rabbit, a puppy, a sleek, long-limbed cat, come to life under your fingers. Slowly his anger oozed away, like blood from an open wound.

Joanne said, "I knew he was worried about money, but I couldn't think why. Then the letters stopped coming to Robin and began to come to me."

He looked up at her face, frowning a little. What was she suggesting? What could be the reason for that abrupt switch from one victim to another? "She's cleaned him out!" he shouted incredulously.

Joanne nodded. "I think so too."

"But, my God! A couple of million in two or three months? That's not possible."

"I don't suppose it was that much. Robin's extravagant. He may have dipped into his capital from time to time. And at least three hundred thousand went into the house."

"But——" He closed his mouth with a snap. If she didn't know he'd given them the house, he wasn't going to tell her now. He picked up the letter and read it again, more attentively. . . . *My friend could easily sell the story to a newspaper—so much human interest and such cute pictures—but she wants to offer you the first chance. If you feel like buying, put an ad in the Sunday* Times *personals, signed Joanne. My friend will find a safe way to get in touch with you.*

Nicholas tossed the letter down, but he continued to look at it, frowning, biting at his mustache. He still didn't get it. Even Rob, who was a fool about money, wouldn't fork over his entire fortune to avoid a scandal. He'd been in scandals before and hadn't seemed to mind especially. Was it possible he'd had the guts to tell this blackmailer where to go? Was that why the woman had turned to Joanne? He rolled the ball of clay over and over in his hands. Joanne thought Robin was broke. If that were true, where had the money gone? Maybe it was something a whole lot worse. Embezzlement? Hit-and-run driving? Rob would pay to keep out of jail. But then why didn't the blasted woman come right out with it?

"Any idea who she is?"

"No, not the slightest."

"You said something about a picture."

"Her face didn't show. Only Robin's."

"Well, I'll find out. I'll put the lawyers to work on it. Now, you're to stop worrying."

She slipped to her feet and stood looking down at him with those child's eyes, so grave and full of trust. (Nicky would fix it. Nicky could do any-thing.) "You're awfully good to me, darling."

"Not at all. This is a family matter." He shifted uneasily in his chair, as if her serene confidence in him were a weight upon his shoulders.

"I hope she won't be too expensive."

Nicholas hoped so too. His careful plans for the future hadn't included blackmail, but, whatever happened, he wasn't going to change those plans. His mind began to shape a campaign, just as his fingers were busily molding the lump of clay.

"Nicky!" cried Joanne. "What in the world are you making?"

Startled, he set the thing on his open palm and studied it with interest: coil upon gray-green coil, a vicious narrow head rising from the center, the ribbed tail standing erect. Without any conscious intention, he had fashioned a very passable rattlesnake, coiled and ready to strike.

The snake's body twisted into a spiral, ever widening, darkening into the blackness of night. He hurried through that swirling darkness. Bullets sang past his head. A siren wailed. He pursued the fleeing figure. It was only a shadow among other shadows, yet something—a known pattern of move-ment, a vaguely remembered outline—filled him with rage and lent speed to his tired legs. The running shape was almost within his grasp; he nearly had the answer to his riddle, when a voice reached him, dimly, across vast stretches of space.

The dream crumbled all about him. He lay still among the ruins, until the steady, soothing voice of Dr. Hatch had swept away the last dark fragment.

## 6

After the aseptic severity of his room in the surgical ward, Nicholas found the new one almost homelike. It was a corner room on the ground floor. The windows were protected by heavy copper screening and by a wrought-iron grille that had little resemblance to bars. One of them looked out upon a green blanket of lawn, shaded by the peppers whose feathery heads he had viewed from the second story. From the other window he saw a group of cottages half hidden among trees and shrubs. Beyond their cheerful red roofs a mountain range stood bold and blue against the sky.

This room had a thick dark carpet on the floor instead of rubber matting. It had a wardrobe for his clothes, a chest of drawers, a table where he could play cards or work at his figurines. One of the shelves in the bookcase held a small built-in radio. The radio interested Nicholas very much until he found that it was strictly an institutional affair. There was no dial, no way of tuning in a commercial station, just a switch to turn the current on and off. Since Crestview did not broadcast to its patients anything but soothing music and inspirational talks, he seldom turned the switch. He wanted war news, market reports, Information Please, and Bob Burns. He wanted Raymond Gram Swing's dry wit and godlike calm.

Every day he asked how the war was going, and every day they told him it was going well for the Allies, but doubtless they would have said the same thing if bombs had been raining on New York City. He was ruthlessly protected from unpleasantness. Even the books Miss Chapin brought from the hospital library were selected for their therapeutic value. Nicholas didn't mind. It was a great luxury, having enough time to read. He was off on one of the best adventures of his life, the discovery of literature. He read Emerson and Plutarch with the same astonished zest. He finished *Pride and Prejudice* and immediately started over again at the beginning, amazed to find that a novel (something he had always considered a mere time killer for idle women) could contain so much information and good sense, to say nothing of first-rate entertainment.

He surprised Dr. Hatch by adjusting himself quickly to inaction. He no longer resented the lack of visitors, news, companionship, now that he understood the reason for it. Anyway, his seclusion was not altogether the fault of hospital regulations. No one but Hero knew where he was. (Everyone thinks you're just getting over an operation, darling, so you needn't worry.)

When he recovered from her more shocking revelations, Nicholas could smile at that. Nothing mattered so long as it didn't involve bad publicity! Still, he was grateful to her. Presently they would let him out of here, and he didn't fancy spending the rest of his days labeled as an ex-lunatic. Hero, he felt, had behaved with considerable tact. She was doing the best she could for him. Presents arrived: hothouse strawberries, delicate confections, books and games and jigsaw puzzles. Every day she sent fresh flowers, which Miss Chapin arranged in vases of some light metal, for glass was a rarity at Crestview.

The nurse explained this when he asked about it. "You see, we have so many depressed patients." For an instant she looked quite depressed herself. "We can't watch them all the time, so we try not to leave anything around that could possibly be dangerous to them."

The entire staff seemed to go in terror of mass suicide. "If one patient gets away with it," said Miss Chapin, "a dozen others try. I don't know how they find out, but they always do. There's some sort of grapevine. I've had patients ask me about a disturbance over in the women's ward before I'd heard about it myself!"

Even Nicholas, who was neither violent nor depressed, had to put up with many routine safeguards against an impulse·toward self-destruction. He shaved himself with a safety razor, but only under the watchful eye of the nurse. She was always present when he ate his meals and never removed the tray without carefully checking silverware and dishes. (You could cut your throat with a bit of broken china. You could open a vein with the point of a silver fork.) His bathroom contained a stall shower, but no tub. (You couldn't very well drown yourself in a shower bath.) The mirror over the washbowl was of polished metal set securely in the wall. Still, it was a mirror, of sorts. Nicholas enjoyed getting reacquainted with his own physical appearance.

He was happy to find that it was not unpleasing. He was a tall, spare old man, big-boned and powerful. His body was smooth and hard, more like that of a man forty-odd than one who had reluctantly passed the sixty mark. The final bandages had been removed from his head, and it was covered with short curly hair, almost black, with only a few gray threads. His beak-nosed face wasn't bad either. Deep lines curved from his nose to the corners of his mouth, but he had good skin and clear, bright dark eyes. A strong, commanding face, thought Nicholas with satisfaction, except for the mouth, which was kind and sweet, like a woman's. At once he began letting his mustache grow out to hide that one evidence of human warmth.

As Dr. Hatch predicted, he soon lost count of the passing days. He couldn't have told whether it was one week or three before Hero paid him a second visit. This time he was up and dressed, if you could call it that. His trousers were freshly creased, his sports shirt of the finest quality, but Nicholas was so used to a collar and tie that he felt disheveled without them, although he understood the taboo. (You could easily hang yourself with a necktie, if you were so inclined.)

Hero wore an elusive shade of gray, the color of fog in the air, unrelieved except for a large handbag in coral to match her lipstick. "Hello, darling," she said. "Thank Heaven they've put you in a decent room. That place upstairs was more like an operating theater!"

Nicholas laid aside his book and stood up. He kissed his wife with far more assurance than he had felt on the last occasion. A bit at a time, Hero's story was coming back to him.

She had (in effect) been born with a gold spoon in her mouth, the only child of Charley Van Norman, sole heir to the stupendous fortune of that brilliant, if disreputable, financier. Her upbringing had been more luxurious than wise. She was a viciously spoilt little monster of seventeen when Charley, like a great many better men, got squeezed in the panic of 1921. An inquiry brought to light a truly amazing record of graft, bribery, and corruption. It was a crash heard round the world. Van Norman was left not only penniless but owing enough money to finance a medium-sized war, and with charges of grand theft hanging over him. He was convicted and sentenced to the penitentiary for twenty years.

Hero's position couldn't have been worse. Her mother was dead. Charley had alienated their relatives. He was the sort of man who has thousands of acquaintances, a few cronies, but no friends. Hero was alone, with no resources except the clothes she stood up in, but she was not Charley Van Norman's daughter for nothing. Raging, bitter, she sold her fur coat and her diamond ring, changed her name, and dropped completely out of sight.

She never spoke of the thirteen years that passed before she turned up in the offices of Seaboard Petroleum. By that time the spoilt brat was quite dead, though the great lady was not yet born. During the two years that Hero worked for Seaboard, rising quickly to the important position of secretary to Nicholas himself, she was a cold, horribly efficient business machine. It could hardly be said that he fell in love with her, but he admired her brains, her pluck, her loyalty to that scamp of a father. Nicholas was lonely. Margaret had been dead for many years. His daughter had married an Englishman and gone to live in foreign parts, where she died of cholera. Robin certainly didn't provide his father with much companionship.

After due consideration, Nicholas decided to marry his secretary, if she would have him. He'd had his doubts about that. She was thirty-two at the time, and he was fifty-six. He remembered his qualms very well, but at that point memory halted. Apparently Hero accepted him, for here she was, Mrs. Nicholas Matheny, his wife. She hadn't yet divorced him for a younger man. She even seemed to be fond of him, but was it the fondness of a daughter, or a friend, or lover? He couldn't tell.

She clung to him almost hungrily for a moment, until the nurse came in. Then she drew away. A faint shadow of annoyance drifted across her lovely face. She stripped off her coat and gloves and tossed them into a chair.

Miss Chapin set a tray down on the table. "The usual orange juice," she said. "I thought you might like some too, Mrs. Matheny."

Hero turned around with a smile. "Oh, thanks. How thoughtful! I can see you're treating him well, Miss Chapin. He's put on weight, and in exactly the right places! . . . They must give you decent food, darling."

"Stuff me like a pig," said Nicholas, grinning.

"He's gained seven pounds," the nurse informed Hero with pride. She moved away from the table and pretended to busy herself straightening up the room, though it was already sufficiently tidy.

With the smallest suggestion of a shrug, Hero walked over to the table and picked up her glass. She stood there, idly examining his books and his figurines. "What were you reading, Nicky?" Her laugh rippled out. *"Alice in Wonderland?"*

"All right," said Nicholas. "Sure, it's funny, but I never had time for inspired nonsense before. I'm enjoying it."

"Of course you are. 'Inspired nonsense'! That's almost an epigram." She sat down, holding the book open on her knees. "This is marvelous. I was wondering just what we could talk about, since I'm forbidden to mention any of the things that might interest you. The war, because you're supposed to think happy thoughts. Business, because you might worry. Though, in your place, I'd worry a lot more if I didn't know what was happening."

"That's true," Nicholas agreed. "How are things going?"

Miss Chapin turned her head. "I'm sorry, Mr. Matheny, but Dr. Hatch said——"

"All right. He's the doctor, but I think my wife's a better psychologist. Never mind the business, Hero. What else can't we talk about?"

"Family matters, unless they're oh, so pleasant! I think I may tell you that Bunny's learning to walk. Let's see, what else? Joanne's feeling better."

"Has she been ill?"

"Oh . . . run down, you know. She's dreadfully thin. Your rest-cure stunt wouldn't do her any harm."

Nicholas said, "How's Robin?"

Hero, who had been turning over the pages of the book as she talked, lifted her eyes. They were clear and empty, like shallow pools of sea water. "I suppose you're wondering why he doesn't come to see you. Robin's . . . away from home just now. Oh, look, Nicky! What's that man doing?"

Outside, on the sunny lawn, a number of patients were taking their exercise. Nicholas often watched them strolling about the grounds in groups of three or four. They might have been perfectly normal citizens walking in a public park, except for the nurses in attendance and the fact that they were much better dressed. The elderly gentleman, who had caught Hero's eye, turned up in a different suit each day. His wizened monkey face looked intelligent and amused, though he always walked alone because of a marked peculiarity in his gait.

"Look, nurse," Hero said. "Why is he doing that?"

Miss Chapin looked. "Oh, Professor Wyndham. He's a darling. Awfully smart, too. I love to hear him talk. He can tell you how a geyser works, and what it was like here a hundred million years ago, and make it sound just like a story."

"But what's the matter with him?"

"Why, nothing, except he feels he has to walk like that—three steps forward and one step back. Nobody knows why. He won't even tell the doctors. His daughter sent him here because he got into so many accidents. Imagine trying to cross the street that way! Besides, she hoped Dr. Hatch could cure him. He may, too. The professor's only been here a few months."

Hero said thoughtfully, "Three steps forward and one step back. How very much like life!"

Nicholas grinned. "Better than Looking-Glass Land, where you have to run as hard as you can just to stay in the same place. That's about my situation."

Hero stood up. She placed her empty glass on the table and bent to kiss his cheek. "Oh, darling," she said in an aching whisper. "Oh, my poor Nicky!" When she straightened up he saw that her eyes were bright with tears.

"Here, what's this?" Nicholas stammered, horribly taken aback.

She didn't answer. She walked over to the window and stood there, looking out. "It's quiet here," she said in a low voice. "Does that ever get on your nerves?"

"Why, no. I like it."

She moved away from the window and began to fuss with the things on his table, pushing a pencil aside, examining the half-finished portrait head of Miss Chapin, fingering the books. "You're not bored, Nicky?" she asked, not looking at him. "It isn't too awfully dull for you?"

"No indeed. Has that been pestering you? I'm not a bit bored." To his surprise, he realized that he meant it. "I enjoy having plenty of time, for a change. You know, it used to stump me how people could sit around all day on their fannies and do nothing. I'm beginning to understand now. I believe I could get to be a first-class loafer, give me time."

Hero walked over to the bed and tested it with her hand. She said, "If there's anything I can get for you . . . anything at all . . ."

Nicholas, because her voice sounded so disturbed and there had been tears in her eyes, tried valiantly to think of something. "You can send some more books," he told her. "And I'd like to try my hand at real modeling clay. Plasticene has its limitations. Oh yes, Miss Chapin said she'd teach me to play cribbage if we had a board."

"I'll see to it. You're sure the food's all right?"

He laughed. "Probably better than you get. Hospitals are favored that way. You ought to see the cream I put on my cereal, so thick it'll hardly pour." That was gross exaggeration, of course. Still, the food was good.

"Cream!" Hero exclaimed. "I haven't seen any real cream for months." She pulled open a dresser drawer and glanced inside, talking rapidly all the while about the inconveniences of rationing, the shortage of beef and shoes and gasoline. Finally she looked at her wrist watch. "I guess I've stayed long enough, Nicky dear. I was warned not to tire you." She picked up her handbag. "Is there a mirror in your bathroom?"

Miss Chapin said, "Right over here, Mrs. Matheny."

Hero went in and shut the door behind her. In a few minutes she came out again, with the coral bag thrust under one arm. In her other hand she carried a small book. "I brought you something, Nicky, and then I almost forgot about it." She came toward him smiling, though her eyes were shadowed. Nicholas couldn't make her out. She was like a person driven by some bitter necessity. She handed the book to him, then turned away to gather up her coat and gloves.

He looked at the worn leather binding. "Margaret's Bible!" He was very much moved. "That was a lovely thing to do, Hero."

She slipped into her coat. "I suppose it's all right, Miss Chapin? The Bible isn't on the proscribed list?" Her voice sounded odd, husky and a little flat. She kept her face averted.

Nicholas wondered what ailed her. Had she been jealous of Margaret all these years? Did she consider the little Bible, which he kept at his bedside to read when he couldn't sleep, the symbol of a superior loyalty? He found that hard to believe.

Hero finished drawing on her gloves. "Good-by, darling. I'll be out again soon. I'll come as often as the doctor, and my gasoline ration, will permit." She stood on tiptoe to kiss him. Her cheek was smooth and cool against his. "Nicky," she whispered, "I'm very fond of you." Her eyes were still unnaturally bright. She pushed the door open and went softly out of the room.

"You look rather tired," said Miss Chapin. "Hadn't you better go back to bed?"

"All right," he agreed absently. While she was getting out his pajamas and turning down the bed, he glanced into the small Bible, smiling with a sort of amused nostalgia. Margaret's maiden name was written on the flyleaf in a round, childish hand. She had entered their marriage in the family register and recorded the children's birth dates: Helena in 1901, Robin, 1908. He turned the page. Under DEATHS she had written the names of her parents and his. Just below, her own passing was recorded in Nicholas' bold scrawl; then Helena's death in 1934.

Something was written on the next line. He held the volume closer. For a moment he thought his eyes must be fooling him. He couldn't grasp the meaning of the words set down there in Hero's upright hand, in a pale, brownish-colored ink. Robin Matheny, August 29, 1943. *Robin . . . 1943*. The Bible fell out of his hands and thumped down on the carpeted floor.


## 7


He was in a long, well-lighted corridor, with an identical row of doors on either side. His arms were twisted up behind his back in such a way that he could scarcely move. Miss Chapin's voice came to him, unruffled, soothing, yet authoritative.

"This way, Mr. Matheny. Come on. You're going back to your room now, Mr. Matheny. Come along."

A door at one end of the hall opened. Three men filed in, attended by a nurse. Moving toward them, from the opposite end of the corridor, was another nurse pushing a wheel chair. A young man lay in the chair, white-faced, golden-haired, beautiful as an angel in an old painting. Nicholas felt an obscure sense of shame. "All right, I'll go. You don't have to hold on to me, Miss Chapin."

She released his arms at once. "The third door on your left."

He was glad to reach the haven of his own room, safe from curious eyes, away from the terrible, clean angularity of that corridor. He took off his clothes and put on his pajamas, as the nurse directed. She tucked him into bed. "How did I get out there?" he asked, bewildered.

"You just suddenly ran out," Miss Chapin informed him. "I don't know why. It was a few minutes after your wife left."

"My wife," Nicholas repeated slowly. "I remember. I thought I could catch up with her."

"I see. I'm going to draw the blinds, Mr. Matheny, so you can take a nap before dinner."

He raised himself on one elbow. "Miss Chapin, how did my son die?"

"What?" She hurried over to the bedside. She looked outraged, as if he had been screaming obscenities at her.

"My boy," he said. "I want to know how he died. He was healthy, like me . . . only thirty-five years old. I can't understand."

"Wait a minute. I don't get this at all. Did your wife tell you? Is that why she was whispering?" The nurse frowned. "But you didn't run out until five minutes later."

"It's written down in the Bible," he said with an effort. Pain was growing strong within him, like the mounting agony of a burn when the first shock wears off.

She gave him a stricken look. The Bible lay where it had fallen, on the floor beside his chair. She picked it up and turned the pages. "Is this it? Joseph Matheny . . . 1916? But I don't see why——"

"That was my father. Look at the last name on the page. Robin . . . twenty-ninth of August."

She said in a gentle voice, "There's no entry after Helena Matheny."

His grief exploded into violence. "Quit acting as if I was a fool!" he shouted. "I can read, damn it!"

"Stop that. Get back into bed."

Nicholas had thrown off the covers and thrust out one leg. Muttering, he drew it back. When they used that tone of voice, you did as you were told. Odd how they contrived to get a sort of moral ascendancy over you. He lay down again. "Robin was a fine healthy boy," he said. "Never had a sick day in his life."

Miss Chapin pushed the open volume into his hands. "You imagined it, Mr. Matheny. See for yourself. There's nothing here about Robin."

Because he was told to, Nicholas glanced at the page. He sat up, blinked his eyes, and looked again. She was right. He examined the other pages in the family record. After a time he raised his eyes. "I don't know," he said in confusion. "My mind plays tricks on me."

"You were awfully tired. I think you dropped off for a few minutes and dreamed you saw his name there. As for the date, you were hurt on the twenty-ninth of August, so naturally you'd connect that day with something bad. You see?"

"Yes, I see." Dreams were funny . . . mixed things up. You'd be walking down Fifth Avenue one instant and home in your California bathtub the next. "I guess that's what happened." His pain vanished. It was only a dream. "Look here, I'm not sleepy. I'll stay in bed, if you say so, but can't I read? Or, look, give me that portrait of you. Maybe I can finish it this afternoon."

Miss Chapin's dimples appeared. She raised the head of the bed and arranged his pillows. "Time for your four o'clock glass of milk, anyway," she said. "I'll go and get it. Don't work too hard."

He looked with critical eyes at the half-finished model. Rather charming, he thought, but definitely not Miss Chapin. The face wasn't round enough; the chin was too pointed. It reminded him of someone else, someone . . . Abruptly the name, and the girl herself, leaped into his mind.

She was coming toward him, across the flying field, from the gate where the cars were parked. Elsa Kuttner, Emil's young daughter. You couldn't mistake those velvet brown eyes, the skin like thick cream, the small pointed face.

She was in a temper. Every line of her body was taut with rage. Her dark gold hair whipped about furiously.

Nicholas was not one to be intimidated by an angry woman. Hit first and hit hard, that was the secret. He strode forward, bellowing, "Hey, what are you doing here? Who let you in? Damn it all, this isn't a free show we're putting on. This is a test flight."

"Mr. Matheny, I've got to talk to you." She stopped right in front of him, her chin thrust out, her fists clenched. She looked so cute, so like an exasperated kitten, that he had to bite his lips to keep from smiling.

Just the same, she had no business being on the field. "I'll talk to you," he roared, "if you don't get the hell out of here."

Elsa stamped her foot. "You needn't make such a row about my coming in. Oh, I know it's supposed to be all very hush-hush, but I've known for years, and I haven't talked."

"What's that? Who told you?"

"Nobody. If a person's got any brains, they don't have to be told things in so many words. They just sort of get the idea. But that's not the point. I want to know what you're going to do about my father."

Nicholas seized her arm. "I'm going to do something about you, young lady. We'll let your father take care of himself."

She shook off his hand. "I thought so. You don't care who gets hurt, so long as you can make a lot more money. Isn't that true? Every day, for eight years, my father's run the risk of getting blown to bits. Why should you worry? You can always hire another chemist. You can hire more pilots if Jimmy Duncan gets killed trying to fly a plane with nothing in the gas tank except sea water and carbolic acid!"

"Eh? What's this?" said Nicholas, quite at a loss.

"Oh, I just said that. I don't know what the stuff's made of." The wind blew a loose strand of hair across her face. She brushed it back impatiently. "Even if they told me, I wouldn't understand. I'm not a good enough chemist."

"Neither am I," he admitted. He couldn't keep up the hard-boiled pose any longer. Besides, she was right, in a way. He hated the risks these people were taking, yet if anything happened, anything untoward, he most certainly would hire somebody else to carry on. Nicoline was more important than any one chemist, any one pilot. He said, "I'm sorry you've been worried, Elsa. Fact is, we try to take precautions. It isn't just luck that your father's still in one piece, and the plane seems to be doing all right on . . . er . . . carbolic acid." He squinted up at the hot, vivid sky. Jimmy was circling the field, getting ready for a landing. The test was almost over. "If that's all you wanted to say——"

"I haven't even begun. Of course I know Father and Jimmy and Oliver don't mind the ordinary professional risks. That's their job. They know what to watch out for and what to do in an emergency, but when they start getting mixed up with thugs and hijackers, or maybe . . . maybe . . ."

She glanced back fearfully. The high angry color faded out of her cheeks. Her eyes looked black and scared and pitiably young. "I was only ten when we left Germany," she said in a low voice, "but you grow up fast there. I saw . . . things. Imagine what this would mean to the Nazis. They must be desperate for oil. You don't suppose, do you, they'd stop at murder, or anything else, to get a really good synthetic?"

Nicholas almost laughed. For a minute she'd had him worried, she looked so darned scared. These refugees couldn't get it through their heads that the

Gestapo wasn't lurking behind every bush. He wasn't afraid of the Nazis, though no doubt they'd like to get their hands on nicoline. Emil said the stuff worked nearly as well as 100-octane, and it was somewhat lighter and enormously cheaper. Best of all, it was not a petroleum product. There was no limit to the raw material from which it could be made. Yes, Hitler'd like to get hold of nicoline, but he never would. Emil had made certain of that.

"Forget it, Elsa. This is America."

She flared up again. "You still think it can't happen here? What about the *Normandie?* What about the Allison Chemical Company fire? I suppose the strikes and race riots and all the rest of it are just accidental? Well, *this* isn't an accident." She drew a crumpled wad of paper from the pocket of her linen dress. "When they start sending threatening letters . . ."

A thin white hand, somewhat stained with chemicals, reached out and grabbed the letter. Nicholas turned around, frowning. He hadn't heard Emil approach and he hated being taken by surprise. "Now see here," he began angrily, "what's all this?"

Emil slipped the paper into his pocket. He addressed his daughter in rapid, guttural German. She answered tartly in the same language. They seemed to be quarreling. After a moment the girl's mouth trembled. She started to cry.

Nicholas waited with growing irritation. Why the hell couldn't they talk English? He had a right to be in on this. Besides, it was rotten bad manners. "I don't talk German," he announced in a tone of fury.

Elsa looked up at him with wet dark eyes. She turned and walked quickly toward the gate.

"What did you say to her?" Nicholas fumed. "Why didn't you tell me you'd been getting threatening letters?"

Emil shrugged. "Poor little one! Nothing, I fear, will erase those early memories. And yet she does not fully understand. They would not have sent a warning. They would have acted."

Nicholas tugged at his mustache. "Who, then? One of the other oil companies? Of course this might break 'em. But how the devil did they find out?"

"Such a secret is difficult to keep, my friend. An incautious word . . . a smile at the wrong moment . . . a feeling in the air . . ."

He was right, thought Nicholas. Sometimes you could almost believe in telepathic waves. "I suppose it's a wonder we've kept it dark this long." His eyes narrowed. Threatening letters! Something wrong with the picture, he felt. He knew big business inside out. Wasn't he big business himself? They didn't go at it in quite that way. "How much did they offer you?" he demanded suddenly.

Emil, whose eyes were on the plane, turned toward him with reluctant courtesy. "Offers? Yes, there have been offers. Naturally I declined."

"How much?"

"Like you, Nick, they conversed in millions." The chemist laughed. "Twenty-five dollars, in sound currency, I can understand. Above that, money is to me figures on a piece of paper."

"Who approached you?"

"I have no notion. Voices over the telephone . . . See, Nick, he is about to make a landing."

Nicholas examined the man's face. The dark eyes were exalted, but the mouth was twisted into a biting smile, as if he were savoring the brilliant irony of his achievement. It was really a fine grim joke that nicoline should have been perfected, in this fateful autumn of 1943, by a man Hitler drove out of the Reich. No doubt that was the sort of justice called "poetic," because it didn't happen as often as it should. He knew pretty well what Emil was feeling. Nicholas felt the same way, and he hadn't done anything except put up the money. Still, his immense satisfaction was clouded by uneasiness. The man had worked eight years and accomplished something truly remarkable. Didn't he have a right to expect fame and fortune?

Nicholas hauled out his handkerchief. He wiped his forehead. "Look here, Kuttner, we thrashed this out once before, but are you sure you realize what you're passing up? There's no limit to the commercial possibilities. I mean after the war, when——"

Emil stopped him. "My friend, I care nothing about your commercial possibilities, and very little for what shall happen to me after the war. I take interest only in winning it. . . . There! A pretty landing, was it not?"

The plane ambled along the runway. It waddled a bit, like a sea gull on land, or any winged creature reduced to the level of earth. "All right, then," said Nicholas. "I'll get busy. If you're perfectly sure?"

"Perfectly. Why not? My salary is already too large, and you add with it other riches beyond the dream of avarice." He laughed and rubbed his hands. "You have given me a chance to pay my debt." His cheeks flushed. The scar which disfigured one of them stood out paper white by contrast.

Nicholas averted his eyes. "I know. I've got a debt to pay too. Different sort, though." He stuffed his handkerchief back into his pocket. "I was born a peasant," he said. "If my folks had stayed in the old country, I'd be tending pigs to this day . . . if there are any pigs left."

The bitterness in his voice made Emil glance at him sharply. "Sometimes, my friend, I forget that your country, too——"

Nicholas said, "America is my country. It's been damned good to me, Emil." As much a part of him as the very blood pounding through his heart was this gratitude to the land which had given him everything he had, even his name (for Matheny was only an approximation of the tongue twister he'd been born with). Of course it hadn't been too easy. He'd sold papers, run errands. He'd been a day laborer, a machinist, a junk dealer, and a lot of other things, before he became Big Nick Matheny, oil operator and multimillionaire. They said money didn't bring happiness, but making something, building something, using the brains God gave you . . . that was happiness, or he didn't know what the word meant.

The only thing he'd missed was schooling. He hadn't had time for that, but fifty years ago book learning wasn't so important. You got wealth out of the ground, not out of a test tube. Anyhow, he learned all he needed to know: how to size up a man or a deal; how to find the joker in a contract or the weak spot in a woman. He'd had a lot of fun. It was a swell show, and now that he was in the middle of the last act, he could still have the satisfaction of paying for his good time.

Nicholas found it impossible to say any of these things, even to Emil, who certainly would understand. All the words had been worked to death by sentimentalists and rabble rousers. You couldn't go on about patriotism, loyalty, gratitude, without appearing to drool, so you kept your mouth shut and tried to pay what you owed.

He looked at his watch. "Since there's been a leak," he said, "we'll have to speed things up. How soon can you get out the reports?"

Emil didn't answer for a moment. "I had intended further tests, but you are right. We should not any longer delay. Make your arrangements, Nick. The reports can be prepared . . ."

Like static crackling into a radio program, Miss Chapin's voice cut through Emil's. "What's the trouble? What are you doing, Mr. Matheny?"

He was sitting straight up in bed. His eyes ached from gazing at the sunlit wall. His mind ached with trying to hang tight to Emil, keep him from slipping off into the gray void.

"Look, I've brought you a nice glass of milk."

Emil was gone. The flying field was gone, and the blue sky, and the hot wind from the desert. For an instant Miss Chapin's round white cap, the curve of her cheek, the red dot of her mouth, took on the form of a huge question mark.

"Miss Chapin, I want to make a telephone call. Is that permitted?"

"Why, I'm afraid . . . I mean I'll ask the doctor."

"You mean it isn't. Well, then . . . My God! This may be important. I don't know. I can't remember enough. If you'd come in just five minutes later——"

"Now don't get all excited. You know that's bad for you."

"See here, if I can't telephone, you can. Call Seaboard Petroleum and ask for Emil Kuttner. Got that?"

"You haven't touched your milk."

Surprised, he looked down at the glass in his hand. With an impatient movement he put it to his lips and drank the milk at one gulp. "When you get Kuttner, tell him where I am and ask him to come and see me right away. Will you?"

"I'll ask the doctor." She took the empty glass and moved away, toward the hall door.

Nicholas said, "I'm allowed to have visitors. My wife——"

"Yes, if they don't upset you. I'll talk to Dr. Hatch about it."

She went away, leaving him alone with his anxieties. He tried to put them out of his mind. (Rest and worry didn't mix.) Anyhow, he had no reason to suppose that the "arrangements," whatever they were, hadn't been carried out before his accident . . . no reason except a recurring dream which might just possibly be more than a dream.

He addressed himself to the portrait of Miss Chapin, with its strange resemblance to young Elsa. Gradually the clay in his hands changed shape, becoming more round at the top, curving into a period at the bottom, like a question mark.

# 8

Nicholas walked sedately along the graveled path, at Miss Chapin's side. The afternoon was unusually fine even for a state which specializes in climate, all blue and gold like a royal banner. A crisp dry wind whispered among the branches of the pepper trees and sent fantastic leaping patterns of shade across the lawn. The air was so exhilarating that Nicholas wanted to run and leap too, though he knew such excesses would not be permitted a man taking a rest cure.

This was his first excursion into the park, and therefore an adventure. The place was larger than he had supposed. His building was only one of several. There was a big three-story structure beyond the row of cottages, and separate quarters for women at the far end of the grounds. The park was surrounded by a white brick wall with ivy clambering over it. "Miss Chapin," he said, "how do you keep your patients from escaping? I don't see any sentries or barbed-wire entanglements."

"This isn't a jail. It's a hospital."

"But a very special kind," Nicholas pointed out.

"Well, yes. Do you know, Mr. Matheny, Crestview's never had an escape!"

He was suitably amazed. "How do you account for that?"

"Oh, various reasons. We keep the disturbed patients separate and watch them pretty closely. There aren't many. We get alcoholics and drug addicts mostly, and cases like yours, injury or illness. They're glad enough to stay until they're well." She laughed suddenly. "Our worst headache is to get people to leave when they're cured! After all, we provide comfort, entertainment, and peace. No family squabbles or servant problems or anything. With such a large staff, the patients even have a lot of freedom."

"I don't get that."

"Well," she said, "if you can keep your eye on a man most of the time, you don't have to lock him in his room so much, do you? We average one attendant to four patients."

"Really! How does it happen I get so much of your time? What's become of the other three guys?"

She glanced up at him obliquely. "Oh, I'm your 'special.' My exclusive attention costs you an extra two hundred a month."

"And cheap at the price," said Nicholas gallantly.

The path curved around a fluttering mass of shrubbery. A few yards past the bend it widened into a circle edged with rustic benches. At a picnic table beneath tall fir trees four men played an animated game of cards. Farther on two nurses stood gossiping beside a wheel-chair. Its occupant was a golden-haired lad with an angel's face. He had a notebook and pencil on his lap, but his hands lay idle. His rapt gaze was fixed on the mountain range which rose steeply behind the sanitarium and stretched off as far as the eye could see, into blue distance. *I will lift up mine eyes unto the hills*, thought Nicholas, *from whence cometh my help.*

All by himself on one of the benches sat the well-dressed elderly gentleman. He leaned forward with a friendly, expectant smile. Nicholas paused beside the bench.

"Would you like to meet the professor?" said Miss Chapin. "Professor Wyndham, this is Mr. Matheny."

"How do you do? How do you do?" The little man hitched himself along the rustic seat, to make room for Nicholas. "Sit down. Sit down. I thought I recognized your face. Big Nick Matheny, isn't it, of Seaboard Petroleum?"

He had a soft, confiding voice, rather like a stage whisper. His speech was slow and very distinct, yet it had an air of intense amusement, as if he were reading aloud some juicy passage from his favorite book and didn't want you to miss a word of it. "We have much in common, Mr. Matheny. Petroleum is well within my province."

"You're a geologist?"

"Paleontologist." He thrust his smiling monkey face toward Nicholas. "I should like to ask you a question, Mr. Matheny. I am curious to know what attitude men in the industry take regarding the rapid depletion of our oil reserves."

"Scares hell out of 'em," said Nicholas, grinning.

"Really? Really? I find that interesting. Why, Mr. Matheny? Forgive me, sir, but you are no longer young. The oil will last your time."

"Perhaps, but . . ."

Professor Wyndham raised his hand. Nicholas fell silent. "I am well aware, Mr. Matheny, that no accurate assessment of the world's petroleum resources is possible. On the other hand, one can make a rough estimate of the *available* supply. Before the war, if my memory serves me, it was supposed that the oil might last another fifty years, taking into consideration the rate of increase in demand, together with improvement in production methods. But consider the terrific acceleration brought about by mechanized warfare! One bomber, Mr. Matheny, making the round trip from England to Berlin, consumes enough gasoline to fill ninety automobile tanks. Just *one* bomber, making just one trip!"

Miss Chapin wriggled her shoulders. "I'm sorry, but my patient isn't supposed to talk about the war."

"We are not discussing the war, my dear girl," said Professor Wyndham, as if he were imparting a delightful secret. "Actually, we are talking about the future of the human race, although as yet no one realizes that fact except myself." He drew forth a gold cigarette case and snapped it open. "Would you care to smoke, sir?"

Nicholas, still deprived of his cigars, was allowed two cigarettes a day. Having never smoked what he termed "coffin nails," the privilege hadn't interested him, but he was glad to accept one of the professor's cigarettes, by way of a polite social gesture. Miss Chapin took a paper book of matches from her pocket and gave both men a light. Then she strolled off to join the other nurses beside the wheel chair.

"Now then," Professor Wyndham continued in a softly portentous voice, "at the present rate of use, how long can the total available supply be expected to last? Twenty years? Thirty? Or do I exaggerate?"

Nicholas puffed at the tasteless paper tube in his mouth. "Twenty, at a guess, depending on how long the thing lasts."

"Ah! And that alarms you? Perhaps you see the end of our mechanized civilization, a return to the pastoral life?" He waved his arm. "These vast cities fallen to ruin; sheep grazing among the piles of stone and rubble; nomadic tribes wandering across the plains in search of game, marveling at the broken, twisted rails, all that is left of a great transportation system; stumbling over cement blocks humped up by frost, relics of a three-lane highway where motorcars once traveled at seventy miles an hour. For, mark this, sir, the coal is going too! And without fuel the most intricate machine is only a pile of scrap metal."

"True enough," Nicholas admitted serenely.

"I wish I had been born last week," sighed the professor. "It would amuse me to watch the swift decline of an era, the Age of the Hydrocarbons! Compared to the Stone Age, or the Age of Iron, only an instant, a mere breath." He leaned back against the rough logs of the bench. "I'm eighty-one. I won't see even the beginning, but you may live long enough, Mr. Matheny."

"No," said Nicholas. "It's an interesting idea, but it won't happen. We'll get fuel."

"Indeed! Indeed! From the moon, no doubt?"

"No. Out of a test tube."

"Ah yes. I am familiar with the story of triptane, but is it not derived from petroleum?"

"I don't know much about it. I'm no chemist, but they tell me you can crack fish or vegetable oils at high temperature and get something that will run a car okay."

"Very good, but at what cost?"

"Sure, that's always been the trouble." Nicholas ground his cigarette butt underfoot. "We'll lick it, though. Do you know what the first handmade automobile cost? It's only a production problem, getting the price down." He had to bite his lips to keep from smiling. They had already licked it, he and Emil, though he wasn't going to tell the professor so.

"Only a production problem!" The little man hitched himself forward. "My word! You industrialists! The modern Children of Israel, and chemistry is your Jehovah!"

"Well, why not? When they can make silk stockings out of coal and airplane bodies from skim milk."

Miss Chapin's flat-heeled shoes crunched on the gravel. "We'd better start back," she said. "You mustn't get too tired your very first day out."

Nicholas rose obediently to his feet.

The professor stood up too. "I shall accompany you, if I may. I have enjoyed our conversation, Mr. Matheny." He started down the path in his curious way, three steps forward, then a step back. "Perhaps we can have another talk tomorrow, if the weather continues fine."

Nicholas was a bit embarrassed until he found that, by taking two steps to the professor's four, he could keep abreast fairly well.

The blond youth looked right through them as they passed by. "Phillip Corey, the poet," Wyndham informed Nicholas. "He will enjoy meeting you, one day when he is not composing. A brilliant lad. Splendid mind!"

"Poor devil. How did he get hurt?"

"The war hurt him, Mr. Matheny."

"Oh, a veteran? Why isn't he at Sawtelle?"

"War produces more than one kind of casualty. Phillip, you see, is both sensitive and idealistic. He burned to go forth and save humanity from the beast. On his eighteenth birthday he enlisted in the Army, but after five weeks of fairly realistic training he became paralyzed from the waist down."

"You mean he fell, or something?" Nicholas asked with some impatience. He was finding the conversation difficult. He liked to look at people when they talked, but the professor's gait kept him always a step behind or a step in the lead, and Nicholas was damned if he was going to imitate the fellow.

"No, no, no," said Professor Wyndham over his shoulder. "The paralysis is of hysterical origin."

"That's funny. He looks calm enough."

"You don't understand." Wyndham, who had fallen behind again, raised his voice a trifle. "I am using the word in its medical sense. Hysteria, you know, may simulate almost any disease, but usually it springs from a repressed feeling of guilt. Poor Phillip, the idealist, found that he was unable to live up to his ideals. However, if one avoids the war, he is a good companion. Phillip was transferred to my cottage recently. And that reminds me, number three cottage lost two of its members last week. We have a vacancy. Should you care to join us, you might mention the possibility to your doctor. I'm sure you would enjoy young Corey and Judge Scott. As for myself, I should endeavor not to bore you too much. . . . What do you think, Miss Chapin?"

They had arrived at the surgical building. Miss Chapin paused in the act of pulling open the door. "I shouldn't give away state secrets, but Dr. Hatch has already suggested putting Mr. Matheny in your cottage. We felt sure you two would get along."

"Excellent! Excellent!" He beamed up at Nicholas, looking remarkably like a good-natured chimp. "This has been a great pleasure, sir. I hope that I may enjoy a walk with you some other afternoon. If I may say so, you accommodate yourself wonderfully well to my eccentricity." He beckoned Nicholas to bend his head and whispered confidentially, "I don't have to do it, you know. But if I stopped, they'd send me home, and I prefer to stay here. So much more amusing!" He nodded his farewell and walked off along the path, taking three steps forward and one step back.

Nicholas stood looking after the little man, scratching his chin thoughtfully. For the first time that afternoon he remembered where he was.

## 9

Nicholas bent over his modeling stand near the window. He was doing a portrait from memory of young Phillip's poetic face. Its special quality eluded him. He was annoyed, too, by a lack of proper light. The day was overcast. Gray sky and a soft feeling of dampness in the air might have suggested rain anywhere except in southern California at this season of the year, but of course it was only high fog.

He wondered why Easterners were so amused by that phrase. It was perfectly accurate. During the dry months, overcast was really ocean fog pouring in at a high level, growing more and more attenuated as it rolled inland. Up here, in the foothills of the tall San Gabriels, high fog was a rarity, though not as unusual as certain health-resort advertisements might lead you to believe. In any case, it made work difficult. Nicholas wasn't sorry when Professor Wyndham opened the door.

"Come in. Have a chair." He added, because the little man had an exaggerated respect for creative effort, "I'll have to quit, anyway. The light's no good."

Professor Wyndham advanced haltingly into the room. "May one look at the portrait?"

"No," said Nicholas. "It stinks. I bit off more than I could chew." He wrapped a wet cloth around the clay face of his model and settled back in his chair, prepared for a stimulating talk. After his long seclusion, companionship was a great luxury. Wyndham never failed to amuse him. Judge Scott was an able raconteur, with the best stock of racy limericks Nicholas had ever heard. The four patients in the cottage were allowed to visit each other. Within certain well-defined limits, they could do pretty much as they chose.

"I have something to show you, Mr. Matheny," said the professor. "What do you think? One of Phillip's poems printed in the *Monitor!* It came out day before yesterday. My daughter was kind enough to send me a copy. Would you care to see it?"

"Yes indeed." Nicholas took the paper, folded to display Phillip's poem, and began to read. Thanks to his recent literary adventuring, he knew the thing was a sonnet. Apart from that, he couldn't make head or tail of it. The words were clear enough, but they didn't seem to have much relation to each other.

"Remarkable thing, isn't it?" said Wyndham.

"Yes. Yes, it is." Nicholas wasn't just being polite. Although it lacked sense in the ordinary way, Phillip's poem affected him profoundly, like a warning, like the foreknowledge of some slow, descending doom.

He was about to read the lines again, when a sound made him lift his head, a furtive rustle, a pattering that might have been the feet of some tiny creature moving among dry leaves. He turned to look out of the window. Rain! Silver lines slanted diagonally past the dark green mass of the pepper trees. The pattering sound grew into a steady drumming on the earth. Water hissed against the windowpane, changing trees and grass into a smeared, futuristic painting.

"Rain!" he cried, with the hushed delight of those who dwell in arid places.

Professor Wyndham blinked. "Why, so it is. . . . I particularly like the sestet. How does it go? 'This bitter cadence . . .' "

"It's coming down hard," said Nicholas. "Quite a shower! Amazing, for this time of year."

"Oh, I don't know. We often have rain in December."

Nicholas swung around in his chair. "December? What the hell are you talking about?"

The professor looked at him with interest. "I fear you are a trifle disoriented as to time. This is the fifteenth of December. I'm sorry if the fact distresses you."

"I can't believe it." Nicholas put a hand to his head. "I was hurt August twenty-ninth. Have I been here almost four months? But that's impossible."

"May I suggest that you verify my statement? A glance at the newspaper you have in your hand . . ."

Nicholas unfolded the paper. He turned to the front page. There it was, in plain print. And a worse shock lay in wait for him among the headlines. SIXTEEN DIE IN COLD WAVE. LACK OF FUEL OIL BLAMED. He skimmed through the story. "Subzero temperatures along the Atlantic seaboard yesterday brought death to sixteen persons . . . thousands of homes and apartments virtually without heating facilities, due to the shortage of coal and fuel oil . . ."

Wyndham's voice came to him softly, as if from a distance. "Mr. Matheny! Are you ill?"

Nicholas said, "Four months! My God, they should have been in production long ago! We got all the bugs ironed out. We had the cost down to six cents a gallon." His eyes wandered down the page. "Drastic cut in gasoline rations . . . nationwide ban on nonessential driving seen . . . war needs to be met at any cost, says Ickes . . ." The paper was full of it. OIL MEN BLAME OPA. "Ceiling prices on crude so low as to force abandonment of stripper wells and discourage wildcat drilling are to blame for the critical decline in oil production, said spokesmen for six major companies today . . ."

He crumpled the paper into a wad and dashed it to the floor. What in God's name had happened? He pulled out his handkerchief and wiped his forehead. An appalling thought had come to him. Was his mind playing tricks again? Had the tests really been successful, or did he just imagine that nicoline was perfected, ready for production?

Professor Wyndham bent over him with an anxious face. "Mr. Matheny, shall I call the nurse? Are you in pain?"

"Wait a minute," Nicholas mumbled. "Keep still." The room had darkened, like a theater when the house lights go down and the curtain begins to rise.

He sat at the desk in his study. An appointment book lay open before him.

The date was printed in bold letters at the top: Saturday, August 28, 1943. Several names were down for the morning hours, but nothing for the afternoon except "Test Fight . . . 2.00."

Nicholas shut the book and handed it to Stuart Hanson, who sat facing him across the desk. Fat, blond, expansive, the secretary seemed, at first glance, as unlike his employer as anyone could be. Yet behind the round face, crinkled with laugh lines, was a brain much like Nicholas' own, save that it lacked initiative. Someone else had to supply the shove that would start him moving.

Hanson fingered the appointment book. "I'll do the best I can, but you know what Washington is these days."

"They'll see me," said Nicholas confidently. "Get in touch with the New York office. Gunther knows everyone. He should be able to get action."

"All right," said Hanson mildly, "but why the great rush?"

"There's been a leak."

"Oh. . . . Who?"

"Can't tell. Too many people had a thumb in this pie. Anyhow, we've got to work fast."

"But why, Nick? What can they do? Unless they get hold of the formula."

Nicholas chuckled dryly. "Kuttner thought it'd be a smart idea to leave out one essential process. Only he and I know what it is. Nobody can steal the stuff; don't worry."

"Then what are you afraid of?"

He didn't answer at once. He hadn't told Stuart what he meant to do. Until plans were matured, the time right for action, he liked to keep his own counsel. "Know how the market closed?" he said finally.

"I've been pretty busy getting out those reports."

"Seaboard was up five and an eighth. Most of the other companies were off a little."

Hanson whistled. "And you're trying to pull in the rest of the stock! What a rotten break!"

Nicholas agreed with him. For three years, ever since Kuttner's experiments had begun to look so promising, he'd been buying up the shares in his company, usually at a premium. It had taken a big chunk of capital, but he had no intention of making a large gesture at the expense of his stockholders. Oh yes, he'd considered all the angles. Seaboard Petroleum would be just as hard hit as the other companies, but even if it went under, he had enough salted away for a comfortable old age. He could leave Hero and the boy pretty well fixed. He'd even made provision for that blasted father of hers.

"I guess you don't understand why I've been pulling in the stock," he said. "I don't want the little fellows to get hurt. You see, I mean to hand nicoline over to the War Department."

Hanson didn't move or speak. His eyes seemed to be turned inward. The room was very quiet, except for a faint rustling which came from the direction of the bedroom. Nicholas glanced up. Through the open doorway he saw a swirl of movement, a flash of color. He put his hands flat on the desk and started to rise from his chair. Just then a gust of wind whipped through the french windows. The curtains bellied out. He sank back, satisfied that the wind, not some eavesdropper, had caught his attention.

"I want fast action, and this is the only way to get it. I'm not going to kid around for a year or two, waiting for building permits and priorities. Too many fine lads might be dying because there wasn't enough aviation gasoline to give them the right air support." He stopped. His plans didn't need defending. Anyhow, this wasn't a matter to shout about, even in the privacy of his own home.

He lowered his voice. "What's eating you, Stuart? We aren't going broke tomorrow. There'll still be uses for oil. Nicoline won't run a Diesel engine. It's no good for heating or power plants, but it ought to release a lot of crude for that sort of thing, and maybe some extra gas for the cars that are lying idle. However, it's too big for us. We couldn't produce a fraction of the volume that's wanted."

Hanson shook himself, like a fat bulldog coming out of the water. "Okay by me," he said. "I was just thinking . . ." He reached into his pocket and drew out a package of cigarettes.

"Thinking what?" asked Nicholas irritably. He wanted a smoke too, but he'd already had one cigar. If he smoked another, he'd be through for the day. He opened his desk drawer and found that the supply of plasticene was gone. Swearing under his breath, he took up the coiled rattlesnake and put a few finishing touches on the wicked head.

Hanson put a lighted match to his cigarette. "Your family isn't going to like this, Nick."

"Why not? They're all taken care of. Even Charley, blast his hide."

"I know, but they're all used to practically unlimited funds." Nicholas gave a snort of derision. "Sure, the income tax takes most of it right now, but that won't last forever. Rob isn't going to like it. Neither is Hero. I'm telling you."

"They can like it or lump it," he said inelegantly. "If Robin doesn't have enough money, he can go to work on his own. Do him good." As for Hero, he thought, she got what she wanted years ago. All the people who snubbed her after the big crash had been brought to heel. She even made them accept Charley, when he got out of the pen.

Stuart said, "There's Joanne. She's always supposed that Bunny would be heir to a large fortune."

"Joanne is scared to death of the fortune. Afraid the boy'll grow up a good-for-nothing loafer like his dad."

Hanson's eyebrows went up. He fell silent. The ash on his cigarette grew longer and longer, until it broke of its own weight and splashed softly over the desk top.

"Rob's got himself in a sweet mess," Nicholas growled. "Joanne was in here just now with an extortion letter. Here, take a look." He fished the blue envelope out of a drawer. "Or maybe you better wait till you've made those long-distance calls. We can talk about this afterward."

Hanson pulled a bronze ash tray toward him and ground out the stub of his cigarette with a savage air. "I'm not surprised. I didn't think she'd let him go that easily."

"She? Who?"

"Didn't you know who Rob was playing around with? Carmelita. That Brazilian dancer out at Marchetti's."

"Good. That makes it easier. I didn't know who it was." He pushed the letter across the desk. "Turn that over to McClintock. He'll know what to do."

"All right. I'll try, but it's Saturday afternoon. Lawyers don't work eighteen hours a day, like we do."

Nicholas frowned. "I can't go away and leave this thing up in the air. I promised Joanne."

"Want me to stay and look after it?"

"No, I'll need you. By the way, Jimmy Duncan is flying us. We're to leave at dawn. See here, attend to those calls now, and I'll get hold of McClintock myself." Stuart didn't move. He looked at Nicholas sleepily, out of half-closed eyes. "Well, what are you waiting for?"

The fat man heaved himself out of his chair. "Okay. It's your show, Nick, but I hope to God you've taken precautions. Have you got guards out at the lab?"

"Kuttner won't have a guard. He says young Grant is worth a dozen ex-marines."

"Who's looking after Jimmy? Who's keeping an eye on that plane? I don't mind telling you I never expect to reach Washington."

"Why not?"

"Too many people have too much to gain by blowing us up before we can get there. The Japs and the Germans, for instance. The other oil companies. I don't suppose Rob would do anything, even if he knew, but I wouldn't put it past Charley Van Norman to stick a bomb in your plane."

"Listen. You and I and Emil are the only ones who know when we're leaving, and how."

Hanson looked down at him with those sleepy, half-shut eyes. "Let's hope nobody else finds out before tomorrow morning." He went out of the room, moving quickly, with a light step unusual in a fat man.

The curtain came down. The room grew brighter. Nicholas found that he was on his feet. Someone was hanging on to his arm.

"Mr. Matheny, where are you going? What's the trouble?"

He looked down at the professor's wizened, anxious face, at the wrinkled hand clutching his coat sleeve. Suddenly he began to laugh. Through the sound of his own wild laughter he could hear shots, a siren wailing. For an instant the floor heaved under his feet. Stuart was right. Someone had found out. Somebody had made damn sure he wouldn't reach Washington.

## 10

"Perhaps we moved you too soon," said Dr. Hatch. He gave Nicholas a cigarette and took one himself. "I thought you'd benefit by having some company, but we can't put up with disturbances in the parole cottages."

Nicholas said meekly, "I didn't mean to cause a disturbance. I just remembered something that upset me a little."

"What was it?"

"Unfinished business." He blew out a mouthful of smoke. "You know, I'm getting used to the coffin nails. Guess I won't take up cigars again, now I'm out of the habit. After all, they're bad for me."

Dr. Hatch wasn't easily distracted. "Still worrying about your business?"

"Yes, I am." Nicholas thought a moment. He couldn't expect help from the hospital staff. They had refused to locate Emil; they wouldn't let Hero talk to him alone. However, he made one more try. "I couldn't have been knocked out at a worse time. A very important matter was pending. For a long time I didn't know whether it had been taken care of or not. This afternoon I remembered. It's still pending."

"Your wife seems very capable," said the doctor, "and surely you have a good organization?"

"This is something I've got to handle myself."

"Would you like to tell me about it?"

"Can't," said Nicholas. "Military secret." Dr. Hatch gave him that look, the considering one which indicated a purely psychiatric interest. "See here, Doc, you might as well admit that I'm an important man and not just having delusions of grandeur. My firm spends enough on research to buy this place ten times over. We get our money's worth. It shouldn't surprise you to hear that we've developed something of military value and that I've got to keep quiet about it."

The doctor reflected upon this. "Well, what do you want? I take it you want something."

Nicholas said, "I want to talk to Emil Kuttner."

"I remember. You asked for him several weeks ago. I'm sorry. We weren't able to locate Kuttner."

"Did you try?"

"Certainly. We were told that he was out of town."

Nicholas began to chew at his cigarette, as if it were a real smoke. He spat out a mouthful of paper and tobacco. "Damn these things!" Out of town? Yes, that might be, only . . . four months? Even if you took into account the confusion of wartime, bureaucratic red tape and all, why such a long delay? "You couldn't find out where he went?"

"No." The doctor grinned at him. "Perhaps your people considered that another military secret."

"Perhaps." He felt let down, though he hadn't really expected much.

"Mr. Matheny, would it ease your mind if we let you have a short talk with your wife about this business?"

Nicholas doubted it. He must try to reach Emil. He must find out exactly what happened. In fact, he had to get away from this place. Ever since the afternoon his mind had been busy with the problem.

"I'll get in touch with her tomorrow," the doctor promised. "Okay? Then let's go on with your memory tests."

Nicholas made a special effort. He repeated ten digits forward and eight back. He solved tricky mathematical problems with a speed that one of the Quiz Kids might have envied. Dr. Hatch went away very much pleased with his progress.

When he was sure the doctor had left the cottage, Nicholas went down the hall to Professor Wyndham's room. It was exactly like his own, though considerably less tidy. Wyndham was a tireless reader and he left his books scattered on the bed, the chairs, the floor, in an impressive state of disarray.

He greeted Nicholas with enthusiasm, although he was preparing for bed and had already removed his dentures. They grinned up malignantly from a plastic case on the table, and the professor's cheeks, deprived of their support, had caved in. He no longer resembled an amiable chimp, but rather the fossil remains of some prehistoric bird.

"Mithter Matheny!" he cried. "Thith ith an unecthpected pleathure. One moment." He snatched up the plastic case and turned his back.

Nicholas removed a complete Shakespeare, a treatise on early Jurassic mammals, a biography of Madame de Staël from one of the chairs and sat down. "Where's that copy of the *Monitor?*"

Professor Wyndham turned around, looking more natural and speaking with his usual precision. "Miss Blue confiscated it. I fear I broke the rules when I allowed you to see that newspaper. I have had cause to regret it. Your doctor gave me a dressing down."

"That's too bad," said Nicholas, "because I'm going to ask you to break some more."

Wyndham laughed softly and rubbed his hands. "You industrialists! Trying to make your own laws, even within the confines of a mental hospital!" He pulled up a chair. His little monkey eyes were twinkling. "Which rules am I required to break, Mr. Matheny?"

"All of them, I expect. You're going to help me escape."

"Escape!" The professor leaped out of his chair. "My dear sir! Are you mad? Are you not aware of the fact that no one has ever escaped from Crestview?" He pursed up his lips, wrinkled his forehead. "I wonder why? Come to think of it, no drastic precautions are taken." Thoughtfully, he tugged at his button nose. "Mental defectives," he pronounced. "Insanity is presumed to be a retreat from life. Doubtless a true lunatic has no wish to escape, so long as he is well fed and comfortable. If he had, the very nature of his malady would prevent him from making and carrying out a plan. He would make a blind rush, and be apprehended immediately."

He sat down again. With a scrawny forefinger he tapped Nicholas on the knee. "We are not lunatics. We can think up a plan and carry it out successfully." He gave an abrupt, dry cough. "That is to say, we could if we so desired. I want no part of it, Mr. Matheny. I am perfectly contented here. No, no, no. We should only land in the disturbed ward." Nicholas was silent. "Er . . . you have urgent reasons for wishing to be elsewhere?"

"Yes. Given a free hand, I believe I can shorten this war by a year or two."

The professor blinked. "May I ask how you propose to accomplish this miracle?"

"By ending the gasoline shortage."

"Ah! That is another matter. Very well. I shall help you. I can do so with a perfectly clear conscience." He stood up and began to pace the room, taking three steps forward, one step back. "Do not interrupt!" he cried, though Nicholas hadn't opened his mouth. "I am thinking. Useless to attempt these locked doors, these iron bars. Hark! . . . I believe the rain has stopped."

Nicholas rose and walked over to the window. Stars winked down at him out of a black hole in the clouds. A wet branch slapped against the wrought-iron grille. "Wind's changed," he said. "Looks like the storm's over."

"Good. Good. We shall be able to walk in the park tomorrow. Mr. Matheny, if I were to create a diversion, do you suppose that you could negotiate the wall?"

"Sure." It was fifty years since he had even thought of climbing a wall, but if the road to freedom lay that way, he'd get across somehow.

"Let me see, I shall need a bit of absorbent cotton, or tissue paper, something that can be ignited by a cigarette end. The best spot will be the picnic ground. Those pine needles should make an excellent bonfire, provided they are not too damp. If so, we shall have to wait." Suddenly his face drooped. "I can get you out, my dear sir, but what then? Where can you go? What can you accomplish without money, pursued by the authorities? You will be apprehended, Mr. Matheny."

"Sure, but not until the job's done. You create your diversion, Professor. I'll tend to the rest."

The lights dimmed, then came on again, as a signal that it was fifteen minutes before bedtime. Nicholas went back to his own room and undressed quickly. Excitement should have kept him awake half the night, but he slept soundly and did not dream at all.

His first waking thought was for the weather. He jumped out of bed and hurried over to the window. The sky was blue. Sunshine had painted the grass a bright yellow. A strong wind hustled down through the mountain passes, whipping the trees about, spreading an untidy litter of branches and dead leaves across the lawn. No one could have imagined a finer day for Wyndham's "diversion."

Nicholas spent an unquiet morning. After breakfast he shaved, had his massage and his talk with the professor. Then he went over his things, choosing the least conspicuous dark suit and a plain white shirt. Over this he meant to wear his reversible raincoat, checkered side out. When his description was broadcast, everyone would remember those gay checks, but the other side was an unremarkable tan which he could wear safely. Without much hope he went through his pockets and was rewarded by finding a five-dollar bill that had slipped past a rip in the lining of his brown tweed jacket. His spirits soared. Providence must be smiling upon this venture, for everything that came into the hospital was searched for pins, money, or other dangerous objects.

He lunched with the other patients in the cottage dining room. He tried to eat a large meal, for he didn't know when another might come his way, but it was hard going. The food choked him. He was sick with excitement, a thing he hadn't experienced since Robin was being born.

After lunch he went back to his room for a final look around. Except for his clothes, the books and games Hero had sent, and his figurines, he had no possessions. The only thing of a personal nature was Margaret's Bible. It was small and flat. He put it into his pocket and was pleased to see that it didn't show at all under his raincoat. For an hour he just waited, pacing the floor, jumping nervously when someone passed his open door. At last Miss Blue rounded up her charges and herded them out into the bright, blustery afternoon.

The park, Nicholas thought, was rather like a room where decorators had been at work, sparkling with fresh new color, although there was a lot of rubbish to clear away. Phillip's wheel chair led the procession. Miss Blue and the judge strolled along behind.

Nicholas fell into step beside Professor Wyndham, whose bright little eyes were glittering feverishly, though his discourse was sober enough—all about conditions on the planet Jupiter. They sounded pretty grim, what with an atmosphere composed largely of hydrogen and helium, and a permanent icecap some sixteen miles in depth. Nicholas listened with interest, in spite of his nervousness, for Wyndham talked about this incredibly distant world as if he had just returned from spending a week end there. It seemed only a moment before they rounded the bend in the path, where it widened into a circle.

"Shall we stop and rest?" said the professor, quite unnecessarily, as they always stopped here in the course of the afternoon walk. He chose a bench near the pine grove. Nicholas sat down beside him. The rustic chairs at the picnic table were vacant. Pine needles and dead branches covered the open space which was usually raked bare. He knew that the boundary wall stood just behind the trees, although it was screened from view by a mass of shrubbery.

Phillip Corey's "special" found a sunny spot to park the wheel chair. Judge Scott, who seemed to be carrying on a gentle middle-aged flirtation with Miss Blue, escorted her to a bench opposite Nicholas. So far as he could tell, their party was alone in this corner of the grounds. He waited tensely for the professor to begin.

The little man took his time. Having finished with Jupiter, he started on Mercury, where the climate was even less salubrious, hot enough on the sunny side to melt lead. Nicholas unbuttoned his coat, feeling warm in spite of the sharp wind. His nerves were jumping at the delay. It was a relief when footsteps crunched on the path. A nurse walked briskly around the bend. He stood up and called to her. "Miss Chapin! Hello there, Miss Chapin."

She stopped, smiling and wiggling her shoulders, evidently pleased to see him. "Why, it's Mr. Matheny! How are you?"

"I'm fine, only I miss my special. I wish you'd come along to the cottage. Nobody plays cribbage with me now."

She laughed. "You don't need a nurse any more, just a playmate."

Looking down at her round, cheerful face, Nicholas felt an instant of panic. She was a symbol of the exquisite care he had been given for four long months, the security he was now tossing away in order to start a crazy adventure which would almost certainly fail. Suppose he couldn't climb the wall? Suppose they tracked him down and brought him back before he finished the job? Nobody had ever escaped from Crestview. It was mad to try. He'd be caught and put in the disturbed ward. Much better give up the whole foolish project.

The professor's voice, asking for a light, gave him an awful jolt. "May I have a light, Miss Chapin?"

Nicholas felt his stomach draw into a hard lump. He couldn't stop it now. She produced a book of matches and lighted Wyndham's cigarette. He hoped she wouldn't notice the stiff grin which was making his face ache.

"Well," she said obliviously, "I must get back. I just came out for a breather."

Nicholas thrust his hands into his coat pockets. The fingers curled, as if he were grabbing at her, trying to hold on. "I suppose you're someone else's special now? I'm jealous." (God, what an inane remark!) "Is the guy young?" (That was even worse. He'd never been self-conscious about his age, and she knew it.)

However, she just laughed. "He's young, but you wouldn't be jealous if you could see him, poor chap. A meningitis case. They're awfully confining. . . . Glad you're so much better, Mr. Matheny."

He couldn't hold her. She was edging away even as she talked. "Good-by," he said, almost with despair. He watched her cross the circle. Her neat figure, in its immaculate white, moved briskly along the path and disappeared behind a late-flowering bush.

"Charming girl," said a voice at his shoulder. He turned quickly. Professor Wyndham drooped one eyelid. At the same moment Nicholas smelled smoke. He heard an angry crackling, more sharp, more insistent, than any sounds the wind made. Smoke whirled gray and thick among the branches of the pines. Little snaky orange flames licked through it.

Judge Scott was on his feet, shouting. Miss Blue grabbed his arm. The professor took one look over his shoulder and dashed straight at them. "Fire!" he screamed. "Fire!"

Nicholas waited just long enough to see him collide with Miss Blue, knocking her over. Then he ran across the picnic ground and ducked in among the trees. Smoke rose like a great bank of fog eddying in the wind. It whirled around him, covered him, so that he melted into it. He became an indistinguishable part of that tenuous, yet opaque, gray curtain.

# PART TWO

# EXCURSIONS

*Saddle my horse.*
*God for his mercy, what treachery is here!*

KING RICHARD II

# 1

Nicholas halted at the edge of the wood. Above him the larches snapped and swayed in the wind. Clouds darted across the sky, like lean gray fish in a tank of sea water. The air had lost its sharpness and felt soft against his cheek. Directly in front of him a slim, dancing birch tipped the white underside of its leaves to meet the coming rain. From this dubious shelter he looked out across the lawn toward his home.

The place had been built, in what was then open country, to please Margaret, who was homesick for her native Vermont. It was a rambling, brown-shingled structure, surrounded by ten acres of hillside climbing steeply from the floor of Benedict Canyon. Years of toil and a lavish expenditure of money had forced the sun-cooked adobe earth to produce quite a fair imitation of the Vermont countryside, complete with wildflowers, birch trees, and a pebbly brook. Nicholas liked the brook. Indeed, he had been very proud of the whole place until Hero pointed out a few of its more glaring faults.

"Some things don't expand gracefully," she said. "For instance, a shoe that looks charming in size four is simply ghastly in size eleven. The same principle, Nicky dear, applies to a New England farmhouse of twenty-six rooms."

She spoke of suitability. "This sort of thing might be all right in some other climate. But really, dear, in a country that's dry as a desert eight months out of the year, your pretty house and your Alice-in-Wonderland woods look like a movie set." Eight months out of the year she was right, but on a day like this, with wind in the trees and rain in the air, the place should have been most attractive. The fact that it wasn't attractive at all, rather than any belated caution, held Nicholas rigid behind the dancing birch.

The grass had grown tall and rough. Curled brown leaves disfigured the ivy clambering over the front veranda. The ruined flower beds were full of weeds. One of the carefully nurtured hard maples had blown down, thrusting a bent limb through a window in his study, lifting torn and broken roots toward the sky. No cars stood in the drive. No gardeners moved about with rakes and wheelbarrows, repairing the storm's damage. Nicholas wondered if the threatened labor draft had become a fact, taking all the servants off to war plants. Anything could happen in four months in a country at war. Yet four months seemed too short a time to have produced this desolation. The house looked as if it had been empty for years. At an upstairs window a loose shutter banged spitefully against the shingled wall. As he watched, a board splintered and tore free, hurtling to the ground.

Nicholas could feel his blood pressure mounting. He was infuriated by waste. Maybe that was why he hated the war so much, why he would have stopped at nothing to end it. All those proud ships, the fine young lads, the good steel, the iron and coal which could never be replaced . . . It sickened you to watch the earth's good things blown to pieces, sent to the bottom of the ocean, wasted and gone.

He started forward. A wet leaf brushed his cheek, like the touch of a warning hand. He remembered what he was and what he had to do. No telling when the Crestview people missed him and sent out an alarm. They might very well be waiting for him behind those blank windows in the still house. Wasn't it the first place they'd look?

He moved back into the wood, picking his way over fallen branches and mud puddles until he came to a point, just opposite his study, where trees and driveway met. A cloud drifted past the sun. Beneath its friendly shadow Nicholas ran across the drive and dodged behind a bush near the french windows.

There he paused again, quite expecting the orderlies to rush out of the house and get him. He'd been a fool to show himself. Why hadn't he waited until dark? Why hadn't he stopped somewhere to telephone Hero and arrange a meeting, instead of running straight to the spot where they'd be most likely to hunt for him? The trouble was he couldn't get used to being a fugitive. The need for caution was strange to him.

Well, he'd been a fool. Nevertheless, he couldn't stand here close to the driveway, in plain view of the servants' cottages. He edged up to the french windows, which served as a private entrance to his rooms. The study, at least, was unoccupied. He reached for his keys, forgetting that he had nothing in his pockets except Margaret's Bible and some change left over from the bus fare into town. However, he didn't need a key. The fallen maple had smashed a small pane right beside the doorknob. One had only to reach through and slip the catch. Nicholas did so, protecting his hand with a handkerchief. He opened the door and stepped inside, closing it quickly behind him.

At once he knew something was wrong. He stood still, looking about him. The study was much as usual. A film of dust lay smooth and gray on the desk top and the polished floor. Still, the room was not in use; servants were scarce. He was disturbed by something less tangible than dust on the furniture, or even the flat silence, for he was accustomed to quiet. It was just a feeling he had, the sort of vague distress people called a hunch. Nicholas had a lot of respect for such intimations, which he thought less mysterious than they seemed. If you made a habit of noticing, observing, you were apt to do it unconsciously and call the result a hunch.

Overhead the loose shutter banged viciously against the wall. Why the devil didn't someone attend to the blasted thing? Were they all out gadding around? His anger rose. There it was again, crash . . . bang.

Nicholas walked out of the room, into a square hall. His suite, and Hero's on the second floor, occupied the whole east wing. A narrow private staircase connected the two apartments. Nicholas climbed the stair and walked through Hero's sitting room to the long upper hall. He followed the sound of the banging shutter until he came to Joanne's room. He knocked twice. After a decent interval he opened the door and went in, feeling like an intruder, though after all this was his house and his shutter.

He walked over to the windows. Just as he reached them the shutter tore loose completely and went crashing down to the ground. Well, that was that. He turned away, very much irritated. Then he noticed how bare the room was. No bottles or jars stood on the ruffled dressing table, no brush and comb, no hand mirror. His own face looked back at him from the triple glass, all blurred with dust. The place was orderly, impersonal, like a hotel room.

Where was she, then? Had Robin finally taken her, and the child, back to their own home in Sherman Oaks? It seemed an odd time for them to go, when Hero would be left alone, except for her abominable father.

Nicholas went back along the hall to Hero's sitting room. The door of her bedchamber stood open. He halted in the doorway, looking about him, filled with an aching dismay. He didn't have to peer into the empty closets, open the hollow dresser drawers, to know at last what was wrong with the house. But where in hell had they gone? He couldn't understand it. He couldn't bear these rooms, so lifeless and deserted, yet with a suggestion of Hero lingering in the air, the piny smell of her perfume, the electric feeling of her personality.

Nicholas went down the stairs to his study and slumped into a chair. He hadn't bargained for the Rip van Winkle effect. He had supposed that everything would be the same as before he went away. (Get on the phone. Bark out orders. Put your subordinates to work digging up facts. Make a decision. Then tell other people how to carry it out.) Of course he'd intended to work through Hero. Now it appeared that he'd have to catch her first.

He got up and went into his bedroom. He pulled open a closet door, half expecting to be confronted by rows of empty hangers, but his clothes were still there. He stripped off the dark blue suit; changed to an equally inconspicuous gray one. He searched through all his pockets, and even pawed over the contents of his dresser drawers, without finding any loose change. He returned to the study and drew aside the tapestry which concealed his wall safe. He had a bad moment trying to remember the combination, but at last it came to him. He twirled the dial, pulled open the heavy door.

The safe contained a number of black velvet jewel cases and a metal deedbox. Here a pleasant surprise awaited him. Tucked into the fat pile of notes and papers he found a packet of currency, one hundred dollars in small bills.

A fortune, under the present circumstances! He removed the rubber band and stuffed the money into his pocket.

The room was growing dark. Fat gray clouds had piled up in the sky. Already the first few drops of an approaching shower spattered the windows. Was there anything else he needed? Nicholas pulled open the top desk drawer. Among the pencils, erasers, paper clips, he saw a little gray-green rattlesnake, coiled and ready to strike. With a sort of grim elation he looked down at the wicked head, the ribbed tail. It was just what he needed: absolute proof that his memories were accurate, not dreams or lurid imaginings.

He closed the drawer and went back to his bedroom. With a storm blowing up, he'd need a coat. The checkered one lay hidden under a pile of leaves, in a gully half a mile from Crestview. Emerging from the closet, with a gray topcoat over his arm, Nicholas heard a sound that rocked him back on his heels. Voices in the hall outside his bedroom door!

"This is my husband's study," said Hero in a clear, rippling tone which carried wonderfully well.

Nicholas heard the latch click. He heard footsteps thump across the floor. On tiptoe, he moved toward the hall, listened a moment, and went out, closing the door softly behind him.

"And this is his bedroom," Hero continued. "Don't forget to look in the closets and under the bed."

"See here, lady," an angry masculine voice protested, "we don't like this any better than you do. We're just following orders."

"But naturally!" she cried. "And I'm just co-operating with you. . . . Isn't he in the closet? What a shame! Suppose you try the dresser drawers. A bit cramped, perhaps, but still——"

"Now, listen here, Mrs. Matheny——"

"I know, I know. You're simply doing your duty, but it's so ridiculous. This is the last place Nicky would come to. My husband isn't a fool."

She flattered him, thought Nicholas, retreating silently up the private stairs, grateful for the thick carpeting underfoot. Just as he reached the top step a door opened below him. Hero's lilting, ironical voice drifted through the hall.

"Shall we try the second floor? It's full of closets and cupboards. For all I know, there may even be a secret staircase, or a priest's hole! Though I must say that would be something of an anachronism in a Cape Cod house, even one that's afflicted with elephantiasis."

Nicholas hurried along the upper corridor and descended the rear stairs. He passed through the big shadowy kitchen, making for the back door. He had his hand on the knob and was just about to turn it when he saw, through the service window, the top of a man's head. The doors were guarded. He was trapped inside the house.

Cautiously, moving on his toes, he slipped through the pantry, into the dining room. There he waited, standing in the dimmest corner. Would they come down the front or back stairs?

The voices, the clattering footsteps, drew nearer. They reached the kitchen. Hero said, in her clear, mocking way, "I know! He must be in the refrigerator. It's large enough to hang a whole steer, so Nicky might be able to squeeze in."

He sneaked out to the hall, around the curving white balustrade of the main staircase, and into the east-wing corridor. He opened his study door. A dark shape stood in the twilight, just beyond the french windows. Nicholas closed the door softly. His position was unenviable, yet he couldn't help smiling. They had sent a small army to subdue him! He mounted the stairs to Hero's suite. They weren't likely to search the upper story again, but to play safe he waited behind the open door of her sitting room.

The sounds of the chase came to him faintly. At last he heard the front door bang shut. He heard a car move off along the drive. Nicholas didn't move. This might be a trap. In fact, he had no doubt that someone had been left behind to pounce on him the moment he showed himself. Was that a footstep in the hall? . . . No. The house was very quiet, now that the wind had died down. He grew tense. What was that whispering noise? A hand brushing the wall? Someone's heavy breathing? . . . No.

With an abruptness that stopped his heart, a light came on in the room.

"They've gone, Nicky," said Hero from the other side of the door. "You can come out now."


## 2


Nicholas stepped forth into the room. "You knew I was here?" he said. "All the time?"

"Of course. Why do you suppose I kept shrieking about where we were to go next?" Hero came toward him, looking cool and faintly amused. She was dressed for the office in black, tailored and very smart. A silvery fur jacket lay across her shoulders like a cape, the sleeves dangling. She had removed her hat, and the beautiful ashen hair was slightly disordered, a thing which became her mightily, thought Nicholas, with a mild stirring of the senses.

She walked right up to him, slid her arm around his waist, and lifted her lovely mouth. "Darling," she murmured, "it's been so long."

Nicholas kissed her. He tried to strike a nice balance between tenderness and ardor, since he didn't know which was expected of him. Like most compromises, this failed to please either party. Hero withdrew herself. She went over to the window and stood looking out into a stormy twilight.

He cleared his throat. "Ah . . . how did you know I was in the house?"

"Margaret's Bible. It was lying on the dresser. You brought it all the way from Crestview, and then forgot it when you changed your clothes." Her voice was toneless. She kept her back toward him.

There it was again, he thought. She acted this way whenever Margaret's name was mentioned. Nicholas sighed. "I'm afraid I don't understand women very well."

"Don't understand women! If you understood me any better, I couldn't endure it. Or do you mean . . . I see. You look perfectly healthy and normal. I keep forgetting." Hero fingered the damask curtain. "So now we're strangers."

"Hardly that. I've got a few gaps in my head, of course." He tried to explain. "It's odd the way your memory returns. The farther back you go, the clearer things are." Maybe that was why Margaret was so much more real to him than Hero: she was farther away in time. Yet he recalled some recent events quite vividly. Unfinished business! Perhaps it was worry that nagged his mind awake. Perhaps his life with Hero had been so complete that his thoughts of her could afford to sleep.

True or not, the idea helped him. He felt more at ease, less harried. Things were working out all right. "You can help to bring me up to date," he said.

She moved away from the window. "We must be patient, I suppose. Are you cold, Nicky? I'm afraid the furnace is shut off, but we still have electricity." She turned a switch. An electric stove, set into the disused fireplace, glowed red, then orange. "Pull up a chair, angel. We may as well be comfortable. You'd better tell me what you came for, since obviously it was not for my sweet sake." She sat down in one of the apple-green armchairs, close to the grate.

Nicholas drew up the other chair. If that's what she thought, he had blundered hopelessly. To cover his embarrassment, he said, "Where is everybody? I got an awful jolt this afternoon when I found the house empty."

"Poor darling. I'm sorry. But how was I to know you meant to stage an escape, in the best melodramatic tradition? . . . We closed the house and took a cottage at the Lorillard for the winter. I found it rather wearing to run a house and a business too. The servants kept leaving for defense jobs. And Joanne hasn't been well. She wants to take Bunny down to the ranch after Christmas. Dr. Jerrold thinks Arizona will be good for both of them. With you away, Nicky, I couldn't see much point in keeping up this great barn of a place. Charley never stays home, anyway. He adores it at the Lorillard, right in the thick of things."

Nicholas could well imagine that. Charley Van Norman had emerged from the penitentiary with a burning ambition. It was his nature to aim himself like a gun and then concentrate every faculty on hitting the target. He had spent the first twenty years of his life passionately pursuing an education. The next twenty years were devoted to a feverish chase after money. When the chase ended, stranding him behind prison walls, he concentrated on becoming a model convict and shortening his time, only to spoil everything by an ill-judged attempt at escape. That was also typical of the man. He tried too hard. He grew tense and that ruined his aim. Would it be so with his latest ambition, which was to make up for lost time and enjoy himself?

"I stand on my constitutional rights," he would say. "I'm alive. I've regained my liberty, and I'm entitled by law to the pursuit of happiness." He worked hard at it. With the aid of Hero's social position and Nicholas' money, he stalked pleasure as if it were a game animal. His white-plumed head, the pink fleshy face like that of a depraved cherub, could be seen wherever there was liquor and laughter and expensive entertainment, from the most exclusive drawing rooms to the most fashionable night clubs. The only way you could avoid him, Nicholas remembered, was by staying at home.

He said, "Charley would be in the thick of things no matter where he lived. With that single-track mind, he'd go on pursuing happiness even if the Japs annexed California."

Hero stood up. She went to the table under the windows, snapped open her handbag, and took out a cigarette case. "You've forgotten so much, Nicky, I suppose you couldn't be expected to recall how I feel about Charley. So I'll tell you. We'll get along much better if you don't criticize him."

"Oh, all right," Nicholas agreed amiably. He had no intention of quarreling with Hero.

She came back carrying an ash tray, which she placed on the low coffee table between their two chairs. "I didn't mean to be disagreeable," she said, "but you and Charley are the only people in the world I care a damn about. It's rather grim for me that you don't like each other. If you didn't at least pretend, it would be intolerable." She lighted her cigarette. "Besides, that was part of our bargain."

Nicholas, somewhat taken aback, remained silent. To cover the awkward pause, he took up the ash tray and turned it over in his hands. It wasn't an ash tray at all, but a shallow bowl of Indian pottery, rust-red clay with primitive designs in brown and cream. Such bowls were common enough in the Southwest, turned out by dozens for the tourist trade, yet he gazed at this one as if it were studded with rubies, for it brought him a memory that was beyond price.

They stood beside the low patio wall, watching the riders clatter off along the moonlit trail, Robin and that fabulous Russian wife of his, Anastasia. Nicholas had asked them to come on this weekend trip because otherwise

Miss Van Norman would have manufactured an excuse. She was far too sophisticated to place herself in a false position.

For reasons which were obscure even to himself, Nicholas had determined on the ranch as a proper setting for what he meant to do, possibly because the place was bought after Margaret's death and held no tender associations for him. Or maybe he felt that his scheme was depressingly practical and should be gingered up with some romantic scenery.

The ranch house stood on high ground, commanding a fine view. The great valley below was filled to the brim with moonlight. Along its farther edge rose the mysterious peaks of the Superstition Mountains. Hero leaned against the adobe wall, looking out upon all this magnificence, breathless and enchanted. Nicholas, rather enchanted himself, looked at Hero. He'd set the stage. He'd managed to get Robin and Stasy out of the house for a couple of hours. Here he was, and here she was, and he couldn't for the life of him get started.

With any other woman it would have been easy. Direct action was the way, he'd found. But he didn't want any other woman; he wanted this one. From the bunkhouse came the soft, plaintive voice of a guitar. *There is a tavern in the town . . . in the town . . .*

"Miss Van Norman," he said.

She turned toward him, politely. The spell of the moonlit desert lingered in her eyes. "Yes?"

"Perhaps you've guessed why I brought you here?"

"Of course. We both needed a change. We've been working much too hard."

"I didn't mean that." Nicholas cleared his throat. "You're a clever woman. You must have noticed, these last few months, that I . . . that we . . ." Why the devil should it be so difficult?

"I know." She gave him a neat, businesslike smile. "For two quite strong-minded people, we get on remarkably well. I've enjoyed working with you, Mr. Matheny."

He walked over to a table which stood in the middle of the patio and poured himself a drink. No wonder it was such a tough job! She was evidently determined to keep matters on an impersonal footing. He made an abrupt switch in his plan of campaign.

"Miss Van Norman, I'd like to ask you a few questions. Please don't take offense. I have my reasons."

"Of course." She seated herself on the low adobe wall. The silver lilies embroidered over her long white skirt flashed briefly in the moonlight. She was so lovely that he had to turn his eyes away and pause to collect his thoughts.

"Have you ever considered marriage?" he asked finally.

"Marriage? As an institution?"

"I mean for yourself."

"Not since I was seventeen."

"Would you mind explaining that?"

"Not at all. When my father lost all his money and went to jail, the boy I was going to marry took to his heels. That cured me of yearning after love's young dream."

"I see. Still, that was a long time ago."

"You take things hard at seventeen. Besides, I've been too busy. For years I've done the work of two men, at half the pay. I've spent my free time studying, reading, taking courses at evening high school."

"Not much of a life for a young woman," Nicholas suggested.

"You're right. I would have chucked it long ago if it hadn't been the most important thing in the world to me. Almost a phobia, I suppose." She rose to her feet. The white and silver dress swirled around her ankles. "I wonder if I can make you understand? I'd been petted and spoilt all my life. I was no more prepared for snubs than I was for poverty. My fiancé wasn't the only one to desert. They all did, the gamblers and yes men, the bluebloods who cultivated us because Charley could do them favors. If I could have murdered them all by pressing a button, I'd have done so with pleasure. Unfortunately, there's no such button, but I'll be satisfied if I can make them crawl."

Suddenly she laughed. "How childish that sounds!" She came over to the table and picked up a cigarette. "A very adolescent reaction. I might have outgrown it if things had been a little easier. But time after time somebody's son or nephew, or a brother-in-law who knew nothing about the business, would be promoted over my head. So far as I could see, their only qualification was the proud possession of trousers. That's the main reason why I went to Seaboard in the first place. You have a reputation for square dealing and not playing favorites."

Nicholas chuckled. "For once it paid dividends."

"I don't know about that. I've certainly tried hard. After all, I gave up a ten-thousand-a-year position to work for Seaboard, at one quarter as much. You see, I knew that at Franklin-Wright I'd never make a penny more than ten thousand."

"And it wasn't enough?"

"Not nearly enough," she answered gravely. "Oh, perhaps if I'd had only myself to think of, but there's poor Charley. I want to make up to him for all he's suffered. I mean to see that he's happy and respected in the few years he'll have left. That's really what I've been working for. Do you think I'd throw it all away?" She flicked the ash from her cigarette. "I don't know what you have in mind for me. Whatever it is, I shan't let you down by running off to get married. You needn't worry about that."

Nicholas took a turn around the patio. "Hero . . . Do you mind if I call you Hero?"

"Not at all."

"I'd like your advice on a certain matter."

After a momentary pause she said, "Why, yes, of course." She seated herself on the wall, looking up at him, waiting.

"Since Rob married again, my house isn't fit to live in. Stasy isn't vulgar, like the other one, but I'm beginning to think she's off her head."

"I know. If you remember, I was there the famous night when she strolled through the drawing room without a stitch on. I'll never forget the governor's face!" She laughed joyously. "Even Rob was a trifle put out. He went around explaining to people that Anastasia was a little absent-minded. And of course, coming from Murmansk, she felt the heat! . . . I see your point. That sort of thing is piquant, certainly, but it doesn't make for a well-ordered household."

Nicholas said, "She won't last long, but while she does I need someone to keep her under control. Besides, I'm lonely. I want a wife, Hero."

She looked at him quickly, then turned her head away. "I'm afraid I can't help about that. People must choose their own wives."

"I've already chosen her."

"Oh! In that case, I suppose you want me to pick out the ring?"

"Not exactly. The fact is she's twenty years younger than I am. She's beautiful and clever, a career woman absorbed in her job. Very ambitious. She doesn't want to get married. How am I going to talk her into it?"

Hero kept her face turned from him. "Are you in love with this remarkable young woman?" Her voice sounded strange, husky, and rather hesitant. He wondered if she were laughing at him.

Regretfully he said, "I guess I'm past the age when one falls head over heels in love, but . . ." He dropped the silly pretense. "Believe me, Hero, I'm very fond of you."

She slipped to her feet. She walked over to the table and rubbed her cigarette end in a small bowl of Indian pottery. Even in the pale light he could see the flush which stained her cheeks. "I've been stupid, haven't I?" She continued to scrub the remains of her cigarette back and forth, although every spark was extinguished. "When the quiz started, I thought you had me slated for a better job."

The resentment in her voice set him back on his heels. "This would be a job, all right. I'd expect you to amuse me when I'm bored, nurse me when I'm ill, listen to me for hours on end without yawning. In short, I want a sort of combination housekeeper, business partner, and devoted friend. Of course that's a great deal too much to ask of any woman." He hurled his cigar butt into a corner of the patio. With his hands thrust deep in the pockets of his white dinner jacket, he strolled back to the wall and stood looking out toward the dark, distant mountains.

Her voice followed him, light and faintly mocking. "Anything else?"

"Yes, by God!" he said savagely. "I don't want a machine. I'd like a woman with some feeling."

"Don't be angry. You've offered me a job. Surely I have a right to know what the duties will be, and the emoluments. Am I supposed to be madly in love with you, although you don't love me at all?"

"Oh hell. Skip it." He spoke gruffly, but his anger was dying. He began to understand how he had blundered.

"No indeed. You've made a very attractive offer. I'm inclined to accept, if you'll agree to my terms."

He smiled behind his mustache. This was the real reason he wanted her, not just for her beauty and youth, though she seemed very young to his tired fifty-odd. She amused him, stimulated him. Her directness was invigorating, like a brisk mountain wind. "All right," he said. "State your terms."

She had come over to stand beside him. Her arm brushed his sleeve. The scent she wore perfumed the air, like pine needles in the sun. "I want money," she said. "Tons of money. And I want power. I want them for the rest of my life."

Nicholas said with considerable irony, "That can be arranged, I guess. Barring a revolution."

"I want a pleasant home for my father to come to when he's released."

"All right. With twenty-six rooms, we should be able to squeeze him in."

"You agree?" she cried, evidently astonished.

"It's a deal. Anything else?"

Hero didn't reply at once. "Nicky . . . May I call you Nicky?"

"Of course." He bit his lips to keep from laughing out loud.

"If that's all I wanted, I could have married it ages ago. But I'm greedy, perhaps because I starved too long. I must have . . . reality in my life, some sort of rock to build on. One's whole world can go to pieces so suddenly. I couldn't bear to have that happen to me a second time."

Nicholas said, "You want the terms down in black and white. Is that it?"

"What? No, no. I'm quite aware that you never break your promises." She laid her hand on his arm. "Can you stand all this dreadful honesty? Don't you want to back out while there's still time?"

"No," he said, "I like honesty."

He heard her sigh. "Then perhaps it will be all right. Even though you don't love me, if we can be honest, if we can trust each other . . ." She added softly, as if to herself, "Love's always one-sided, anyhow."

Nicholas jumped. "Eh? What's that?"

She looked up at him gravely. "Didn't you understand? I never should have stated my terms if I hadn't been able to agree to yours." She moved away a few steps. Her eyes turned toward the enchanted, moonlit valley. "I'm not a machine. It's just that so few people are worth caring for. When I'm lucky enough to know someone really admirable—someone strong and splendid, a Charley Van Norman or a Nicholas Matheny—why, then I care a very great deal."

Nicholas put his hands on her shoulders and swung her around so that he could see her face. She meant it. Her eyes and the tones of her voice, everything about her, told him it was true. "My God, Hero, what have you been up to? Testing me out, or something?"

"No, certainly not. I meant exactly what I said. I want money and power, only not at the expense of my own integrity. That's a pretentious word, but I can't think of any other. If I hadn't been very fond of you, Nicky, I'd have said no at once."

"My God! I believe you would!" His arms dropped to his sides. What a clumsy fool he'd been! "You were always so businesslike and impersonal . . . I didn't know, or I'd have gone at it differently." He stormed at himself, "A hell of a cold-blooded way to propose marriage."

"Not at all. It struck me as being rather mature and intelligent." She laughed softly. "Though perhaps a bit too dignified. Aren't you ever going to kiss me?"

The moonlight dimmed to a faint orange glow. Rain spattered the windows. Hero stirred restlessly in her chair. "Darling, if you're not using the ash tray . . ."

He looked at the small clay bowl in his hands. Other memories came crowding into his head: Hero, stately and beautiful in her white wedding gown; Hero presiding at his dinner table, charming his guests with her wit; Hero tossing aside dignity, along with her party dress, when the guests had gone and they were alone together. She had been all that he expected, and more. She had never given him a moment's uneasiness. How on earth could he have forgotten?

He set the bowl on the table and rose to his feet. He took the cigarette away from her. Roughly he pulled her up into his arms and kissed her as he had that night at the ranch, as Hero deserved to be kissed.

Her coat slipped from her shoulders and fell unnoticed to the floor. "Why, Nicky," she murmured. "Why, darling, you've come back to me!"

### 3

The stormy twilight darkened into night. Rain thrust at the window with inquisitive fingers. Hero lifted her arm from under the yellow satin puff and switched on the bedside lamp. "I'm hungry," she said, yawning.

"So'm I. What do we do about it?"

"Get busy with the can opener, I'm afraid. Unless you want to risk going to a restaurant. Too bad you're such a striking-looking man, Nicky dear. I've always been proud of the way people turn to stare at you, but it might be a trifle inconvenient, under the circumstances." She turned over on her stomach and reached for her stockings. "Oh, my poor clothes! Did you have to throw them all over the floor?"

"I'm sorry."

"How ungallant!"

"Hypocritical," said Nicholas. "I guess it had better be the can opener, if you don't mind." Anxiety slashed like a cold wind through the warm blanket of his contentment. "I can't afford to take risks. Too many things I've got to do."

"What things, Nicky?" Hero wriggled about under the satin quilt, drawing on her stockings. "This room's like a refrigerator."

He said, "First I want to get hold of Emil Kuttner. Should have done it right away, but you distracted me. I want to see Hanson and have a talk with McClintock. By the way, did he straighten out that business of Robin's?"

"What business?" She jumped out of bed and shivered into her black wool dress. "It's lucky we stocked up on canned goods last year. I can offer you baked ham and asparagus tips. Or would you prefer smoked turkey? I think some's left, although the last cook had a predilection for it."

Nicholas raised himself on one elbow. Strange, he thought, how physical intimacy quickened your perceptions. An hour ago he wouldn't have felt nearly so certain that Hero was being evasive. "Tell me," he said.

She went over to the dressing table, took a compact out of her handbag, and powdered her face delicately. "Tell you what, angel?"

"Why you don't want to talk about Robin."

She applied lipstick to her mouth, very carefully, taking her time. "Let's get something to eat first. We have such a lot to discuss, I hardly know where to begin."

"Has anything happened to him?"

"Why, Nicky, what makes you think——?"

He interrupted. "I had a dream, Hero. Rotten thing. I dreamed the boy was dead and you'd written it down in Margaret's Bible."

She closed her handbag with a snap. "But . . . how extraordinary!" She walked around to his side of the bed and sat down on the edge of it. "Darling, you know I'm extremely fond of you." She took his hand, held it against her cheek. "I want to do what's best. They say you have to be protected from shocks, but, Nicky, I don't know. You're so strong . . . sturdy-minded. I am too, and I feel I can face anything if I know the whole truth. I should hate having bad news kept from me."

Nicholas said in a husky whisper, "All right. Let's have it."

Tears glistened briefly in her eyes. She stood up. "He died the same night you were hurt." Hero walked around the end of the bed, past the dressing table, and into the other room. She came back in a moment, with her furs huddled about her shoulders.

Nicholas said, "How did he die?"

"He was accidentally killed. There was an explosion at the laboratory. Of course you don't remember."

"What was Rob doing there?"

"We don't know. Perhaps he found out, somehow, that there was danger. Perhaps he meant to warn you and was too late. Nicky, he didn't suffer. They said it must have been almost instantaneous. There are worse ways to die."

Nicholas was silent. After a time she came and put her arms around him. "Darling . . . oh, darling." Her voice grieved for him.

He said, "All right. I'll get up now." Clumsily he patted her shoulder. "Don't worry about it." Sorrow could wait. Just now there was room in his heart for nothing but a leaden rage. They had tried to kill him, and they'd killed his only son. He didn't know who they were, but he meant to find out, and then . . . well, he'd know what to do. He dressed, going through the motions mechanically. He knotted his tie with steady fingers. He didn't realize that Hero had left the room until she came back, carrying a steaming cup of coffee. She set it down without a word and went away again.

Nicholas drank the coffee. It scalded his throat but failed to warm the coldness deep within him. He folded the satin puff neatly and smoothed the rumpled counterpane. Then he gathered up his top-coat and walked down the stairs. Hero was moving about in the dining room. He dropped his coat on one of the hall chairs and went in to her.

She was arranging silver and napkins. "Nicky, you'll eat your dinner? It's all ready."

Women, he reflected, always felt easier if they could get you to swallow something. It was their first thought, their surest remedy, in sickness, sorrow, disaster, or death. "Yes, I'll eat." He sat down heavily. "We'd better have a talk."

She set a loaded plate in front of him. He picked up his fork and went to work, as if the food were a pile of debris which must be removed. "I suppose you know what's back of all this? Stuart must have told you."

Hero sat down opposite him. Candles flickered between them, making her eyes shine. "You mean the nicoline formula? Yes, I know, but Stuart didn't tell me. I found the papers in your safe."

Nicholas looked at her curiously. "How did you know what they were?"

"Angel, have you forgotten? Seaboard hired me partly because I had a smattering of chemistry. One of the free courses offered by the Los Angeles

Evening High Schools, you see. My other great qualification was a recent, though not very intimate, acquaintance with Portuguese. Lucky I was never called upon to use it!"

Nicholas said, "Tell me just what happened that night. The night I was hurt."

"I wish I could. After all, Nicky, I wasn't there. I knew nothing about it until the police came and woke me up." She added gently, "Perhaps if you'd given me your confidence . . . but you didn't tell me anything except that you were leaving for Washington early in the morning. Afterward Jimmy Duncan told me you meant to leave from our own field. I've never understood why you were at the laboratory, way down at the other end."

"I stopped for Kuttner, and all the reports and samples. You see, we were going to turn the stuff over to the War Department."

Hero paused with a forkful of turkey halfway to her mouth. "How like you, Nicky!" She lowered the fork, setting it carefully on the edge of her plate. "And then at the last minute everything blew up in your face. But that's not like you. You've always had such wonderful luck."

"This wasn't bad luck; it was dirty work."

"What makes you think so?"

He smiled slightly. "Someone talked. Seaboard shot up five points. Emil got a threatening letter, and before that he'd had offers for nicoline—anonymous, of course. Who do you think would want the formula that bad? Our competitors? Do you think they'd go so far as to blow up the lab, if they didn't get it, and try to shoot me?"

"What?" she cried. "Nicky!" Hero half rose from her chair. "Someone tried to shoot you?"

"That same night," he explained, "just a few minutes before the explosion."

She sank back in her chair. "You dreamed it!"

Because that was the exact truth, Nicholas lost his temper. "Like I dreamed Robin's death, I suppose?"

"Oh, darling," she murmured.

"Are you certain he wasn't shot?"

"Quite. . . . Oh, Nicky, I see what you're getting at, only it seems so fantastic."

"We're at war," he said.

"I know. I thought, of course, the explosion was just an accident. Those things happen. After all, nicoline was still in the experimental stage."

"Was it?"

She leaned forward, frowning a little. "You mean it wasn't?"

"Jimmy Duncan did a test flight that afternoon. We were all set and ready to go. Someone took a lot of trouble to stop us and damn well succeeded.

Four months! We've got a critical oil shortage, people dying of cold in the East, even essential driving cut down. After four months there should be enough nicoline to supply all the cars that still have tires. Why not? It wouldn't take long to convert a few plants, once you got hold of the metal. There's plenty of raw material, God knows. You saw the formula. The stuff only costs six cents a gallon. Why aren't they making it? I was stopped, but where the hell is Emil?"

Hero pushed back her chair and stood up. Her napkin fell to the floor. "Emil," she said, "Emil Kuttner. German."

"Yes, with a drop of Semite. That makes all the difference. You should see his face when someone mentions the Nazis."

Hero said, "Did you trust him, Nicky? I'm very sorry, because Emil tricked you."

Nicholas scraped up the last bit of food on his plate, choked it down, and put his napkin to his lips. "Why do you say that?"

"Because he did. That formula isn't worth the paper it's written on. Do you suppose I've been asleep all this time? Naturally I had our chemists go to work on it. They tried over and over again, with about as much effect as if they were using Coca-Cola instead of gasoline."

Nicholas looked up at her. "What chemists? Where is Emil?"

Hero shrugged. "You have a guess. Emil disappeared the same night you were injured, darling. Odd, don't you think?"

"No." He pushed his plate away violently. "Emil and I were the only ones who knew anything about the process that wasn't written down. So Emil disappeared, and I was left for dead. In fact, right now I'm as good as dead, for all the help I can give you." He slapped his hand against the table. "Emil's disappeared," he shouted, "and I can't remember, God damn it!"

Hero came around the table and gripped his shoulder. Her fingers dug through coat and shirt, bruising his flesh. "You'll remember. You're getting better all the time, Nicky. It will come back to you."

"Maybe," he said without hope. "I don't know. . . . Hero, I chased a man. At least I think I did. He ran out of the lab and I chased him. I had my hands on his coat, and then the explosion knocked me down."

"Who was it?" she whispered.

"I couldn't tell. Too dark."

She released his arm. "Nicky, Emil may have been all you thought, but the Nazis have curious methods. What if Emil had relatives in Germany or one of the occupied countries? Perhaps, in the end, he couldn't bear to think of what would be done to them."

Nicholas said stubbornly, "He wouldn't have sold out to the Nazis. He'd have killed himself first."

Hero stepped back a pace. "Oh! Oh, I hadn't thought of that."

He pushed his chair back and got to his feet. "We'll have to find out. How about Elsa? What's become of her?"

"Elsa? . . . Oh, I remember. He had a daughter. A very intense young thing, with terrific dark eyes and a lot of dirty-blonde hair. I don't know. I had forgotten her."

"She'll have to be found. Put Hanson to work on it, or . . . By the way, where is Hanson? Has he disappeared too?"

"I haven't seen him for ages," she said indifferently. "I imagine he's at the same place. He had a flat overlooking Silver Lake, didn't he? However, I have plenty of good people. We'll find the girl, don't worry. Darling, would you like some coffee?"

"Thanks." He paced the room, his hands dug deep in his pockets. He'd have staked his life, quite literally, on Emil's good faith. And yet he was nagged by that dream, something familiar about the running figure, some trick of movement that he almost recognized.

He stopped beside a window, looking at the dark glass threaded with slanting silver lines where the rain had touched it. If he could bring himself to believe that Emil had sold out, everything else fitted. He wouldn't let Nicholas see the anonymous letter. Why not? He'd been furious at Elsa for mentioning it. He refused to have a bodyguard. (I've taken my own precautions. Oliver's worth a dozen hired guards.) Rather fishy, that, when you stopped to think about it. And not a bad stunt to blow up the lab and make off with the whole business safe in your head, while the only other person who shared your secret lay dying of a cracked skull, or so you thought.

Nicholas made an angry sound in his throat, half groan, half bellow.

Hero, coming in with the coffee tray, paused beside him. "Don't, Nicky. Don't worry so. This is very bad for you." She set the tray down. Her arms went round him. She rubbed her soft cheek against the sleeve of his coat. "Why didn't you wait, darling? That officious doctor promised me a private talk with you. We could have thrashed this thing out just as well, and you wouldn't have been under such a strain."

Nicholas took his hands out of his pockets. He stroked her soft hair. "I had to get away. I've got a job to finish."

"I'll do it," she said. "Tell me. I'll do anything you say. If Emil's alive, I'll find him. If not, I'll get hold of the daughter. By the way, does she know the rest of the formula?"

He shook his head. "Even the assistant didn't know. What was his name? Grant. Oliver Grant. Emil never told anyone but me."

"Or so he said." Hero walked over to the table. She picked up the coffeepot, filled one of the thin china cups, and set it down beside his plate. "I'm sorry there's no cream. Canned milk, of course, but I thought you'd prefer to have yours black." She filled her own cup and sat down, crossing her slim

legs, leaning comfortably against the high-backed chair. "Come and drink
your coffee, angel. We ought to start pretty soon. It will take at least an hour,
in this weather."

"Start where?"

She looked at him over the rim of her cup. After a moment she said, "I'll
have to take you back, Nicky. You must know that."

"Back? To Crestview?"

"Why, yes. You can't stay here alone, with the furnace shut off and no
servants. Besides, they might come after you again. And if you go out, you'll
certainly be picked up."

"I'm not a criminal," he protested.

"No, darling, but officially you're an escaped lunatic. It comes to the same
thing."

Nicholas picked up his coffee cup and drained it.

Hero said rather anxiously, "You're not going to be difficult, are you, dear?
Surely Dr. Hatch explained that unless you finish out the rest cure you might
have dreadful relapses later on? You wouldn't want that. Nothing could be
more important than getting your health back, darling."

He put his cup down. Love, he reflected, was sometimes more hampering
than enmity. Hero's wifely solicitude, though endearing, might be the ruin of
all his plans.

She added, "Besides, what can you do that I can't manage ten times better? I don't have to keep out of sight."

"All right. You win."

Her face cleared. She gave him a warm smile. "I knew you'd be sensible,
darling. We'll have a long talk on the way out. You can tell me just what I'm
to do."

"Sure," he agreed. "How about the dishes and stuff?"

"Ivan will be back tomorrow. He'll clean up. He stayed on as caretaker,
you see, but I gave him a week off to visit his son at Hueneme. That's why
the house is in such a state."

Nicholas smiled, well pleased. Ivan had been his chauffeur for eighteen
years. He could count on Ivan, if the need arose. Hero's cup, he noticed, was
half full. "Finish your coffee," he said. "I'll go get my overcoat."

"Do you want to bring my hat, too? I left it upstairs."

From the archway he glanced back at her, the sleek yellow head elegantly
framed by the carved chair, the slender arm lying on the table, the coral-
tipped fingers curled around the handle of her cup. Each lovely line of her
body expressed repose, yet one of the narrow black suède pumps was beating out a nervous rhythm against the Chinese rug.

Nicholas went on through the archway, scooped up his coat from the chair
where he had left it, and walked rapidly down the hall to his study. He closed

the door behind him and ran to the french windows. With his coat collar huddled around his ears, he stepped forth into the streaming darkness.

## 4

It was an ill omen, thought Nicholas, that his first hours of freedom should have been spent robbing a safe and stealing a motorcar. The fact that both were his own property, while it gave him an agreeable immunity from the police, didn't change the character of his actions. Still, he couldn't afford to be squeamish. When he walked out on Hero, he renounced all the useful machinery of wealth. He was like a pilot forced down behind enemy lines, walking away from the wrecked plane into certain danger, with only his two legs to rely upon instead of wings and instruments and flashing speed.

He didn't know what steps might be taken to catch him. Probably they would not be drastic. Nicholas at large was a menace to nobody but himself, and Hero disliked publicity. Yet she was certain to try, in a discreet way, of course. Women, he thought, always took the personal view. He could count on Hero to be more concerned about her husband's health than about her country's welfare.

And she'd be quite right. What could he do, stripped of his money and power, alone against a hidden enemy? The sensible course was to go back to Crestview and finish the rest cure. He set his teeth and faced the driving rain. How could you rest when your only son lay dead and his murderers went free?

He crossed the slippery drive, pausing at the edge of darkness where the woods began. Thick, low-hanging clouds tossed back the city lights in a diffused red glow, like flames behind smoke. When his eyes grew accustomed to this faint evil light, he saw the car, Hero's long black coupé, parked at the front veranda.

Nicholas ran toward it, splashing through shallow puddles, crunching over sticks and wet leaves. He climbed into the driver's seat. Hero, most obligingly, had turned the car so that it faced downhill, and she had left the key in the switch. He released the hand brake. The car rolled silently along the dim, curving driveway. A few hundred yards from the house the road dipped in among some evergreen trees. At that point he turned on his lights and started the motor. Soon he was off the estate, racing down the canyon highway toward Beverly Hills.

His conscience hurt him only a little. Hero wasn't stranded. She had plenty of other cars to choose from and, unlike Nicholas, she was in possession of the keys. Hero really ought to approve of his taking the coupé, if only as a health measure. On such a night he would be most unwise to tramp about for hours, wet to the skin. Besides, if his memory served him, there was a highly respectable precedent for what he had done. . . . *Go into the village over against you, and straightway ye shall find an ass tied, and a colt with her: loose them, and bring them unto me.*

*And if any man say ought unto you, ye shall say, The Lord hath need of them . . .*

At the end of the canyon road he turned left into Sunset Boulevard. He felt tired, yet exhilarated. He liked rainy nights, and it was good to be moving again, though he wasn't too sure of his direction. The executive in him cried out for someone to whom he could give orders. He reached the Strip and slowed down, looking to right and left until he found a drugstore.

Nicholas parked at the curb and went straight through the store to a telephone booth at the rear. He opened the fat directory and found a sizable section devoted to people named Hanson. It was a long chance. After four months, Stuart might be anywhere. However, if he had moved on, the telephone book was not yet aware of it. He dialed, quite expecting an impersonal voice to inform him that his number had been disconnected. Instead the bell rang methodically. He let it go on a full minute before he put up the receiver and consulted the directory again, making a mental note of Hanson's address. None of the family had ever been invited to pay him a visit at his mysterious flat in town, so Nicholas didn't know where the place was. He asked the druggist for a map and located the street, a short curly one, wavering into the hills from Silver Lake Boulevard.

Outside, he hesitated in the shelter of the doorway. No use dashing out there now, since Stuart wasn't home, yet time was vital. He couldn't squander it just waiting around. Across the street, cars were stopping before a faded red sidewalk awning. This small bustle of activity attracted attention in a street otherwise nearly deserted. Nicholas watched a handsome blonde run laughing across the wet walk, her long skirts lifted unnecessarily high. His eyes wandered to the discreet sign on the awning. Marchetti's. Hadn't he heard the name somewhere? Yes, by God, that's where Robin's blackmailing slut of a dancer hung out!

Nicholas turned up his coat collar and plunged forth into the rain. Marchetti's doorman ushered him into a lobby which was rather like that of some fashionable dressmaker. It had the same air of spurious refinement, the same dove grays and shadings of rose in the color scheme, the depressing naked elegance.

He shrugged out of his coat and allowed the captain to lead him inside. The place was built like an arena, in tiers around an oval dance floor. The air was full of smoke, the light dim and bluish. He declined the offer of a table near the orchestra. It was, he knew, a fine tribute to his tailor, but he preferred a less conspicuous spot and sat himself down behind a pillar on the second tier.

Presently his waiter appeared. Nicholas ordered a dry sherry. "By the way," he said, "you've got a dancer here? . . . Foreigner of some kind?"

"Yes, sir. Antoine. He'll be on in ten minutes, sir." The man started to move away.

"Just a minute. He's got a partner, hasn't he?"

"Why, no, sir. Antoine is a tap dancer. Oh, were you thinking of Pablo and Carmelita? I'm sorry, sir. They aren't with us any longer." He got away before Nicholas had a chance to ask where the team had gone.

While he waited for the fellow to come back he glanced about him. The couples at the near-by tables were laughing quite a lot and leaning forward, their eyes fixed on the orchestra platform. At the moment it was occupied by a small piano and an enormous woman who banged away and pretended to sing. She was obscenely fat, disastrously middle-aged. Nicholas couldn't imagine what such a woman was doing in a place like this. Her voice might have been good once. Now it was ruined by drink and tobacco and age. The laughter gave him a clue. Her songs were the sentimental ones that had been popular when Nicholas was a boy, yet she managed, by a trick of intonation, a flick of an eyebrow, a fleshy grimace, to turn them into something filthy.

He hated her, but he couldn't drag his eyes away. He was leaning forward like the rest, gazing at the creature in a sort of appalled fascination, when the songs ended, the lights came on. She stood up, bowing and smiling, and looked straight at his face.

Nicholas ducked back behind the pillar. He was suddenly very anxious to get his information and get out of here. The man at the next table kept staring at him. Two girls sent him coy glances over their shoulders, until he put on his most ferocious scowl. Young hussies! Ought to be turned over somebody's knee, he thought.

At last the waiter returned. He set down a small-stemmed glass. From under his coat he whisked something that looked remarkably like a letter and held it out to Nicholas.

"What's that?"

"For you, sir."

"There must be some mistake."

"No, sir. She said the dark gentleman sitting alone by the pillar."

"Who said that?"

"Beulah, sir."

"And who the hell is Beulah?" He didn't wait for an answer. "Give it here." At first he hadn't noticed that the envelope was square and a peculiar shade of blue. He ripped the thing open, took out a sheet of matching paper, and read the penciled scrawl. *Come back and see Beulah, honey. Beulah's got something to tell you.*

Nicholas looked up at the waiter's blank face. "The woman who sang?"

"Yes, sir."

"How long has she worked here?"

"Quite a while. Seven or eight months. Beulah's very popular, sir."

Nicholas stuffed the note into his pocket. He picked up the sherry glass and drained it. She might know something. That's what he came for, to get information, yet he felt a strong reluctance to see that fat face again or listen to the husky, ruined voice.

As he sat there hesitating he became aware of a small uproar near the entrance. A rather large, extremely noisy party was just coming in: three glittering ladies, two sleek, neurotic young men, and a boisterous oldster with the face of a dissipated baby under his waving plume of white hair.

Nicholas jumped up. Of the two evils, he preferred Beulah to an encounter with Charley Van Norman. "All right, let's go. Where do I find her?"

"This way, sir."

The fellow trotted off between a row of tables. Nicholas followed, stooping a little, trying to make himself small, for Charley had sharp eyes. One of the old fool's hobbies was target shooting, and he was damned good at it. You had to have a fine eye for that sort of thing. The waiter opened a green baize door near the orchestra platform and stood aside.

"Turn to your right, sir. Number five, next to the last door."

Nicholas pushed a bill into the man's hand. He walked down a musty corridor that smelled of paint, cigarette smoke, and sweat. No one was about except a thin, bald-headed man in ill-cut evening clothes, who leaned against one wall gazing sadly at the floor. He didn't so much as glance up when Nicholas brushed past him. Perhaps he was stunned by the noise of the orchestra. In the confined space of the hall it was terrific, almost too much to be borne.

Nicholas pounded on the door of number five and was told, with raucous good nature, to come in. Beulah sat before a dressing table, touching up her fleshy mouth. Several changes of costume dangled from hooks along one wall. Shoes, undergarments, and crumpled pieces of face tissue littered the floor. Beulah herself was arrayed in a pale blue negligee, dripping soiled chiffon ruffles. His eyes rested for an instant on a huge, imperfectly covered bosom, which reminded him of the pink underbelly of a nursing sow. After that he looked steadily at a point just below her left ear.

She noticed his discomfort. All the great soft mass of her shook with silent laughter. "Don't you mind Beulah, honey. I been around show business so long clothes don't matter no more, except somethin' shiny to catch the customer's eye, and the less the better."

Nicholas couldn't think of any appropriate remark, so he said nothing.

The creature continued to laugh. "Maybe you think Beulah's shape ain't what it used to be, but so what? Some likes it fat, some likes it lean. No accountin' for tastes, is there?"

He quite agreed. "I believe you have something to tell me?" he asked with considerable stiffness.

She left off daubing her mouth. "Beulah can tell you plenty. I been waitin' a long time, but I got patience. Take things how they come, that's show business. When he gets good and ready, I says to myself, Robby's pa'll be around wantin' to find out what Beulah knows."

Nicholas said, "Were you acquainted with my son?"

"I'll say. Better'n you was, at a guess." She pointed at a flimsy door set in the clapboard partition. "That there was her dressin' room. Lita an' me was good friends. She was always runnin' in and out, and she liked to shoot off her mouth. Even if she didn't, a fella can't keep their secrets with only that strip of cardboard in between."

He walked over to the partition. At this end of the corridor, with Beulah's door closed, the noise of the orchestra was not much louder than a neighbor's radio. He put his ear to the wall, but heard nothing. "Who's got that room now?"

"Antoine."

"Can he hear what we're saying?"

"Could if he was there. Why'd you think I picked this time? He's on for the next eight minutes. Take a chair, why dontcha? Push that stuff on the floor."

"Thanks," said Nicholas. He continued to stand. "I recognized the blue stationery."

"Thought you might. That's why I snitched it from Lita. I had an idea it might come in handy."

He said, "Who wrote the blackmail letters? Did you?"

"Hell, no. Lita wrote them letters. But you got it all wrong, mister. She wasn't after money. Lita wanted to get him back." She gave a fat, greasy chuckle. "Poor silly kid was in love. Didn't have the sense to know he was just killin' time till his wife got through breeding. Lita figgered if she busted up his marriage, she could be number four." Beulah pursed up her mouth and made calf's eyes. " 'Robby loves me, Beulah,' she'd say, 'only he's heir to this goddam fortune,' she'd say, 'an' what can he do? His ole man cracks the whip. My poor Robby ain't got no choice but to go back to that sniveling fool.' Lita kidded herself that way. Couldn't stand the idea he was fed up, I guess. You Mathenys sure got what it takes."

Beulah gave him a considering look that turned his stomach. "Wisht I was twenty years younger, or you was around eighteen. That's the kind that goes for Beulah nowadays." She heaved out a plaintive sigh. "Funny thing, the older I get, the younger *they* get."

Nicholas pulled a bill out of his pocket. "I'm glad to have this matter cleared up," he said. "I appreciate the trouble you've taken."

Beulah leaned over to pull off her dirty blue satin mules. She didn't appear to notice the bill. "What's cleared up? Beulah hasn't even got started."

"I'm in a hurry, and our friend next door will be coming back. I shouldn't care to——"

"We got lots of time." The woman hurled her slippers into a corner and shoved her feet into high-heeled pumps. "Don't you want to know where his money went to? Ain't you interested in how he come to get bumped off? Beulah knows. She'll tell you about it, honey. Always glad to do a favor for a nice, generous gentleman."

Nicholas said, "How much?"

"Beulah's awful poor, honey, and not gettin' any younger, or she wouldn't take a cent. Not a cent. Glad to do you a favor, and besides . . ." She straightened her back. The horrible simper left her face. The lumpy features hardened, became still and stern. "Besides, I hate the guts of those goddam Japs. I'm American, a hundred per cent. If you was hard up too, I'd tell you for nothin', and welcome. But the way it is, if I can do a good turn for you, and the country, and myself——"

"How much?" said Nicholas.

"Oh hell, Beulah ain't greedy. Make it five grand. That's chicken feed to Nick Matheny, but it'd help me out a lot right now."

He laughed out loud. Chicken feed! At the moment poor Beulah could buy and sell him ten times over. He stopped laughing and chewed his mustache. If he wrote checks, would they be honored? Exactly what arrangements had Hero made? He swore at himself. What a fool he'd been to spend their time together making love, instead of finding out the things he needed to know.

Beulah was watching him closely. "Is it a deal?"

He shrugged. "Sorry."

"Make it three."

"I'd have to think that over."

Beulah got to her feet. The negligee flopped open, with untoward results. Nicholas lowered his eyes.

"God," she said, "So that's how you get to be a millionaire! All right, listen, I'll sell for one grand. Take it or leave it."

"I don't have my checkbook with me. Could you——?"

"No, I couldn't. Beulah don't like checks. Too easy to stop 'em. I'll take cash, and small bills, too."

Nicholas continued to look at the floor. Would it be possible to raise a thousand dollars in cash, at short notice? Schemes flashed through his mind, all of them highly improbable. He didn't know where to turn. Bankers, law-yers, friends, he couldn't go to any of them without the risk of being handed over to the authorities as a dangerous maniac. He was in an awful fix.

Into the silence which filled the room a sound of knocking fell like a shower of pebbles tossed into a still pool.

"Hey, Beulah! Are you decent?" a jovial voice called out. "Can you spare a few minutes for Charley?"

# 5

Nicholas hurled himself at the door in the partition. It flew open, striking a solid object which proved to be a chair. He slammed the door shut behind him and wedged the chair under the knob.

From the next room Charley's voice came to him distinctly. "What's going on in there?"

"Don't you pay no attention, honey. That's just Antoine. He's always squabblin' with them boy friends of his."

"I'd better lend a hand. Get out of my way, Beulah."

Her voice hardened. "Aw, keep your pants on. It's none of your business."

The corridor was empty except for the bald-headed man, who still lounged against the wall. This time he lifted sad eyes as Nicholas approached him. His mouth fell open. The cigarette hanging from his lip dropped to the floor. "Jeez!" he cried. "Robby's ole man!" He ducked into a runway leading to the orchestra platform.

Nicholas hardly gave a thought to this eccentric behavior. He was intent on getting out of a place where everyone appeared to know him by sight and take a violent interest in him. He paused in the lobby to collect his coat. Did the hat-check girl look at him a shade too closely? Was there a touch of irony in the doorman's suave good night?

He dodged a speeding limousine. With undignified haste he clambered into Hero's car and started the motor. He was halfway to town before his outraged heart slowed down to a normal pace. At Silver Lake Boulevard he turned to the left and drove on at a crawl, peering out through the gentle rain until he came to a sign (not quite so cleverly concealed as most of them) that said Lake Vista Drive. The grade looked steep. He shifted into second. The car hummed smoothly up and up, twisting around snakelike turns, until the road leveled off on a flat hilltop. It ran straight on for a few hundred yards, then went plunging downward on the other side.

Nicholas came to a stop under a street lamp. He'd seen a lot of fine homes, but nothing that resembled an apartment house. From this height the view across the city was splendid in spite of the rain, but he would have exchanged it gladly for one legible street sign.

He started the car, slipping cautiously over the edge of what appeared to be a precipice but was actually a moderate grade dropping away from the light. A wet claybank rose up in front of him. The road made a hairpin turn, dipped to the right, and forked. Nicholas halted again, quite at a loss.

Before he could make up his mind which way to go, Providence sent help in the form of a raincoated girl who was being dragged uphill, at the end of a leash, by two hilarious red setters. He lowered the window and called to her, "I beg your pardon. Is this Lake Vista Drive?"

"No, this is Cliffside. You've come too far. Lake Vista ends at the top of the hill. . . . Hey, stop pulling my arm out by the roots. Angus! Davy! . . . What number are you looking for? Twenty-three thirty-six? That's in the court. You're all right. You can go in from this end just as well."

"I see," said Nicholas, thoroughly bewildered. "Thank you very much."

"Angus, for heaven's sake!" The girl had already been dragged past his car. "Straight on," she shouted over her shoulder. "You can't miss it. Practically all glass."

When he reached the court Nicholas saw what she meant. It was really a double row of houses, one above the other, climbing the steep hillside, with a flight of steps in between. Since each unit had a large studio window facing Hollywood and the sea, the effect from below was very glassy indeed.

He panted up the stairs, pausing a moment at each landing to catch his breath. At last he came to 2336, on the third level. He rang the bell and waited. Inside, the telephone began to peal. There was no response to either summons. Damn the fellow, thought Nicholas. Didn't he have sense enough to stay home on a night like this? Exasperated, he jabbed at the button again before starting back down the stairs.

From within a voice lamented, "Ring out, wild bells, to the wild sky. The night is dying. Let it die."

"Stuart!" Nicholas shouted. "Is that you?"

He heard springs squeak, a loud thump, a muttered curse. He waited, biting at his mustache. Fellow must be drunk, he thought, or else Hero was right when she said he'd gone off his trolley. Footsteps pounded across the floor. The door opened.

Hanson stood there in his pajamas, his face a pale blur in the uncertain light. "Nick!" he said in a tone of amazement. "Or am I seeing things?" He shivered. "Not that it matters. Ghost or man, you're welcome." He stepped back, out of the doorway.

Nicholas walked in. "Did I wake you up?" Nothing, he reflected, made you feel so superfluous as disturbing another person's sleep. "Never occurred to me you'd have turned in so early."

Hanson switched on a lamp. He looked at his wrist watch. "Hell, it isn't early. It's late. I must have slept through the alarm again." He pulled a flannel robe around his shoulders. "Put a match to the fire, will you, Nick? Make yourself at home. I'll be with you in a minute." He hurried across the room and up a flight of stairs to the balcony which ran along one wall, opposite the studio window.

Nicholas found a paper book of matches on a table. He lighted the crumpled newspapers stuffed under a heap of logs in the brick fireplace. He drew up a chair and huddled close to the flickering heat of the young, tender flames. Kindling flared up briefly. The logs caught. He removed his damp overcoat and stretched out comfortably, letting the benign warmth soak into his tired bones. He didn't think at all, just sat and rested.

Stuart called to him presently, "Do you want to come up, Nick? We can talk while I eat."

Nicholas climbed the steep pitch of the stairs. A small, glittering white kitchen lay straight ahead. Stuart was at the stove, turning slices of bacon in an iron skillet. He wore a coarse blue shirt and dungarees.

"Why the disguise?" asked Nicholas. "Or is this a fancy-dress party?"

Stuart looked up with a grin. "How do you like my outfit? Becoming, don't you think? Especially since I've taken off twenty pounds." He scooped part of the bacon onto a plate, laid the rest on slices of bread, covered it with more bread, and wrapped his sandwiches in oiled paper. "Hungry, Nick?"

"No, thanks. I've eaten."

Stuart broke three eggs into the frying pan. "Sorry I can't stick around. We've got a hell of a lot to talk about, but I'm late already. I'm on the grave-yard shift now."

Nicholas sat down on one of the hard kitchen chairs. "I don't get it. What sort of work are you doing?"

"Running a punch press out at Lockheed. Sure you don't want an egg?" He brought his plate over to the table, went back to the stove for the coffee-pot. "You needn't look so staggered. It's wartime."

"But, my God, a man with your qualifications! In your own line you're invaluable."

"Thanks, Nick. Maybe you could prove it to 'em. I can't." He filled his coffee cup and began to eat his breakfast. "But tell me, how come you're in town? I understood . . ." He hesitated, evidently embarrassed.

"If you knew where I was, why didn't you come to see me?"

"Hero said you weren't allowed to have visitors. Anyhow, I didn't know where you were. I gathered it was a sanitarium, but we've got quite a few in California. Hero and Dr. Jerrold made all the arrangements and did it on the quiet, for obvious reasons. The accident was bad enough." He glanced up briefly. "Or the so-called accident. We couldn't hush up the fact that you were hurt. Seaboard went off fourteen points when the news leaked out. We didn't have any trouble pulling in the rest of the stock." He spread butter and marmalade on a thick slice of bread. "You look great, Nick, better than before this happened. They must have fixed you up fine." He grinned. "There I go, stating the obvious. Of course you're all right now, or they wouldn't have sent you home."

Nicholas said, "They didn't. I got out over the wall."

Stuart dropped his fork. "Huh? Escaped? How come?"

"I've got a job to do. I couldn't stay loafing around a sanitarium. Not after I remembered."

"A job? Oh, I get it. The nicoline business. Lord, but that seems a long time ago." His eyes had the strange blankness that comes of looking into another place and time. "Funny, all that afternoon I kept yelping that we wouldn't get to Washington. We," he repeated. "They'd have got me, too, if my wife hadn't died that day."

Nicholas stood up and began to pace back and forth, as if the small white room were a cage. "Who was back of it, Stuart?"

"Don't ask me."

"Wasn't there a police investigation?"

"Sure, but nothing came of it. Not surprising, since we had to keep mum about all the pertinent facts. I wanted to hire private detectives for the job, but Hero wouldn't stand for it. You see, at that time we still thought we had a hot military secret on our hands."

Nicholas stopped beside the table. "I've got to find out," he said. "The war isn't won. Not by a long shot. And there's a fuel shortage. Nicoline's more vital than ever."

"I know, but didn't Hero tell you? The formula's no good, Nick, and Kuttner's disappeared."

"Then we'll have to locate him." Hanson was silent. "Look here, are you going to help me? If not, say so. I haven't any time to waste."

"Why, sure, anything I can do . . . you know that." He spoke with the false heartiness of one who has long since abandoned hope.

"All right. First, you can get a check cashed for me. I'm on the track of some information, but it'll cost a thousand dollars."

Stuart hesitated a moment. "I can let you have it, Nick. Give me a day or two. I don't keep that much of a balance."

"I'm not asking for a loan. I just want a check cashed."

Stuart buttered another slice of bread. "Afraid that's out."

"Why?"

"Well, if you must know . . ." He got up, walked over to the stove. With his back to Nicholas he said, "Hero had you declared incompetent. She had herself appointed guardian." He picked up the skillet, banged it down again.

"You can't get hold of a thin dime without her okay."

"I see." Nicholas drummed on the table with his finger tips. This was bad, yet he might have expected it. To carry on a business like Seaboard Petroleum, you had to have clear legal authority. He didn't blame Hero. In her place, he'd have done the same thing. "Here's the trouble. She's fussing about my health. Wants me to finish the cure." He thought a moment. "Might not be a bad idea. It looks as if my hands are pretty well tied. Now, if you and Hero would work together . . ."

Stuart gave an abrupt, barking laugh.

"Well, why not?"

"Ask her."

Nicholas looked at him sharply. For the first time he noticed a change in the man, a change too startling to be accounted for by a mere loss of weight. The round rosy face was almost haggard. There were new bitter lines around the sweet-tempered mouth. "Stuart; what's happened to you?" He got no answer except a slight shrug. "Why aren't you with Seaboard any more?"

"Didn't Hero explain? I forgot my place."

"What? Don't be a fool."

"That's a fact. I presumed on my position, or so she thought. I'll tell you about it someday, when we've got more time."

"You'll tell me now," Nicholas bellowed, "and be quick about it."

Hanson came back to the table. He sat down and poured himself another cup of coffee. "You won't like it, either. I had the impudence to ask Joanne to marry me, after——" His cup clattered against the saucer. "Hell, Nick, I forgot you didn't know."

"You mean about Robin? Hero told me this afternoon." Odd how the fact of Robin's death kept hitting him in the face. For some reason he couldn't seem to take it in, perhaps because he'd been out of his head at the time. He'd missed all the immediate horror, the grim, slow-moving panoply of funeral rites, flowers, condolences. Maybe that's why people went in for such things, to help them believe in the incredible finality of death, so that, believing, they might go on from there.

Hanson was looking at him closely. "You saw Hero today? Then why come to me?"

Nicholas said, "Tell me about Joanne."

"Oh, nothing much to tell." He glanced at his watch. "I've been in love with her so long I can't remember when it started. Of course I never let on. We were both married. Then my wife and . . . well . . . her husband died practically the same day. I guess I acted like a fool. I'd waited four years. I could have waited a while longer."

"I see. You lost your head and blurted it out. When? The day after the funeral?"

"Not quite. I champed at the bit for nearly a month." Stuart pushed back his chair. He carried the coffeepot over to the stove and set it on an asbestos mat above a low flame. From one of the cupboards he took a lunch box, a thermos bottle. "I'm afraid I'll have to cut this short, Nick, though I'd like to stick around and talk. But I don't care much for absenteeism, do you?"

Nicholas said, "A month! I can imagine how she reacted. Joanne was devoted to Robin. Why, she——" He stopped, remembering the day in his study when she gave him the extortion letter. Her behavior was remarkable for a wife who loved her husband, but suppose she hadn't loved him? That's just how a wife would behave who merely wanted to avoid a scandal, who was only doing her duty for the sake of her child. (Robin loves me. It's hard to fool a person you love.) Not a word about her own feelings. (I don't expect him to be faithful. He's like a drug addict when it comes to women.) Tolerant, detached. Was that the language of love? Nicholas thought not.

"She was very polite." Stuart poured hot coffee into the thermos bottle. "She said perhaps someday when she was over the shock, and we had a chance to know each other better . . ." He rammed the cork tight. "I thought she meant it. Guess I was wrong."

"Why? What happened?"

"A couple of days later Hero gave me two months' salary and the air. The whole family moved in to town. By some strange chance, nobody's ever home when I call."

Nicholas frowned. "You let that stop you?"

Stuart finished packing his lunch box. He snapped the catches shut. "No," he said. "No, that isn't what stopped me. By another odd chance, there weren't any good openings for me in Los Angeles. Several in the East, but I wanted to stay here. Your wife's quite a psychologist, Nick. She knows damn well I can't ask Joanne to share the ninety cents an hour I make running a punch press." He started toward the stairs, the lunch box swinging by a strap. "You couldn't have handled the thing better yourself."

"Stuart, wait a minute."

"Can't. Make yourself at home, Nick. Get some sleep. We'll thrash everything out when I get home in the morning. So long." He ran, whistling, down the stairs. The front door banged shut.

Nicholas stood still, frowning. He didn't like this yarn. Something phony about it, he thought. Hero wouldn't care if Joanne married again. Why should she? And Hanson was perfectly eligible. He was a decent fellow, intelligent and well mannered. His family was almost as good as Joanne's, certainly a lot better than Hero's. Either Stuart was lying or Hero knew something about him which made the marriage undesirable.

He examined the rather untidy kitchen. She had always maintained that Stuart kept a girl here. Could that be it? He looked at the uncurtained windows, noted the absence of a tablecloth. He walked over to the back door and looked out through the wet glass. This door was on the other side of the house from the main entrance. It opened on a small stoop. From the stoop wooden stairs went up the hill and down.

Mighty convenient, he thought, for an illicit love affair. She parked her car at the Cliffside entrance, where it wouldn't be seen by anyone looking for the proper Lake Vista address. If an irate husband or sweetheart came pounding at the front door, all she had to do was run up to the kitchen and down the rear stairs. Nothing to it.

Nicholas turned off the light and descended to the living room. He looked in vain for any sign of a feminine presence. None of the women he knew would have tolerated this haphazard furniture. Indian rugs lay askew on the floor. Modern pieces in blonde wood were mixed up with the awkward overstuffed chairs of twenty years ago, and all the windows were bare.

He walked over to the door and bolted it. Then he went back to the fireplace, took a log from the wood basket, and placed it on the heap of dying embers. The room was getting cold, or was the chill inside of him? He had wanted to believe in that girl, because if Stuart was lying, if he couldn't trust Stuart, then he would be quite alone.

A sound outside made him lift his head. Someone was coming down the stairs. He waited, hardly breathing, for the footsteps to go on past the door. They hesitated, stopped. The bell rang. Nicholas stood very still, so still that he could hear the voices, although they were low pitched.

"Not here, I guess."

"Huh. Wouldn't open the door if he was. We better go in and look around. It was a straight tip."

Metal jangled against metal, as if the fellow were taking a bunch of keys out of his pocket, skeleton keys, perhaps.

"What if it's bolted?"

"Then we'll try the back. Kitchen doors are a pipe."

Nicholas waited no longer. He lifted his overcoat from the chair, gently, so that the buttons should not rasp against wood. Moving swiftly, yet without a sound, he ran up the narrow steps toward the kitchen.

# 6

He woke with a start and sat up in bed. He was in a strange room, a hotel room, by the look of it. You couldn't mistake the cold cheerfulness of the furniture, the determined neatness that resembled a store window rather than a place to live. Nicholas turned sick eyes from the bare glass-topped dresser to the windows curtained in bright cretonne. The room was comfortable and pleasant enough, but he had no idea where it was or how he came to be there.

A telephone stood on the bedside table, with a cardboard folder propped against it. On the front cover, along with a spray of yellow California poppies, was the name of the establishment. He was in the Hotel Winthrop, on Beverly near Vermont. *Every room with bath. Park free in the basement garage.* Had he done so? He couldn't remember. Those men had come snooping; he ran up the stairs, into Stuart's kitchen. After that . . . what?

He lay back against the pillows. (Take it easy, now. Don't try too hard. It'll all come back soon.) He'd been crowding himself, that was the trouble. After the protected life of the hospital, all this running about and excitement was too much of a strain. Better go slow for a bit.

Nicholas opened the folder and studied the breakfast menus inside. After a while he took up the phone. A pleasant voice wished him good morning.

"Good morning. What's the time?"

"Ten thirty-five, sir."

"Thanks. Look here, I'm a little under the weather. Touch of flu or something, maybe. I'd appreciate it a lot if I could have a tray sent up." He waited, listening to the sound of a flurried consultation at the other end of the wire. Finally the voice asked, grudgingly, what he would have.

He ordered a modest breakfast and a newspaper. Both arrived, in due time. He ate slowly, sitting up in bed with the pillows at his back. He read the editorials and war news, carefully avoiding a front-page story about the fuel situation, for he must give his mind a rest. This sudden gap in his memory was a clear warning, like a brief twinge of pain. He tried not to wonder who had betrayed him last night. Hanson was the most likely, since he was the only person who knew where Nicholas was, yet anyone might have guessed—Charley or Beulah or the bald-headed man. Other people might have recognized him, for all he knew.

He put the matter firmly out of mind while he showered and dressed. He felt fine after his long sleep, rested and full of energy. An automatic elevator at the end of the hall took him down to the first floor. The moment he stepped into the lobby it all came back to him. Why, of course! He'd driven straight out Silver Lake Boulevard and stopped at the first hotel he came to. He registered as John Flannery, paid for his room in advance, and went straight to bed. That's all there was to it. Much relieved, he stepped into the hotel barbershop and got a shave. It was almost one o'clock when he finally descended to the basement garage and climbed into Hero's car, but he didn't feel that the morning had been wasted.

He drove up a steep ramp and turned into Beverly Boulevard. The rain had let up, for a time, although the sky was still gloomy. Nicholas looked at his gas gauge. The tank was three quarters full, fifteen gallons or thereabouts.

He drove on, uncomfortably aware that he couldn't get any more when that was gone. At Rossmore he turned to the right and parked in front of the Kuttner house. It looked strange. The rose trees bordering the walk had been clipped back to their gnarled dark trunks. Someone had torn out the Cherokees that used to clamber over trellises on either side of the door. Nicholas rang the bell with fear in his heart. Elsa had loved her roses.

The second ring was answered by a limp rag of a woman in a blue cotton dress. She looked at him in silence, without hope.

"Is Mr. Kuttner in? Or his daughter?"

A fretful, aged voice came whining out through the hall. "Cecilia! Who's there, Cecilia?"

"Somebody for Kuttners."

"Tell them to stop bothering us. I'm sick and tired of it."

"You waked my mother," the woman said in a tone of weary reproach. "The Kuttners don't live here any more. They left more than three months ago. I don't know where they went." She started to close the door. Perhaps his face reflected her own discouragement, for she was moved to add, "If you wrote a letter, maybe the post office could forward it."

"Cecilia!"

"Yes, Mother. . . . I'm sorry, but we've been bothered so much." The door was closing. "Their name's still in the phone book and people get the address that way. I wish they'd get the new books out." The door shut, softly but irrevocably, in his face.

He walked back to the car. Climbing in under the wheel, he caught a glimpse of himself in the rearview mirror and laughed suddenly. No point in being doleful, he thought. If it was that easy, Emil would have been found long ago. He drove on up the street until he came to a drugstore. He shut himself in the phone booth, called Seaboard Petroleum, and asked for Oliver Grant.

"What department, please?"

"Chemical Research."

"I'll connect you."

Ten minutes later, having talked with three different girls, Nicholas learned that Mr. Grant was no longer with the company.

"Where can I reach him?"

After a lengthy wait a fourth girl suggested that he consult the telephone book. "Mr. Grant opened his own laboratory several months ago. I don't have the address, but I think it's in Santa Monica." She rang off.

Nicholas slammed the receiver back in place. Damn these soulless corporations, he thought with a wry grin. He called Information. No, they didn't have any chemical laboratories listed for Santa Monica . . . no Oliver Grant . . . no Elsa Kuttner.

He stamped out of the place, exasperated, yet with his jaw set stubbornly.

He wasn't licked. He still had Beulah, provided he could raise some money. Sitting crouched over the wheel, he put his mind to work and got the answer—those velvet boxes in his safe at home. He could pawn the new brown diamond studs, the old pearl ones, the rings he never wore, the old-fashioned gold watch chains. He drove on toward Hollywood. Rossmore made a jog and became Vine Street. A red light halted the crosstown traffic at Santa Monica Boulevard.

Santa Monica! Had that girl meant the town or the street? When the signal changed he made a left turn, drew over to the right, and ambled along the boulevard, examining every store and building, with a fine disregard for the traffic piling up behind him. It was a hundred-to-one chance, of course, but he was on his way to Beverly Hills anyhow and hadn't much to lose. For once luck was with him. A few blocks west of Vine he found it, a one-story brick building with large gilt letters all across the front:

## THATCHER-GRANT TESTING LABORATORIES

Nicholas drew in to the curb and parked. He crossed the sidewalk, pulled open a heavy plate-glass door. The office was big and handsomely furnished, with venetian blinds at the windows and a thick pearl-gray carpet on the floor. The girl at the desk was telephoning. He closed the door softly and waited.

"Why, no, we haven't seen him," she said. Her face was turned away from the door. He could see only part of a creamy cheek, a fall of dark gold hair. "Yes, of course. What's your number?" She reached for a pencil. "All right, if he comes in I'll let you know." She put the phone down, jumped to her feet, and walked around the end of the desk.

Nicholas said, "Elsa."

She turned her head. For a moment she stood rigid and still. Then her hand went out toward the telephone.

Nicholas moved swiftly. Before she could touch the dial his fingers clamped down on her wrist. She looked up at him. Her eyes, velvet brown like Emil's, were full of hate. He held on to her thin wrist, too shocked to say anything. He had no words, no sort of weapon, to use against hatred striking out at him from the face of a friend's daughter.

Elsa didn't struggle. She turned her head away, took a deep breath, and let out a shout. "Oliver! Help!"

Nicholas let go of her arm, so abruptly that she staggered back. He picked up the telephone pad. The number she had written down was his own private wire at Seaboard. Beneath it she had scrawled "Mr. Van Norman." He ripped off the top sheet and stuffed it into his pocket.

The inner door burst open. Oliver strode forward, sandy hair bristling, eyes glaring behind his thick spectacles. "What's up?" He halted a few feet from Nicholas. "Why, it's Mr. Matheny! I thought . . ." He hesitated, looking at the girl from under lifted brows.

Elsa stepped close to him and began to whisper.

Nicholas couldn't distinguish a word, but he could make a shrewd guess. "That's true," he said quietly. "I was in a sanitarium and I escaped, but you needn't be frightened. I'm not exactly a raving maniac. I just got a clout on the head and lost my memory."

They stood with their shoulders touching, silent and watchful. The air drifting in through the doorway behind them carried a familiar odor: the raw, stinging smell of chemicals, the unmistakable pungency of crude oil, reminding Nicholas of his own laboratories. He went straight to the point. "I've come to find out what happened to your father, Elsa."

Hatred flamed up again in her dark eyes. "Why don't you tell *us?*"

"Hush, darling." Oliver slipped his arm around her thin shoulders. "He just got through telling us he doesn't remember."

Elsa said, "Oh, I see. It's just slipped his mind that my father is dead."

Nicholas took a step forward. "Dead? Are you sure?" The moment he said it he was abashed by the strangeness of such a question. "I mean . . . I was told he disappeared."

"Of course. Certainly he disappeared. A person's apt to, you know, when they get blown to pieces."

He closed his ears to the futile irony of this appalling statement, but he listened to the pain in her voice. Blown to pieces! True or not, he couldn't doubt that she believed it. He looked at Oliver. The young man's face was not so hostile, but it had a wary, shut-in expression that he liked even less.

"We don't really know," Oliver told him in a slow, careful voice. "The police found his car parked near a bus terminal and decided he must have skipped out. They drove Elsa nearly insane with questions, trying to find out why."

Elsa added with helpless fury, "When I told them the truth, they just laughed. What's the matter with policemen? Why do they always have to be stupid, or else brutal?"

Oliver said patiently, "They want facts, Elsa. You had no proof. If your father hadn't destroyed that poison-pen letter——"

"What did the letter say?" Nicholas interrupted.

"You ought to know," she raged. "You wrote it yourself, didn't you?"

He sat down on the edge of the desk. He felt weak, a little ill, as if he were taking a physical beating from her angry young vitality.

She added in a sullen tone, "It said if he didn't stop work and get out of town, he'd be sorry."

"I see. The usual thing. Why wouldn't he let me see it?"

"He told me it would embarrass you."

"So you jumped to the conclusion that I'd written the thing? Really, my dear girl!"

Her eyes wavered.

Oliver said, "You see, she got the impression that Mr. Kuttner recognized the handwriting."

"And you wouldn't do anything to protect him," Elsa cried. "You just laughed at me when I asked you to. 'This is America,' you said. Now I understand. This is America, where a man with a lot of money will do anything to get a lot more. He'll hire a brilliant scientist to invent something, and then kill him so as not to have to share the profits."

Nicholas, horrified as he was, very nearly smiled. No wonder the police hadn't believed her tales, if she went on like this!

"Isn't that true?" she insisted.

"No. There wouldn't have been any profits to share. Your father and I were going to Washington to turn the nicoline process over to the government."

"I don't believe that."

He sighed. "I could prove it, if I had more time."

Elsa's brows drew together. She looked a little embarrassed, a little uncertain.

Oliver said, "That's interesting. Mr. Kuttner never mentioned any such scheme to me. It's too bad you have so little time, sir. I'd like to see those proofs."

Nicholas looked at him sharply. What was his game? Every time the girl started to weaken, he jumped in to stiffen her resistance. Perhaps he was covering up for himself. Oliver wasn't supposed to know all the processes that went into the making of nicoline, but a smart young man who was on the spot and knew his job could find out a great deal. He left Seaboard some months ago and set up his own business. If the laboratory equipment was as good as the office furniture, it had cost him plenty. And any number of people would have paid well to get hold of Emil's formula, or to get it destroyed, for that matter.

Oliver saw him glance suspiciously around the room. "Not a bad layout, is it, sir? My partner, Bill Thatcher, put up most of the money, and Elsa and I do the work."

He was mighty quick to defend himself, thought Nicholas, from a charge that hadn't even been made.

"I mean," Oliver continued, "she's running the office until I get well enough established so we can be married."

Elsa said in a passionate voice, "He means I would have starved if he hadn't given me a job here."

"Starved! Surely your father—"

"Oh yes, Father carried insurance and he had money in the bank, only I can't touch a penny of it until he's presumed dead. Seven years! When everybody at Seaboard was so busy hushing things up, they never gave a thought to how I was going to live for seven years. All they cared about was stopping an investigation. Father ran away, they said. As if he'd go away for four whole months and leave me to starve and worry and . . . Don't you see?" She pressed her hands to her eyes. The diamond on her third finger winked coldly at Nicholas. She said in a low voice, "That's why I know he's dead."

"Yes, I see." The police would have laughed at such a statement, but to anyone who knew Emil it made sense. "I'm afraid you may be right." She turned her back on him and moved away a few steps. Her head drooped; her arms hung limp and discouraged. Nicholas said, "It's up to us to carry on now. That's what he'd have wanted, don't you think so?" Elsa didn't answer. He looked at Oliver, standing quiet and alert in front of the half-open door. "You worked with him. You were in on most of the experiments and you knew what line he was taking. Couldn't you go on from there and work out the rest of it?"

Oliver gave a soft, ironical laugh. "I thought that's what you really came for."

Elsa swung around. Her eyes sparkled with fury. "You don't care a damn about my father. You only wanted to make a lot of money out of him and then—"

Nicholas lost his temper. "That's enough," he thundered. "I'm sick of listening to this nonsense. Can't you think about anything but money? Hell, I sunk millions of dollars in your father's research work. I never got a dime of it back and I don't expect to. Haven't you heard there's a war going on?" He jumped to his feet and raged up and down the room. "The country needs fuel. If I live long enough, the country's going to get it. There's just one way to stop me. The way Emil was stopped. They killed my son, Elsa, and they damned near killed me. I'm not squawking. If a few more people have to die to get nicoline into production, so what? It'll be cheap at the price."

He halted in the middle of the room. Pain stabbed through his skull, blinding him for an instant. He swayed on his feet.

Elsa gave a low cry. Oliver ran to him and seized his arm. "You'd better sit down, Mr. Matheny. Over here."

Nicholas murmured, "Cheap at the price. I've got a right to say that. I'm at the head of the list."

"Elsa, get him a glass of water. Take it easy, sir."

Nicholas lay back in the cushioned chair. He drank the water Elsa brought him. The pain left as suddenly as it had come. "Thanks. I'm all right now."

"Don't you want a doctor?"

"No. It was nothing."

Oliver said, "You ought to go back to the hospital, Mr. Matheny. You don't look very well."

Nicholas smiled. "I'll go back when the nicoline formula's in the hands of the government. When I've finished with the dirty rats that murdered Emil and killed my boy."

"Who do you think . . . ?"

"I don't know. I mean to find out." He added with weary exasperation, "I haven't much time. A pity to waste it snarling at each other."

Elsa scuffed her foot on the pale gray carpet. "What did you want us to do?"

"You might start by telling me what happened after the test flight."

Oliver said, "We checked the instruments and got Jimmy Duncan's report. Then Mr. Kuttner sent me in to town to cash a check for him and phoned Elsa to pack his bag. I picked it up on my way back and brought along some sandwiches. We didn't have time to go out to dinner. There was an awful lot to do. We worked until after three. I got sleepy and started making mistakes in my figures, so Mr. Kuttner sent me home." Oliver smoothed his hair back with the palm of his hand. "I didn't know he'd been threatened. It never occurred to me that I shouldn't leave him alone."

"Where was his car?"

"Right outside the gate, where we always parked."

"Watchman on the job?"

"No, he was down at the other end, keeping an eye on Jimmy's plane. I let myself out. The gate locks automatically, if you remember. Was it locked when you got there?"

Nicholas didn't know. His head was spinning with conjecture, a waste of energy since he had so few facts to go on. The gate may or may not have been locked. Oliver might have left at three, or he might have hung about waiting to shoot down the only other person (when Emil was gone) who knew the secret part of the formula.

"I'm afraid that's all I can tell you, sir."

Elsa said, "Why don't you finish the story, Mr. Matheny? You were on the spot when it happened."

"But, darling, Mr. Matheny can't remember." Oliver's voice was soft, controlled. Was there a very faint tone of satisfaction in it, or just the suggestion of a sneer?

Nicholas stood up. This is where I came in, he thought. Alone, the girl would have been easy to handle, but he couldn't do anything with that careful, enigmatic young man, short of sticking a bomb under him. Well, why not try? He said, "You're right. I don't feel well. Maybe I'd better go back to the hospital. This thing is beyond me. Perhaps we'll never know exactly what happened. Unless . . . Oh, I've got it!"

They stood with shoulders touching, united against him, though Elsa wasn't angry now, just puzzled and unhappy. Watching them, he said, "Best thing I can do is turn the matter over to the FBI."

Oliver seemed quite unmoved. "Yes, why don't you, sir? That is, if you really want the facts brought to light." His face was impassive. His eyes, behind the thick glasses, told nothing. He was either entirely innocent or most annoyingly clever.

Defeated, Nicholas turned away. He went out of the door and crossed the sidewalk to his car. With his foot on the running board, he glanced back. Elsa was plainly visible through the plate glass. She stood at the desk, holding the telephone in one hand and twirling the dial with the other.

## 7

The scrap of paper in his pocket rustled as he climbed into the car. A futile gesture, that had been. No doubt Elsa remembered the number. If not, all she had to do was call Seaboard and ask for Van Norman. Oh well, it didn't matter. Charley was a good guesser, but Nicholas had always managed to keep one jump ahead of him.

He turned at the next cross street and drove up to Sunset. The sky was overcast. A misty dampness in the air indicated that the storm was not yet over. He passed the Strip and entered Beverly Hills, keeping well within the speed limit, for he couldn't risk being stopped for a traffic violation. Anyhow, he was enjoying the mild gray day. After so many months of harsh sunlight, it rested you to see delicate colorings and blurred outlines. In the canyon he even slowed down a bit to admire the sycamores arched over the road, their branches mottled in green and pearl, the ground beneath them rust red with fallen leaves.

He turned into the hill road leading up to his estate, but when he reached the main gate caution sent him on around a bend, toward the service entrance. A low brick wall and a high mat of shrubbery fenced the place at this side. Nicholas didn't drive in, although the wooden gate stood open. He turned the car and parked just below the entrance, in case he should want to get away in a hurry.

A narrow asphalt road plodded up the steep slope, skirted the edge of a hilltop, and came out on fairly level ground behind the servants' quarters. Nicholas paused to consider his next move. Evidently Hero was determined to send him back to the hospital. She'd be tactful about the means she used, but Charley was helping her, and Charley was quite capable of setting the police on him or putting guards around the house. Might be a good idea to have a talk with Ivan first.

He left the road and walked past the neat back doors of the cottages. Ivan's was the last in the row, next to the garage. He knocked at the kitchen door. There was no answer. After a moment Nicholas turned away. Ivan, he realized, would not be here even if he'd come back from Hueneme. He'd be at the house cleaning up.

Just beyond the cottages, road and driveway met. A wide strip of concrete curved through the apricot orchard, passed the kitchen entrance, and then swept on around the east wing. Nicholas took a short cut through the orchard, avoiding the open drive. Halfway to the house, he felt a drop of rain on his cheek, then another. A good brisk shower was falling by the time he reached the end of the wing and stopped beside his study windows.

Everything was exactly the same as yesterday afternoon. The fallen tree leaned drunkenly against the wall. The room inside was empty. He put his hand through the opening in the french window and turned the knob.

Dust still lay thick on the wide mahogany desk, the polished floors. The house was quiet. He heard nothing but a dismal patter of rain, a stealthy rustling among the dead leaves that littered the concrete driveway. He went straight to his safe and took out a handful of the small velvet boxes. Just to make sure, he opened the top one. It contained a ring of heavy silver, set with a square turquoise, souvenir of a trip to the Navajo country.

He snapped the lid shut and examined the other boxes. When he came to the last one he tossed them all back and shut the safe. His first watch, kept for sentimental reasons, the cameo pin bought for his mother's birthday out of a boy's slim earnings, Margaret's wide, old-fashioned wedding ring . . . the whole lot wouldn't fetch a hundred dollars. He might have known that Hero would leave nothing of real value in an unoccupied house. Jewels and silver probably reposed in some bank vault. Even though the place was still full of expensive things, you couldn't very well cart off Persian rugs and Hepplewhite chairs to the pawnshop, or could you?

Nicholas walked out of his study and down the hall. Rugs, he seemed to remember, were not valued according to size. Some of the small ones in the drawing room were costly antiques. He was sorry he hadn't paid more attention to Hero when she chattered about Bokharas or Ispahans. He didn't know one from the other.

He came to a stop just inside the door of the long, white-paneled room. Except for a flat, even coating of dust, the parquet floor was bare. Hero had neatly foiled both moths and marauders. Nicholas leaned against the wall. He couldn't help laughing at himself. Big Nick Matheny, with his fine house, his stocks and bonds, his ranch in Arizona, and his billion-dollar oil company, and he couldn't lay hands on a few hundred in cash, couldn't even get at his own rugs and silverware! What an uproarious joke!

His amusement faded quickly. So much depended on those few hundred dollars, at least if Beulah really knew something. Maybe she was just doing a little chiseling. Come to think of it, that was extremely likely. Discouragement settled like a dense fog all around him. He couldn't see any way out of it.

A sound overhead disturbed the quiet. Was that a footstep in the upper hall? He waited. Yes, somebody was coming down the stairs. Nicholas pressed his back against the ivory paneling. The steps were light but sharp, like the sound of a woman's high heels. They passed the drawing room and continued on toward the front door. Cautiously he leaned forward, twisting so that he could look into the hall. A slim black-clad figure stood at the open door, silhouetted against a gray curtain of rain. At first he thought it was Hero standing there, pulling on her driving gloves. Then he saw the dark hair hanging loose under a small black hat. Joanne!

He was delighted to see her. Without thinking, he walked into the hall, shouting her name. Joanne whirled around. A white bundle fell out of her arms and squashed to the floor. A dreadful thing happened. With a choked cry she turned and ran. Her heels slipped on the wet boards of the veranda. Her purse flew out of her hands, spilling its contents into the puddles on the walk. Almost within reach of her car, she stumbled and went down on her knees.

Nicholas hadn't moved. He stood in the hall, his eyes blurred as if the rain were driving straight into them, dismayed at what he had done.

Joanne scrambled to her feet. She seized the door handle, shook it. Then, with a frightened whimper, she looked back over her shoulder at the handbag, the compact and key ring and cigarette case, which lay at the bottom of the steps. Slowly she lifted her eyes to Nicholas' face.

He cleared his throat. "Damn it, Joanne, I had no business jumping out at you like that. I'm awfully sorry I frightened you." She didn't answer; just looked at him with those big scared eyes. He added in a gentle voice, "Better not stand out there in the wet. You'll catch cold." A little color was seeping back into her cheeks. He went on talking. "I was so glad to see you, I didn't stop to think."

Suddenly she moved, came running back up the walk. Nicholas went to meet her. He picked up her scattered belongings, rubbing them dry with his handkerchief before he dropped them into the black suède purse.

"Nicky," she said, "I'm ashamed of myself."

"Now wait a minute. I'm the one that ought to feel ashamed." He took her arm. They went up the steps and across the veranda. "It'd scare hell out of anyone to think they were alone in the house and then have some fellow rush out and shout at them." He laid her purse down on the hall table and closed the door.

"Well, it was rather startling. . . . No, that's not quite honest." Her face was troubled. "You see, I heard them talking last night, Hero and Charley. They said you'd run away from the hospital and that— Oh, Nicky, how could I?"

"That'll do," said Nicholas. "I don't blame you. How could you know whether I'd be in my right mind or not? Look here, you're not afraid now?"

"Oh, darling, the minute you started talking to me I realized that Hero was right and Charley must be mistaken."

"What's that? . . . Yes, I see." He stooped to pick up the white bundle she had dropped. It wasn't, he observed, a bundle at all, but a child's teddy bear covered with soft white fur. He touched the pink button nose with his fore-finger. "Something for Bunny?"

"Don't you recognize it? One of his birthday presents. I've never had a chance to thank you, Nicky. . . . Oh, what a silly thing to say. Darling, I understood. You never expected to get back from that trip, did you? Isn't that why you picked out presents for the next ten birthdays?"

He stroked the silky white fur. "You're too subtle for me. Look, I was in a tearing hurry. I just told that fool of a clerk to send out some toys and charge 'em to me."

Joanne began to laugh. "Did you, by any chance, forget to tell her Bunny's age? Half the things were more suitable for a child of eight or ten. A magician's outfit, and a mechano set! I thought you must have had premonitions, or——" She broke off, shivering.

Nicholas said, "You're cold. I guess you ought to go home and take off those wet clothes. I was hoping we could have a talk, but maybe some other time would be better." He hadn't intended his voice to sound so wistful, but there it was.

She took the teddy bear out of his hands and set it on the table beside her purse. "Let's go into the library. Ivan keeps a fire laid in the grate, in case we want to come and browse among the books. We can toast our feet. I might even make us a nice hot cup of tea!"

The library, he thought, was one of the best rooms in the house, comfort-able, used, full of warm color. He put a match to the fire and pulled up easy chairs side by side. Joanne took off her wet pumps. She rested her narrow, silk-clad feet on the bronze fender.

Nicholas stretched out too. His sense of urgency was gone, or at least slumbering. He'd been so driven. This was a great luxury, to sit at peace with someone he liked and trusted, talking of children's toys and cups of tea. He said with perfect good humor, "So Charley thinks I'm off my head, does he?"

"He said you were dangerous. Charley's such a fool."

"I wonder. Perhaps he meant that I was dangerous to his plans."

Joanne laughed. "He hasn't any plans, except for amusing himself."

"Yes, that's just it. What did he say?"

"Nicky, I wasn't eavesdropping, you understand. They were arguing and raised their voices."

"You don't have to explain, my dear."

"Well, Charley told Hero that he'd seen you in a night club but you ducked out before he had a chance to speak to you."

"True enough. I had business there."

She gave him a rather impudent grin. "You don't have to explain, either, darling. . . . Anyway, he said they'd have to catch you because you were dangerous. He asked Hero where you'd be likely to go next, and she said Stuart Hanson's apartment."

"I see." At least he knew, now, who had sent those men to get him the night before. He was extraordinarily glad it wasn't Stuart.

Joanne leaned forward. The smile was gone and she was frowning anxiously. "But then Hero said Charley was all wrong. Far from being dangerous, you were the one who was in danger. What did she mean?"

"Hero's concerned about my health. Thinks I left the hospital too soon. She's right, of course, but I had to do it."

"Why, Nicky? Oh, I'm sure you had good reasons, but what could be more important than getting your health back?"

He told her. Before he knew it, he was blurting out the whole story. Joanne listened in silence. If she had interrupted, asked questions, he might have stopped himself in time, but she was so still he almost forgot her, obsessed as he was with what he had to tell. Only when the yarn was finished did he notice how white and strained her face had grown. He could have kicked himself. Hero said the girl wasn't well. It was a crime to shove this extra burden on her.

"Well, that's that, and I should have kept my mouth shut. Only, you see, Bunny's my heir. A year-old child. If anything should happen to me, you and Hero will have to carry on my work."

Joanne's dark eyes were shadowed. "I can't understand why Rob was there," she murmured.

"Nor I. Hero thinks he got wind of something and tried to warn me, but he was too late."

"Or perhaps . . . too early?"

She kept her face turned away from him. Her voice was expressionless. He could only guess at what was in her mind. All that day a vague dread had crouched at the back of his thoughts. Now it leaped forth into the open. "What are you suggesting? Damn it all, Robin wasn't mixed up in this thing. If that's your idea, forget it." The violence of his feelings lifted him out of his chair and sent him stalking about the room. "Rob had his faults, God knows. He was idle and dissipated. You couldn't trust him with a woman. But he wasn't a thief, Joanne, and he wasn't a murderer."

Nicholas paused. His own voice echoed in his ears. Why was he shouting? Whom was he trying so hard to convince?

Joanne stood up too. Her coat fell back from her shoulders. In her stocking feet, in her straight black dress, she seemed smaller, fragile and very thin. "Don't, Nicky. There's no reason to torment yourself. Of course Robin didn't have anything to do with it. People can't murder themselves, and he was murdered." She said this with a kind of hurt distaste, like a well-bred child forced by circumstances into some incredible piece of rudeness. "Didn't they tell you, Nicky?"

"I thought . . ." he stammered, "the explosion . . ."

"Oh no." She clasped her slender hands together tightly. "Robin wasn't hurt by the explosion, except for a few bruises. He was strangled, Nicky." She looked down at her clasped hands. The firelight glittered on her rings, the plain band of platinum, the extravagant diamond. "Somebody choked him to death," she said in a voice so low that it was little more than a frightened whisper.

# 8

Nicholas walked over to a small liquor cabinet built into the wall between high bookcases. He filled two whisky glasses with cognac. He didn't need the stuff himself. The fact that Robin had been murdered was less unendurable than a suspicion that he had sold out to the enemy. Joanne, though, looked ready to faint. He made her sit down again. He thrust the brandy glass into her hand.

"I guess I was too hard on the boy. I wanted him to make something of himself. I didn't much care what he did, so long as he did it well, but Robin never took enough interest in anything to work." He leaned against the mantel, one hand cupped around his glass to warm it. "Maybe if I'd tried harder . . . but I got disgusted and gave him up as a bad job." He sighed heavily. "Wish I had it to do again. Probably make the same mistakes, though. Parents always want their kids to be just like them and get sore if the youngsters turn out different."

Joanne said, "Robin was too much like you."

"What? We were different as night and day."

"No," she insisted. "Actually, Rob was like you in many ways. Some people thrive on opposition. If your family had been rich and influential, Nicky, I'm sure you wouldn't have become an empire builder. It wouldn't have been a good enough fight to interest you."

Nicholas gulped down half of his brandy. "You think I made things too easy for him?"

"I don't suppose you could help it. He told me once that when he was in college he got quite steamed up about aviation. He said you rushed out and bought him a plane, hired instructors . . . Oh, maybe I'm wrong, but I think you were too anxious to help. If you'd opposed him, if you'd thundered and bellowed and threatened to cut him off with a shilling, he might have succeeded just out of sheer obstinacy."

Nicholas sighed again. "I expect you're right. I tried everything else." He said, "Were you very fond of him, Joanne?"

She tilted her glass so that the liquor ran in oily scallops around the rim. "Why do you ask?"

"Well, I"—he cleared his throat—"I think a lot of you, Joanne. I'd like you to be happy. You've had a pretty dirty deal, but that's over. When a thing's finished, better put it behind you and go on from there."

"You mean I'm not to grieve too much for Rob?"

"Well . . ."

"It's all right, darling." She leaned over to pick up her pumps and slip them on her feet. "Of course I loved him in the beginning, but it must have been rather a poor sort of love. It didn't survive the first disillusionment. You see, we'd been married only three months when I found out he was . . . keeping another girl."

Nicholas swore. "Why did you stick?"

"I wonder if I can make you understand. Great wealth is a little like royalty. It puts an obligation on you. I used to read history a lot, and I always felt sorry for the queens, just producing heirs and being neglected while their husbands did as they pleased, but now I understand. Marrying Robin was like marrying the heir to a throne. It had to be for good, whether I was happy or not. Do you see? I wasn't a private person any more. I was a link in a dynasty . . . daughter of Nicholas, wife of Robin, mother of Bernard. Is that drivel?"

"No," said Nicholas, "it isn't drivel."

"I don't mean just the money, so much as the business. All those wells and refineries, the pipe lines and tankers reaching out all over the world . . . so many millions of wheels that would stop dead if we didn't produce the oil to keep them turning . . . so many thousands of people who would be out of a job if we didn't provide work for them. Sometimes I think the company doesn't belong to us at all. We belong to the company." She flushed a little under his attentive eyes. "I'm afraid I have a tendency to dramatize myself."

"No, you're quite right. We've got a bear by the tail. If I can put over this project of mine, it'll be even worse. A lot less money, and more responsibility."

"Why? What would happen?"

"I'm not sure. Probably the formula would be turned over to several private companies who have plants that can be converted, or they might make the stuff themselves. After the war, I suppose nicoline would be in the public domain. In any case, it'll play hell with the oil business. I wonder, would you mind too much?"

"Mind? I should say not. I'd far rather bring Bunny up to tackle a good tough job than to sit tight conserving what other people have built. Although, really, my feelings have nothing to do with it. The country needs nicoline. That's all that matters."

He could have hugged her. The future, at least, was safe. He could trust it to Joanne and her boy.

She said, "We've got to find the missing part of the formula."

"Find it?"

"Why, yes. Surely it must be written down somewhere. Such an important secret."

Nicholas said, "Emil wrote it out for me, and I destroyed the paper when I'd learned the whole thing by heart. It was a devilish job, like memorizing something in a foreign language. I might never remember." He drank the rest of his brandy, but it failed to warm the cold fear within him. "That part of my brain may be gone for good. Perhaps——"

"Nicky! I've just thought of something." She stood up. Her face sparkled with excitement. "I helped take care of you part of the time, when you were so ill. We had a lot of trouble making you stay in bed. Well, one afternoon I came down to relieve Miss Westcott, and she was lying on the floor unconscious."

"They told me I had a habit of beating up my nurses," he murmured, very much abashed.

"She wasn't really hurt." Joanne set her brandy glass down on the table. "This is the point. When she came to, she said you were determined to get up and write something. When she tried to stop you, you hit her. And, Nicky, I did find pencils strewn around, and a sheet torn off the scratch-pad. Perhaps if we were to search your rooms . . ."

"Worth a try, anyhow." Nicholas was beginning to share her excitement. "Here, you'll need your coat." He held it while she slipped her arms into the loose sleeves.

The study was damp and cheerless. He turned on all the lights. "Where do we start?" He looked at the gray film on the mahogany desk top. "Sure you want to help? It'll be a dirty job. I thought Ivan was supposed to keep things up."

"I'm not afraid of a little dust, Nicky. Ivan's visiting his son. Hero expected him back today, but she had a wire instead. The boy has flu, it seems, and Ivan won't leave until he's out of danger."

"I see." Nicholas walked over to the safe. He turned the dial, swung the door back. "This is the obvious place, so it won't be here, but we have to make certain." He took out the deedbox and a handful of loose papers. "You might look through these." He noticed the velvet jewel cases. An idea struck him. "By the way, how are you fixed for money?"

Joanne smiled. She laid an affectionate hand on his arm. "How like you, Nicky! Always thinking of other people, bless you! I have enough, though. Apparently that blackmailer didn't get Robin's money after all. He'd been speculating. Mr. McClintock says some of the investments are turning out all right, so you needn't worry, darling. Bunny and I are well taken care of. Just the same, it was lovely of you to ask."

He bit his mustache. Maybe he was a vain old fool, but all this praise lavished upon his undeserving head made it impossible to say that what he really wanted was the loan of a thousand dollars. He tried, but the words lumped in his throat and stuck there.

Joanne sat down, with the papers heaped in her lap. Nicholas went methodically around the room, looking behind pictures, lifting the edges of the rug. He removed chair cushions and dug deep in the crevices of the upholstery, finding quite an assortment of buttons and small coins, but no papers. Joanne finished with the contents of the safe. Nicholas put her to work at the desk drawers, while he tackled his bedroom. He was thorough, poking into jars of talcum and tooth powder, tearing the bed to pieces, even examining the cuffs of trousers and the toes of his shoes. The hiding place couldn't be very elaborate. He'd been too ill, too short of time, to do anything fancy like ripping up floor boards. It had to be something simple, yet ingenious, a madman's hiding place, cunningly contrived.

He stood still, his eyes shut, trying to think of such a spot. When that failed, he went around the room handling every loose object, in the hope that one of them might jolt his memory awake. Nothing happened. The time between his injury and the brain operation was completely dead for him.

He washed the grime from his hands and went back to the study. Joanne answered his unspoken question with a shake of her head.

"Where was I," Nicholas asked, "when you came down? Was I back in bed?"

"Yes. Well, not really in bed, just lying on top of the covers as if you'd fallen there."

"Could I have hidden it anywhere else? Upstairs, or in the library? Did I have enough strength?"

"I don't know." She looked dubious. "All those books, Nicky! It would take forever."

He scratched his chin. "Didn't I say anything that might give us a clue?"

She hesitated a moment. "Well, you kept asking for Stuart Hanson."

"Did I, for a fact? Now, that's interesting. Maybe I wanted to tell him where I put the thing. Did I have a chance?"

"He spent nearly an hour with you when he came home from the office that night. But if he knew, wouldn't he have told Hero?"

Nicholas thought this over. "I gather I wasn't too coherent. Suppose I mumbled something about Hamlet, without explaining that I'd hidden a valuable paper in the book." He went to the desk and picked up one of the telephones. "Anyway, I can ask him."

Joanne stood up quickly. "Of course I was guessing. We don't know the paper exists at all."

"That's true, but I can't afford to pass up any chances." He began to dial Stuart's number.

She said, "I'll wait for you in the library." Her voice sounded lifeless and cold. She almost ran from the room.

He had no time to wonder about this abrupt withdrawal, for Stuart answered the first ring.

"Nick! I thought you were never going to call. I've been hanging over the phone all afternoon. What happened? Why didn't you stick around?"

"Charley figured out where I was and sent a couple of thugs to get me. I left by the back door."

"Oh, I see. Where are you now?"

"Out at the house. Stuart——"

"I got the money for you, Nick. Small bills. Okay?"

Nicholas heaved a sigh that must have been perfectly audible at the other end of the wire. He was jubilant, not only because of the money (though he could certainly use it), but this was proof of Stuart's loyalty. Thank God he was no longer fighting alone.

Nicholas liked to pay his debts promptly, if possible. He said, "Can you bring it out here?"

"Well, I haven't an awful lot of gas, but——"

"Joanne's with me."

"Oh. I'll be right out." The receiver clicked. The line buzzed vacantly. Smiling, Nicholas put the phone down and went back to the library.

Joanne bent over the fire, raking the scattered embers into a heap. They glowed red; they put forth small brave flames. She stood the fire tongs in their rack beside the bronze fender and sank into her chair. She looked tired and rather ill.

"I'm afraid I've worn you out," he said. "How about another spot of cognac?"

"Thank you, this is plenty." She picked up her glass, which was nearly full, and took a small sip. "Nicky."

"Yes?"

"Nicky, I . . . if I were you, I wouldn't trust Stuart Hanson too much." She said this with difficulty, as if the words hurt her throat.

"Why not?"

She tilted her glass, watching the brandy run round the edge. "Perhaps it's just a feeling I have."

"Nonsense. What have you got against him?" She didn't answer. "Look here, Joanne, I gather Stuart hasn't made any secret of the way he feels. You must know that he's in love with you." She still wouldn't look at him, but she blushed rose red. "Of course, if you don't like the man, that's enough reason for a brush-off, but do you have to kick him in the teeth besides? Was it necessary for Hero to fire the poor guy and try to hound him out of town?"

"Nicky!"

"Didn't you know that?"

"I thought he left of his own accord. And I thought I knew why. . . . Nicky, what's he doing?"

"War work. Punch press or something."

"Oh no! Stuart? With his brains? How awful!"

Nicholas said deliberately, "I'm not so sure. Do him good to sweat off some of that fat. He's already lost twenty pounds." He'd expected to get a rise out of her, but she was silent, motionless, except for those nervous fingers twisting the brandy glass around and around. Exasperated, he went on, "Don't be a fool, Joanne. Stuart's one in a million, and he loves you. I've got a sneaking hunch you're not as indifferent as you like to pretend."

Joanne lifted her head. "Indifferent!" She laughed softly, bitterly. "I don't know how it happened. He was so kind. All those months before Bunny came, when I was so ill, he'd stay with me. We played millions of games of Chinese checkers and Russian bank, evenings when Rob was with his dancing girl and you and Hero were away. We had a chance to get well acquainted. He seemed to have all the qualities I admired. I thought he was honest and loyal and completely fine." The blush faded from her cheeks. Her eyes looked sick and scared. She whispered, "That's what I thought."

"Oh, you changed your mind?" She didn't answer. "Why, Joanne? What are you afraid of?"

She rose to her feet. "Afraid?" The glass fell out of her hand. It smashed to bits on the fender. Like dark tongues of flame, the brandy licked out over the floor. Joanne didn't even glance down at it. "Yes, I'm terribly afraid. You see, they both died practically the same night. First his wife, then Robin."

Nicholas cried out, "Joanne! Good God!"

"Was that just a coincidence?" She glanced at him, then looked away quickly. "Robin was strangled."

"Joanne, think what you're saying!"

"I've thought," she whispered. "He knew I'd never divorce Robin. He waited a long time . . . years. Then his wife died and he was free. People can wait too long, Nicky." She cleared her throat. "They can bottle things up until there has to be some kind of explosion. Don't you think it was odd? First his wife . . . then, a few hours later, my husband."

Nicholas shouted, "I don't believe it!"

Joanne turned her head from side to side, as if it ached unbearably. Tears beaded her lashes. "I don't want to believe it either."

A gust of wind caught the open door, slamming it shut. Lightning flickered briefly at the windows. Far off, in the direction of the hills, thunder echoed like a rolling drum.

## 9

Nicholas looked at her intelligent forehead, the honest dark eyes and dauntless chin. He was beginning to understand Joanne, he thought. She was a fact-facer, one of those people with a horror of self-delusion who often go to the other extreme, believing only what they don't want to believe. Still, she must have something more to go on than wish fulfillment in reverse.

He said, "What makes you so sure?"

Joanne blinked the tears out of her eyes. "He didn't go to Arizona until next day. Stuart had a reservation on the night train. He must have pulled all sorts of wires to get it at such short notice. And then he canceled. Hero happened to be coming downstairs, and she heard him at the hall telephone."

Something flickered in Nicholas' head. Like the lightning outside the windows, it was gone in an instant, leaving no glimmer of light behind. He said, "Well, what then? He wasn't making any secret of it, or he wouldn't have used the hall telephone."

Joanne sighed. "He couldn't hope to keep it a secret. You can check on a train's passengers." She looked at Nicholas from under level brows, her eyes black with pain. "What made him change his mind . . . all of a sudden, when he had everything arranged?"

"I can think of a dozen reasons."

She said, "Stuart knew about the extortion letters. You told him, didn't you? That same afternoon?"

"Yes, I guess I did, but . . ." Nicholas frowned. He tried to remember what Stuart's reaction had been. (Oh yes, Carmelita. I didn't think she'd let Rob go that easy.) He said, "Surely you don't suppose he went into a murderous rage over those letters? Robin's behavior wasn't any news to Stuart."

"Yes, but it might have made him feel . . . well, more justified."

He looked at her curiously. "You really think that?"

Joanne's eyes wavered. "Oh, I don't know. Put in so many words, it does sound incredible. I was so sure. Now I don't know what to think!" She began to wring her hands. "If I've been wrong . . ."

Nicholas said, "I think we'd better have a talk with Stuart. Ask him to explain a few things and give him a chance to defend himself. That's only fair, isn't it?"

"I suppose so."

"He's coming out. Ought to be here in half an hour."

"Coming here?" Joanne cried. "Why didn't you tell me, Nicky?" She snatched up her coat. Her hands were shaking. "I can't stay. I can't see him."

"Here, wait; you want to find out the truth, don't you?"

"Yes, of course, but that's not the way." She hauled the coat over her shoulders and walked rapidly out to the hall.

Nicholas followed, swearing helplessly at himself. He'd been a little premature in supposing that he understood Joanne better. "Can't you give the man a hearing?" he grumbled. "I thought you liked him."

"I do. I love him, Nicky. That's just the trouble." She paused in the hallway to pick up her hat, her purse, the child's white teddy bear. "Stuart wouldn't have to do anything except look at me and say it wasn't true. Don't you see? I'd be the easiest person in the world for him to fool." She fumbled in her bag, dropped her car keys on the floor, and stooped for them before Nicholas had a chance. He watched her in amazement, this intrepid daughter-in-law of his, who could face anything except the idea of being governed by her own illusions.

She hurried toward the white-paneled door. He opened it for her. "Nicky?"

"Yes, Joanne?"

She looked up at his face with that childlike trustfulness which always made him feel such a humbug. "You'll tell me the truth, when you find out?" (They couldn't fool Nicky. Nicky was too smart.)

"Of course," he promised, as if it were perfectly simple. He looked out between the white pillars of the veranda, through a gauze curtain of rain, toward the trees massed blackly against the sky. Already the stormy afternoon was darkening into twilight. Another day was almost gone.

He went down the steps with Joanne. He took the keys out of her hand and unlocked the car door.

"Don't stay out in the rain, Nicky. I'll——" She stiffened.

"What's the matter?"

"I thought I heard a car coming up the hill. Good-by, darling." She slipped into the driver's seat. "Take care of yourself." The motor choked, then caught. Spray fanned up from the front wheels as they struck a puddle in the drive.

Nicholas went back to the veranda. He waited a few minutes under the shelter of the porch roof. Joanne's car disappeared behind the trees. The sound of its motor grew faint, ceased altogether, but no other car rounded the bend in the driveway. He heard nothing but the whisper of the rain, a guttural dripping of water from the eaves. Shivering, he crossed the porch and went into the empty house. He snapped back the night-latch button, so that when Stuart arrived he could get in. He shut the door and walked along the hall to the east wing.

Back in his study, he stood in the center of the room looking about him, wondering if he had missed any possible hiding place; wondering, too, at the sturdy vitality of hope, which can live in the human mind like a bug in a wall, nourished only with dust. He knew quite well that the paper he sought probably existed only in Joanne's eager imagination, fed by his own necessity, yet he behaved as if it were real.

Where would you be likely to hide a thing of value if you were ill, out of your head, yet desperate and determined? Not in a sickroom, for the sick have no privacy. You'd want a spot beyond the reach of nurses and servants with a mania for tidying up, yet accessible to a trusted hand, for this was an object which had to be found as well as hidden. Who would he have chosen to find it? Stuart, perhaps, or Hero. Stuart's rooms were in the other wing, but Hero's were at the top of a private stairway. He could have reached them without much fear of being seen and hauled off to bed. He went back to the hall and climbed the stairs.

Hero's sitting room was cold and rather dark. He walked around a table, skirted the dim bulk of an armchair, and opened the bedroom door. He ran his hand along the wall until he found the light switch. Color and form leaped out of the shadows, as if he had created them with a wave of the hand.

This common everyday miracle always pleased him. He had no patience with those fools who yelped about the simple life while they sat snug and lazy in their modern homes, served in a thousand complex ways by the products of other men's ingenuity. From bitter experience, Nicholas knew what the simple life meant: ceaseless toil, a mind-destroying concentration on the animal necessities, keeping warm and fed and halfway clean.

He walked around Hero's pretty frilled dressing table and slid back a strip of paneling which masked her jewel safe. He had no trouble remembering the combination. The small door swung back. There wasn't much inside: a few oddments of jewelry, a letter or two, a packet of telegrams. He examined these curiously and was touched to find that they were the messages he had sent her when he was out of town. The poor love letters of a man who never has time for such trifles! He put them back, ashamed that he had given her so little to treasure, aside from material things. The packet struck against something lying at the back of the safe.

Nicholas reached inside and drew out the obstruction. It was a cube-shaped box, covered with gaudy lettering and pictures, like the box containing a child's game. In fact, that's what it was, a child's toy, for the label read, CHICO THE MAGICIAN . . . HIS INK.

Funny thing for Hero to keep in her safe, he thought. He turned the box over. On the other side he read, *Directions for using disappearing ink*. The letters seemed to run together. He shook his head and blinked rapidly. *Use only with Chico's special pen inclosed in box. Write slowly and distinctly, keeping the pen full of ink. Writing will disappear within ten minutes. To bring back, warm with the hand or hold under an electric light bulb.*

Nicholas transferred the box to his left hand. He closed the safe with care, slid the panel back. He turned off the light and walked softly through Hero's sitting room, as if someone were ill in the house. He went down the stairs and into his bedroom. Margaret's Bible lay on the dresser where he had left it the day before, after he changed his clothes. Still walking softly, he entered his study and sat down at the desk. He pushed the telephone aside, placed Bible and ink bottle in front of him. He switched on the strong desk lamp.

With hands that shook a little, he turned the pages of the Family Record until he came to the deaths. He held the sheet close to the light. Nothing happened. He was beginning to breathe less painfully, when he saw a faint discoloration on the white page. Pale, creamy hen tracks appeared. They grew darker; they spread and became letters, traced slowly and distinctly in Hero's firm, upright hand. *Robin Matheny, August 29, 1943.*

The Bible fell out of his hands. It dropped to the floor with a protesting thump, as books will when they are ill-used. Why had she done it? He remembered her strange behavior that afternoon in his room at Crestview. She had been affectionate, concerned for his comfort. She had given him the Bible reluctantly, as if forced by some strong compulsion. But why? To give him a shock, to hold back his recovery? He could think of no other reason.

With the instinctive movement of long habit, Nicholas reached across the desk for the cigars which were not there. He pulled out the drawers, one after another, and rummaged through them. He couldn't even find a bit of plasticene to occupy his fingers, except for the small coiled rattlesnake. He picked it up and slammed the drawer shut.

The flat, narrow head stared up at him without malevolence. After all, a rattlesnake attacked only when its life was threatened. Any creature can turn violent in self-defense. Was that it? Did Hero feel herself threatened? (I want money. I want power.) Well, she had both. So long as he was confined at Crestview, she had absolute control over Seaboard. If her chemists worked out the rest of the nicoline formula, she could use it for Seaboard's private profit. (I'm greedy. Perhaps because I starved too long.) If they failed, the secret would be locked up with Nicholas in a mental hospital, where it need not harm the company's interests. But she had to keep him there until the war was over. (Do they treat you well, Nicky? Is the food all right, the bed comfortable? You're not unhappy, are you?)

Poor Hero, he thought. Poor girl, torn between her love for him and the terrible, lashing drive of her ambition! His fingers closed on the small green snake. The clay was dry, now, and brittle. It broke in his hand, cracking right through the center. Yet the two halves did not fall apart. They were held together by a core of something white and tough.

Nicholas stripped off the plasticene, revealing a tightly rolled bit of paper which had been worked into the broad, flat base of the snake's coils. His heart pounded with excitement; his ears sang. He unrolled the paper and spread it out under the light.

One glance was enough. He began to laugh, softly at first, then with a violence that hurt his throat. He'd found it, and it wasn't a damn bit of good to him. Seaboard had the rest of the formula, and Seaboard was Hero. He couldn't do a thing without her help, and he knew beyond any possible doubt that he'd never get it.

The biting irony of his position struck him like a blow in the face. Feeling weak, a little dizzy, he slumped back in his chair. This abrupt movement very probably saved his life. He heard the sound of a shot. A bullet bored through the window, shattering the light bulb a foot away from his head. Darkness poured into the room.

He started up blindly. The desk lamp smacked against his forehead. Nicholas staggered. His foot caught on the chair leg and he fell sprawling, half stunned.

*The second bullet crashed into the window. Broken glass tinkled down on the brick steps. A siren screamed. He was running, running after a man who fled through the darkness. Rage gave speed to his legs. Fury kept his tired heart going until the earth heaved under him.*

He lay still where he had fallen. The air was gray with dawn, or was it twilight? His eyes felt gritty, as if they were full of dust. Someone bent over him. He lifted his hand. His fingers closed on a loose fold of cloth, rough and substantial like tweed.

"Hanson," he said, "what the hell are you doing here?"

**PART THREE**

# RETREAT

*I prithee,*
*Harry, withdraw thyself; thou bleed'st too much.*

KING HENRY IV

# 1

The room was filled with a gentle rosy light from the lamp on the bedside table. The pillows were soft under his head. A down quilt covered him from foot to chin. The door stood open. Along the hall, as if poured through a funnel, came the sound of voices which had aroused him.

"Hanson! What are you doing here? How did you get in?"

"Same way you did, Charley, through the front door."

Nicholas pushed back the quilt and swung his legs off the bed. His mind was playing tricks on him again. He seemed to hear those words repeated over and over. *Hanson, what are you doing here? Hanson . . .*

He stood up. His head throbbed. What the devil had happened to him? Oh yes, he'd had that dream again, and just before . . . Good God, the nicoline formula! He hastened into his study. Enough light came through the bedroom doorway to reveal the overturned chair, the desk lamp lying smashed on the floor. So it wasn't a dream, at least not all of it. Someone had tried to shoot him. The knowledge was steadying. He could face real bullets with more aplomb than the vague terrors that lived only in his mind.

Those angry voices pursued him into the study.

"I don't have to explain what I'm doing in my own home. It's different with you, Hanson. A discharged employee! I've a good mind to call the police."

"You and who else, Charley?"

Nicholas walked over to the desk. For an instant he thought the formula was gone. Then he saw it lying beside Margaret's Bible, a slender white tube, rather like a cigarette. The paper, tightly rolled for so many months, had curled back into shape. He thrust it into his vest pocket.

At once he began to worry. Suppose he were caught and taken back to Crestview, his clothes searched, the scrap of paper lost or burned? Just at the thought, cold sweat started out all over his body. What if he got killed? That fellow who kept taking pot shots at him might be luckier next time. The little tube of paper began to feel like a stick of dynamite in his pocket.

Charley's voice stabbed through his anxiety. "I saw a light in Nick's room when I came up the drive. Is he here? I want to see him."

"Nick? I thought he was in the hospital."

"What's the use of lying, Hanson? We know he was at your place last night."

"That so? It's news to me."

Nicholas walked around to the other side of the desk. He righted the chair, sat down, rummaged through the drawers for paper and envelopes. His inkwell was dry, but he found an indelible pencil. He wrote:

**MRS. ROBIN MATHENY:**

*Inclosed find part of the Kuttner formula K-37 (nicoline). Get the remainder from Seaboard Petroleum, Dept. of Chemical Research, and deliver the complete formula to the Fuel Administrator, or the War Department. This letter authorizes you to act for me in all matters pertaining to the above formula.*

*(Signed)* NICHOLAS MATHENY

He dated the letter August 28, 1943, the day before his accident, hoping to God there was no way to determine the age of indelible pencil markings. On a separate sheet he wrote:

**DEAR JOANNE:**

*I'm sorry to put this responsibility on you, but I can't see any other way. You must attend to it yourself. Trust no one, not even Hero. Please try to do something for Elsa Kuttner. She is destitute, working for Thatcher-Grant laboratories. Don't be too hard on Stuart. I think you're wrong about him. God bless you and the boy.*

NICKY

He put both letters and the precious tube of paper into an envelope and sealed it down. On the outside he wrote, *For Joanne. To be opened in the event of my death or incarceration.*

He got the safe open, with some difficulty because it was in a dark corner and he dared not switch on a light. He stuffed the envelope into his deedbox, underneath the other papers. He closed the door, replaced the tapestry. After a moment's thought he went back to his desk, wrote down the combination, and addressed another envelope to Joanne at the Hotel Lorillard. This one he slipped into his coat pocket. If anything happened to him, someone would probably see that she got it.

Nicholas took a deep breath and started for the hall door. This time he didn't mean to run away. A radical change had taken place. His mind was no longer the sole repository of an important secret. They couldn't destroy nicoline just by getting rid of him. The most urgent part of his job was done. Now he could afford to take chances.

In the hall he was met by voices that were like flying fists. "Get out of my way, Hanson. I know he's in there, and I intend to see him." . . . "You stay where you are, or you'll get hurt."

Nicholas went softly up the private stair, past the door of Hero's sitting room, into the long upper hall. At the top of the main staircase he paused. Light blazed from the crystal chandelier, gleaming white on the paneled walls, yellow on the polished oak floor. Against all this brilliance Charley stood like a silhouette in his long black overcoat, his shock of hair waving defiance. Stuart faced him, looking solid and formidable in his brown tweeds. He had taken up a position near the entrance to the east wing, between Charley and the hall telephone.

Nicholas moved quietly down the curving stair. Halfway down, he paused again. "What do you want with me, Charley?"

The blond head and the white one both jerked around. Two pairs of eyes looked up, startled. Charley had a smile on his face, but that didn't mean anything. He was so set on being jolly that he'd adopted a perpetual grin. Nicholas often wondered if he took it off even when he went to bed.

"Nick!" he cried. "I knew you must be here, but this madman wouldn't let me see you."

"How did you know?"

"What? Oh, feminine intuition." Charley laughed. "Not mine, Hero's. She said you'd come back here. After all, where else could you go?"

Nicholas descended another step. "You've chased me all over town. I want to know why."

Charley's grin turned deprecating. "Why, Nick, old man, surely that's obvious? You're not well. We have to get you back to the hospital before you do yourself a serious injury."

Stuart said, "Just the famous Van Norman altruism."

"Now, look here, Hanson, no need for that. You can't realize what bad shape Nick's in, or you'd be with me. Do you know what they told us? He's likely to have relapses, if he doesn't get proper care. Epilepsy, or paranoia . . . no telling what might develop. If you have any regard for Nick at all, you'll help me persuade him to go back."

Stuart looked up at Nicholas. "Is he lying?"

"No, but I figured it was worth the risk."

Charley lifted a pale, well-manicured hand to adjust the white scarf folded about his throat. "Nothing could be worth such a risk. I don't understand you, Nick. Haven't you any consideration for Hero? Good Lord, man, she doesn't want her husband shut up in an asylum for the rest of his life!"

"No," said Nicholas, "only for the duration."

The fixed grin wavered. "What do you mean by that?" He started toward the staircase. Stuart moved too, just enough to block the way. Both men halted, as if this change of position had been a figure in some slow, stately dance.

Charley got his smile back. "You know," he said pleasantly, "I'm beginning to think you have an ax to grind, Hanson. Maybe it's to your interest for Nicky to kill himself or go off his head again."

"Sure. It's swell for me, having Hero in the saddle." Stuart laughed ironically. "I'm nuts about running a punch press, at ninety cents an hour."

Charley unbuttoned his coat. He drew a fine linen handkerchief from his breast pocket and wiped the palms of his hands. "Nick, old man"—his voice became appealing—"don't pay any attention to this fellow. He thinks he's got a grievance, but I ask you, when a man is incompetent and has to be discharged——"

Nicholas said, "I know why Hanson was fired."

"You know? In that case, I shouldn't think you'd want to have anything to do with him."

Nicholas moved down the stairs. He halted a short distance from the bottom. "What do you want, Charley?"

"I told you." He shifted from one foot to the other. Stuart took a step forward. Charley continued to smile, but his eyes grew wary. "I don't know what's got into you, Nick. I'm afraid you're not yourself. My poor girl's nearly out of her mind, too, worrying about you. As if she didn't have enough trouble already, handling the business! I promised her I'd get you back to Crestview safe and sound. Why be stubborn, Nick? Why put all this extra burden on Hero?" His voice became soft, wheedling. "You know she thinks the world of you. All she wants is for you to get well. Is that asking too much? Hero would do anything for you."

"Would she?"

"Of course. And I think you might do this one small thing for her." He slipped the handkerchief back in his pocket, with an air of finality, as if he had disposed of the argument. "Well, how about it, old man? Shall we get started?"

"No," said Nicholas.

Charley dropped his wheedling manner. He turned brisk. "I know what's bothering you. The business. But honestly, Nick, you couldn't do any more than we're doing. Hero says you're all upset about the war effort, but I assure you, we're doing our part. We brought in two new wells in the Del Rey field last week," he said energetically. "We've let loose all our trade secrets, even the Brompton process for hundred-octane. We've kept all our stripper wells going at a staggering loss, and we're going to drill in the Sunnyvale field, although it's ten to one against bringing in any profitable wells there. What more could anyone do?"

" 'We'?" said Nicholas. "What the hell do you mean, 'we'? You've got nothing to do with Seaboard."

"Why, yes, I have, Nick. As a matter of fact, I've been helping out. You left things in pretty bad shape. Frankly, buying in the stock at a premium was a terrible mistake, especially at this time. What got into you? Somebody had to straighten out the muddle, so Hero put me in charge of finances."

Nicholas came down to the foot of the stairs. He said, "Hero put *you* in charge of finances?"

"Well, certainly. I know my stuff, and Hero had to have someone she could trust. Suppose it ever got out that Seaboard was shaky? I've got a job on my hands as it is, with the losses we've been taking, and no capital, and the surtaxes." He thrust both hands through his hair. "My God! The taxes!" he cried in a tone of genuine agony. "More than ninety per cent!"

"We're fighting an expensive war," said Nicholas.

"That's no excuse for confiscating private property. If I couldn't find ways to get around it, we might very easily go to the wall. But you've no idea what a lot of juggling I have to do."

Nicholas moved forward. He could feel the muscles of his face contract in what might have been taken for a smile but was really a grimace of intolerable rage. "You've been doctoring the books to beat the income tax?"

"Certainly I have. This crazy tax law doesn't give us any choice. It's that or go broke. But you don't have to worry, Nick. I'll keep Seaboard off the rocks, and the Treasury experts won't ever catch up with me, either. I know a trick or two they never heard of."

Nicholas said, "You thief." His arm shot out. His fist crashed into the smug, grinning mouth. Charley staggered. His arms flew up. "You jailbird." Nicholas hit him again. He went down, collapsed in a heap on the floor, and lay still.

## 2

"That's enough. Here, you can't kick a man when he's down."

Nicholas tried to jerk away, but Stuart held fast to his arm. "I built it," he stormed, almost sobbing with fury. "I built it right. Oil stinks, they used to say, but not Seaboard. Not my company. There isn't a man on earth can claim I ever cheated him out of a single penny."

"That's so, Nick. Everybody knows you're straight as a die. Calm down, now."

"Income-tax evasion, by God!" Nicholas shouted. "He couldn't have thought up anything worse. Cheating the government, when we're up to our necks in war! Let me go, Hanson."

"No, that's enough. It won't help matters to kill him."

Nicholas felt a stab of pain go through his skull. He left off struggling. His knees trembled. The angry blood roared in his ears. "Stuart," he said in a quieter voice, "Hero didn't know. She wouldn't stand for that."

"Nick, you'd better sit down. Let's go in the library where it's warm."

Nicholas allowed himself to be helped across the hall. He dropped into an armchair, panting for breath. Stuart piled logs on the dying fire. He took the hearth broom and swept up the scattered pieces of Joanne's broken glass. He fetched brandy from the liquor cabinet. "How about a spot of cognac? Do you good, Nick. I guess I'd better go see if you cracked any important bones." He went out to the hall.

Nicholas lay back in the chair and closed his eyes, but his thoughts would not relax. They raced about like hunting dogs trying to pick up a scent. He had to prevent that crook from ruining Seaboard, but how? Even if he could bring himself to inform against his own company, no one would pay any attention to an escaped lunatic, beyond getting the poor devil sent back to the asylum. He had no authority to dismiss the man. His only hope was an appeal to Hero. She must be ignorant of what was going on. Quite aside from moral scruples, she was too shrewd a businesswoman to commit a fraud which would certainly be discovered sooner or later and drastically punished. Yet where Charley was concerned she was blind, infatuated, unlikely to believe anything against him. Nicholas set his jaw obstinately. He'd find some way to convince her.

Stuart came back from the hall. "He's all right. Sleeping peacefully."

Nicholas put his empty glass down on the table and got to his feet. "Let's go, before he comes to."

"Where, Nick?"

"Marchetti's, first of all."

Hanson blinked. "That's a night club, isn't it?"

"Right." Nicholas put on his overcoat.

"Well, you're the boss. Oh, wait a minute; that's the joint where Rob's girl used to dance, isn't it? What do we do there?"

"We give your thousand dollars to a disreputable woman named Beulah." He walked through the hall without a glance at the black-clad figure huddled on the floor.

Stuart followed him, shrugging into his coat. "For value received, I hope?"

"I hope so too." Nicholas opened the door and stepped out on the veranda. The rain was over. A fresh cold wind drove masses of cloud hurrying across a sky which was almost black, yet translucent, like deep ocean water patterned with swirling foam. He looked at his watch. A quarter to seven! It couldn't have been much after four when Joanne left. He said, "Did I pass out for a while?"

"You took a nap while I was searching the grounds."

"Oh. Did you find anything?"

Stuart turned to close the door behind him. He said, in a carefully noncommittal voice, "Hero's car was parked at the service entrance."

"Yes, I know. I left it there. Had to have a car, so I helped myself to the Packard last night."

"So that's it. I was wondering. We can use mine for this expedition. Then I'll bring you back here to pick up the Packard before I go on to work."

Nicholas paused, with his foot on the running board. "I forgot about that. You ought to get some sleep."

"I'm all right. I dozed this afternoon, while I was waiting for you to call. Climb in, Nick." He stepped on the starter button. The engine hummed. "I'm going to see this thing through. That is, if you want me."

"You bet I do."

Stuart pulled out from behind Charley's vivid yellow convertible. They rolled down the curving driveway, around the bend, into the dark strip of woodland.

"Stuart, I wish you'd tell me something."

"Sure, Nick. What is it?"

"The night I was hurt, weren't you going to Tucson on account of your wife's death?"

"Sure."

"Did you go?"

Stuart gave him a quick glance, then turned his eyes back to the winding road. "Don't you remember? No, I suppose not, after that crack on the head. Why, I had a reservation on the evening train, but that business of the truck drivers' strike boiled up, and you asked me to stay over."

"So I did." It was coming back to him, the conferences with his lawyers, with the union delegation, the WLB representatives. "We spent the rest of the night wrangling, didn't we?"

"With ten minutes off for sandwiches and coffee. You arranged to have one of the company planes fly me to Arizona, remember? We managed to get away from the office a little before dawn."

Nicholas said, "Ivan drove us out to the field, I suppose."

"That's right. You let me off at the main gate. Kuttner hadn't turned up yet, so you went on to the lab to see what was keeping him. You told me not to wait, Nick. Bragwell had his plane all ready and you said I might as well get going. I wish to God I hadn't. I should have gone with you, but it never occurred to me there'd be trouble at the lab. I thought if there was any monkey business, they'd try it on Jimmy Duncan's plane."

"We all thought so. We had armed guards all around the hangars and the main gate, and nobody at the lab. I tried to get Emil to accept a guard, but he didn't like strangers messing around there, no matter who they were. He said Grant was a crack shot, worth a dozen ordinary men, but the young fool got sleepy and Emil sent him home. At least," he added thoughtfully, "that's how Oliver Grant tells it."

Stuart made a sharp left turn and swung the car into the canyon highway. "Grant!"

"Would that surprise you?"

"I don't know. Of course he had a swell opportunity."

Nicholas said, "He was very hostile when I talked to him this afternoon. He's set up his own laboratory, with a lot of expensive equipment. I noticed he was in a tearing hurry to explain that his partner found most of the money. . . . On the other hand, Emil trusted him, and Emil was plenty suspicious. He learned that in Hitler's Germany."

"Grant's a clever chap, Nick."

"Yes. Maybe he fooled Emil." Nicholas sighed. "I hope Beulah can put us on the right track. Oh, by the way, Stuart, how soon did you and Bragwell take off?"

"Within five minutes. Dawn was just starting to break, I remember. Why?"

He didn't answer. In that dream of his (which wasn't a dream at all) a plane rose from a near-by field, just after the first shot. Its engines covered the noise he made when he began to run. Bragwell's plane, he thought. The times checked to perfection. And Bragwell wouldn't have taken off without his passenger. Stuart was in the clear. He let out a sigh of relief. Not that he'd ever had any serious doubts on that score, but he needed proof for Joanne. He must check with the pilot, of course, or better yet have Joanne talk to him. Let her convince herself.

He said, "What was Bragwell's first name?"

"Let's see. They called him Marty, short for Martin, I suppose. What are you getting at, Nick?"

"I want to talk to him. He might have seen something. Maybe he's in the Army, though, by this time."

"Not a chance. Poor guy had a bum leg. I couldn't see that it interfered with his flying, but they wouldn't take him. You can get in touch with him easy enough. He's got a ten-acre farm near Van Nuys. I know, because he talked about it all the way to Arizona, when I was trying to catch some sleep." He swung to the left into Sunset Boulevard. In a few minutes, they entered the Strip. "Where is this joint?"

"Middle of the next block."

Stuart made a forbidden U turn and parked just beyond the marquee. "I hope they serve food in here. I haven't eaten since nine this morning. How about you, Nick?"

"I had breakfast around eleven." The doorman bowed them into the gray-and-rose lobby. "We can't eat here, though. It's one of Charley's hangouts."

The captain came toward them, smiling. "Never mind," said Nicholas. "We have business backstage."

The smile vanished. "Oh. Go around to the side entrance, then."

"We'll go this way. Come on, Stuart." Nicholas brushed past the man. He led the way, between rows of tables, down to the green baize door, and along the smelly corridor to Beulah's room. He knocked, waited a moment, and knocked again.

A voice behind them said, "Looking for Beulah? She's home sick."

Nicholas turned quickly. He found himself face to face with the bald-headed man in the ill-fitting dinner jacket. The fellow turned pale, but this time he didn't run away, for Stuart had a firm grip on his arm. "What's the matter? What are you scared of?"

"You're Rob Matheny's old man."

"Well, what of it?"

"Nothing, only I heard you was dead."

Nicholas laughed. "Not quite. Who told you that?"

"I don't know. One of the fellows."

"Who are you, anyway?"

"I play the sax."

"I see. Where does Beulah live?"

"She's got an apartment at the Caro Nome. That's on Fallview, just off of Sunset."

"Thanks a lot. What's the matter with her, do you know?"

The bald-headed man snorted with laughter. "Give you three guesses. It isn't the first time Beulah's been hung over." He reached up and scratched his shiny pate. "But it's the first time she ever tried to wiggle out by claiming she had a bullet in her. Usually calls it flu. The boss is sore as hell."

"A bullet!"

"That's what she says."

Nicholas didn't wait to hear any more. He thrust a bill into the man's hand and walked rapidly down the odorous hall.

### 3

The phone booth stood in an angle near the entryway, half hidden by a dragon screen. Nicholas, reaching for the directory, paused with his arm outstretched. What was Beulah's last name? He cursed himself for a fool. That's what came of doing things in a rush. He'd been too anxious to get away from Marchetti's, a place where he was known, a place frequented by Charley Van Norman. Of course he could phone them and ask for her name and number, but he hated to leave so obvious a trail. Already the poor woman's life had been in danger, probably on his account. He didn't want to add to her peril.

Through the small window in the booth he could see his table and the back of Stuart's head. A fat, elderly Chinese was setting down two cups and the preliminary pot of tea. It would be several minutes before their dinner arrived. He called the Lorillard and asked for Mrs. Matheny. After a moment he heard Joanne's soft, well-bred voice.

"Joanne," he said, "this is Nicky."

"Darling! Where are you?"

"I'm phoning from a restaurant. Tell me, is Hero there?"

"No, she just left."

"Where could I reach her?"

"She's on her way out to the house. Charley called, and she went off in a terrific hurry. I've been anxious about you, darling. Are you all right?"

"I'm okay. Joanne, will you do something for me? Call the house in about half an hour and ask Hero to wait there for me. I want to see her tonight, but I have something else to do first. Will you do that?"

"Of course."

"By the way, are you alone?"

"Miss Mitchell's here . . . Bunny's nurse."

"In the same room?"

"Why, no, she's—"

"Never mind. Have you got a pencil and paper handy?"

"Yes."

"All right. I left something for you in my safe out at the house. If anything should happen to me, you go and get it, but go alone. Be sure nobody knows what you're doing. Here's the combination. Write it down and learn it, then destroy the paper. . . . Got that?"

"Yes." She repeated the numbers correctly. "Oh, Nicky, please be careful. Don't let anything happen."

"I'll take care." He glanced over his shoulder. Stuart hadn't moved. He was smoking a cigarette, sipping his tea.

"Joanne, I found out about Stuart. It's all right."

"Oh, you mean . . . Oh, Nicky!"

"He was with me all that night. We had a strike threat to deal with. The minute he spoke of it, I remembered. He went to Arizona in a company plane. They took off at least five minutes before the explosion."

"Nicky! Are you sure?"

"Just about. You can check with the pilot. His name's Martin Bragwell and he's got a farm near Van Nuys."

For a minute or two she didn't say anything. Perhaps she couldn't. When she did speak her voice was so low that it was difficult to distinguish the words. "You didn't tell him what I thought?"

"No, and I don't intend to. If you want to tell him, that's your affair." The fat waiter was approaching their table with a loaded tray. "I've got to go, now. Yes, I'll be careful. Good-by, Joanne." He put up the receiver. From his coat pocket he drew the envelope containing the combination of his safe, tore it to shreds, and dropped the pieces into a trash basket under the shelf.

He left the booth and slipped into his chair, looking with distrust at the bowls of food on the table. There was the inevitable rice, a pastry roll full of minced chicken, a sort of hot salad made of infant pea pods and water chestnuts, gray, sticky rectangles which proved to be almond duck.

Nicholas ate his full share of these strange viands, though he had never understood the American passion for what he termed "funny food." He was hungry enough to eat anything, though he would have preferred a steak and a baked potato.

Stuart said, "Did you get her?"

"No. We'll have to go around there. It isn't far. I was talking to Joanne."

Stuart set his teacup down with care. He looked steadily at Nicholas, across the table.

"That'll be all right now, I think."

"What have you been up to, Nick?"

"A spot of matchmaking." He grinned. "I'm pretty good at it. Talent I didn't know I had." He helped himself to another serving of rice. Stuart continued to look at him expectantly. He added, "I just cleared up a misunderstanding. Let it go at that, will you, Stuart?"

"Looks as if I'd have to." He picked up his fork. "Darned nice of you to bother, with all this other stuff on your mind."

"Okay. Let's get on with it."

They finished the meal in silence. Outside the wind blew fresh and cold from the ocean. Clouds hustled across the sky. In one of the black pools between them a round yellow moon lay like a reflection on still water.

Stuart drove along the boulevard to Fallview, located the apartment building, and parked in the nearest vacant space. The front door opened directly into a long corridor. Nicholas paused beside a double row of mailboxes set into the wall.

"Here it is. Beulah Westmore. One o eight—that'll be near the back." The house was not so squalid as his brief acquaintance with Beulah had led him to expect. The hall was airy and well carpeted. Through an open doorway he caught a glimpse of immaculate white paint, furniture upholstered in blue damask.

He stopped at the door of 108 and knocked. A savage voice ordered them to go away. Nicholas called, "Is that you, Beulah?"

"Who wants to know?"

"Nick Matheny. May I come in?"

"No. I wouldn't let you in if you was God in a wheelbarrow!"

"Don't be a fool. I've brought the money."

A very considerable change had come over Beulah in the past twenty-four hours. Nicholas wouldn't have supposed the jolly, vulgar creature could be so sullen and suspicious. After a pause she said, "How do I know it's you?"

"Can't you recognize my voice?"

"No. Anyway, anybody can change their voice. Listen, what color paper do I use?"

"Blue."

"What shape envelopes?"

"Square."

"How much did you bring?"

"A thousand dollars."

"What for?"

"Now, see here," Nicholas bellowed, "I haven't got all night. For God's sake, open that blasted door and let's get down to business."

This display of temper seemed to reassure Beulah. There was a rumbling and scraping, as if heavy furniture were being dragged across the floor. Apparently she was removing her barricades.

"Okay. I'll let you in, but watch your step. I've got a gun." The key turned. They heard her jump back. "Come in slow. I got you covered."

They went in slowly, stopping just inside the door. Beulah crouched behind a large wing chair. Only her eyes showed, and the hand that held the gun. "Who's that with you?" she snarled.

"My secretary, Mr. Hanson. He's all right."

"How do I know he is? He better stick his hands up. You lock that door and stand in front of it. Don't move, either of you."

She came out from behind the wing chair and poked her gun at Stuart's back. He stood with his arms in the air, looking dreadfully unhappy, while Beulah patted his pockets with her left hand. She did this awkwardly, with much groaning and swearing. The grimy red velvet robe slipped off her shoulder, revealing a mass of gauze bandage, striped with adhesive tape.

"How did it happen?" Nicholas inquired sympathetically, although he had to bite his lips to keep from smiling.

"Happen! What d'you mean happen? This wasn't no accident. He was waitin' for me someplace around, when I got home last night. Plugged me going up the walk to my own front door! I'd of been a goner, only one of them lousy little brats next door left her kiddy cart on the walk and I fell over it. That's how come I got winged instead of a bullet in my head and curtains."

"I see. Is it very bad?"

"Sure it's bad. Hurts like hell. I'm in awful agony. . . . You can sit down now. Over on the couch. Shove that stuff on the floor."

Stuart removed a heap of soiled chiffon underclothing, a pink girdle, and two bath towels. He and Nicholas sat down side by side. Beulah's apartment did not fulfill the promise of that clean, airy hall, but no doubt she was the sort of woman who would create a mess wherever she went.

"Of course," she went on, "it could of been a whole lot worse, but I got a crease in my arm you could lay two fingers into. Believe me, I don't aim to stir outa that door till they got him under lock and key."

"You talk as if you knew who did it."

"You bet I know." Beulah started to swear. Nicholas, who thought he knew all the impolite words in the English language, learned a couple of new ones, and a fine Italian phrase as well. Among other, choicer, expressions, he caught the words "cotton-headed old fool . . . him and his undertaker's coat."

"So it was Charley Van Norman! How do you know that?"

Beulah left off swearing. The exercise in self-expression must have done her good, for her annoyance faded, gave way to greed. "I better start at the beginning. You say you brought the money?"

"Yes. Hanson's got it."

"All right. Give it here." She flipped through the roll of bills. "That's okay." Beulah sat down and crossed her enormous legs. She stroked the bills lovingly, as one might fondle a kitten. "I guess I oughta apologize for actin' so ornery when you come to the door. Beulah's been here alone the whole lousy day, without nobody to talk to or nothin' to drink, an' gettin' more scared every minute. When you knocked, I thought sure it was Charley come to finish poor Beulah off." Her vast bosom heaved. She was laughing soundlessly. "I'd sure like to see his face if he knew you was here, and Beulah was gettin' to tell her story after all."

"I hope he doesn't know," said Stuart mildly. "We'd prefer to get out of the place alive."

Nicholas said, "That's right, and the sooner the better. Let's have the story."

"Well, lemme think. It all started when your Robby fell for Lita. She wasn't no tart, y'understand. Lita was so goddam refined she might as well been dead. But she's a good-looking piece, and Robby was nuts about her. Kep' bringing her joolry and stuff, but she wouldn't take it. 'I ain't the sort that takes expensive presents offa men,' she'd say, real refined. Robby'd go away mad, and she'd come in my room and cry. 'He'll be back,' I usta tell her. 'You're doin' all right for yourself. Another couple years and he'll be all set to take you down to the county clerk.' "

Beulah shook with silent laughter. She slapped her thigh. "I was away off. He come around to it in six weeks. 'Lita,' he says, 'I'd go to Reno like a shot if it wasn't for my ole man. He's nuts about her and the kid. If I was to try anything like that,' he says, 'it'd be just too bad. We'd have to live on your salary, because I couldn't earn a dime if I was to starve for it.' "

Nicholas felt his face getting uncomfortably warm. He said brusquely, "You can skip that part."

"Listen, mister, Beulah's telling this story. You shut up, if you want to hear the rest. Where was I? Oh yeah—well, they yapped and yapped. I'd go do my turn and come back, an' they're still at it. He'd walk the floor while she done her turn, and then start all over again. Lita says, 'It's funny all the dough your ole man's got, and you ain't got a thin dime. What's the idear? Don't he trust you with money?' Rob says, 'Listen, baby, I got better'n two million bucks in my own right, on'y it's where I can't get at it.' She asks how come, so he tells her. 'We got a war on, honey,' he says, 'an' before it's over, we're gonna run short on oil,' he says. 'I been socking every penny I got and all I can borrow into wildcat drilling.' "

Nicholas turned his head. "Know anything about that, Stuart?"

"News to me, Nick. I'd heard about the girl, but if Rob was wild-catting, he kept it under cover."

"What do you mean 'if'?" Beulah interrupted with some indignation. "I'm tellin' you I heard him say so."

Stuart said, "I knew he was hard up. He tried to borrow fifty thousand from me."

"Did he get it?"

"Nick, I never had that much money in my life, all at one time. As you know, my expenses were pretty heavy. Besides, he wouldn't explain what he wanted it for and made me promise not to tell you. I didn't like the look of it. I supposed the girl was bleeding him."

"Not her," Beulah cut in. "Lita never took a nickel off him. I know why he wanted it. He was having trouble with one of his wells. Said he lost a bit and had to do a fishin' job, whatever that is. Must have been somethin' expensive." Beulah gave an oily chuckle. "He says to Lita, 'I dunno what the hell to do. Guess I'll have to slap a mortgage on the house. I even tried Fatso, but he turned me down.' " She glanced at Stuart. "Why'd he call you that? You don't look fat to me. Just nice and chunky."

"Why didn't he come to me?" Nicholas fretted. "I'd have been tickled to death to help him." He felt a thrill of pride in the boy, for the first time since Robin was out of short pants. Maybe he'd been foolish, overextended himself, but at least he'd done something on his own, something worth while. He'd risked everything he had trying to get oil for his country.

Beulah said, "I can tell you why. Lita wanted to know the same thing. 'Why don't you ask your ole man?' she'd keep saying. 'I'll see him in hell first,' Rob'd say. 'This here's my baby. He ain' gonna get his mitts on it.' Honest, he acted like he was jealous of his own father! I didn't get it, and neither did Lita. That's what they rowed about."

"He quarreled with her?"

"I'll say."

"When was this?"

"Couple months before he got his. It'd been goin' on a long time, but that's when the lid blew off. Y'see, he swore up and down he'd get a divorce and marry Lita the minute he was outa the woods. The pore kid fell for it. But she nearly went nuts when he got in deeper and deeper, and it looked like he was gonna lose his shirt. She kep' nagging at him. 'Go ask your ole man. If you love me,' she'd say, 'you won't throw away our happiness just because you got too much pride to ask your old man.' I told her she was a damn fool, but Lita never had the sense to shut up, and of course he got sick of it. They had an awful row one night, and he quit comin' around. She stood it a week, and then she started writin' them letters."

Beulah reached for a package of cigarettes. "This shoulder's killing me," she remarked. "Might help if I had a drink, but I ain't got a thing in the house." She looked hopefully at Stuart, but he only shrugged. She stuck a cigarette in her mouth, lighted it. "I tried to stop her. 'Look,' I says, 'can't you tell he's fed up? Where you made your mistake,' I says, 'you hadn't oughta slep' with him.' She yelps, 'But we're gonna get married, Beulah.' 'That's what you think,' I tells her. Poor Lita. She couldn't take it in. 'Robby loves me,' she'd say. 'It's only this goddam money that's stoppin' him. If he wasn't heir to no fortune,' she'd say, 'he'd get a divorce in two shakes.' "

Beulah exhaled a cloud of smoke. She leaned forward in her chair. The creature was enjoying this, thought Nicholas. She reminded him of some repulsive animal happily worrying a carcass.

"So then," she continued joyously, "Lita cooks up this business of the kid. 'That oughta fetch him,' she says."

"You mean it wasn't true?"

"Huh? Listen, Lita's a dancer. Dancers can't have kids. If she'd really been that way, she'd of done somethin' in a hurry. . . . Well, darned if he doesn't shoot her letters back unopened! So then she gets desprit. 'I bet his wife don't know about me, Beulah,' she says, 'and what if I was to tell her?' 'Go ahead,' I says, 'and that'll be the end of you and Robby, and a good thing. I'm gettin' so I puke every time I hear the guy's name.' But y'see, she's about off her head by that time. 'He won't know I done it,' she says. 'I'll pertend I'm somebody else just out to get money. An' I'll send her that pitcher you took at the flat. That oughta start her thinking.' "

Nicholas thrust out his arm to look at a wrist watch that wasn't there. Beulah saw the gesture. "Okay, I know you think Beulah's shootin' off her mouth, but this stuff's all part of it. Y'see, Robby got a peek at one of them letters. He was fit to be tied. Come around to the place that night, yellin' his head off. Lita was scared. Tried to pertend she didn't know nothin' about it, but Robby was wise. 'Who else would of wrote it?' he says. 'You done it, this time. Where d'you suppose I saw the goddam thing? Laying right on my ole man's desk!' "

Beulah paused to stub out her cigarette, leaning forward so that her robe slipped open. Nicholas averted his eyes from the generous display of skin and a wisp of torn lace which appeared to be the inadequate top of Beulah's nightdress. More ragged lace showed where the robe failed to meet over her massive knees.

"They had it hot and heavy for a while," she continued with relish. "Then Lita starts to whine an' cry. First thing you know, they're slobbering over each other! I like to died. Beulah couldn't tell you to this day if he was really nuts about her or if he just had too much to drink. Anyway, he stuck around till closing time." She paused again, evidently for dramatic effect. Her eyes moved triumphantly from Stuart to Nicholas. "That's how Rob happened to be there when Charley come lookin' for him."

She got her effect, all right, thought Nicholas. He nearly jumped off the couch. Stuart shouted, "Charley? What did he want?"

"You keep your pants on, honey. Beulah's gonna tell you. Beulah always gives a fella his money's worth." She gave him an insinuating wink. The red velvet robe shivered with her silent laughter. "Where was I? Oh yeah, Charley he comes rushing in and hollers at Rob, 'Where the hell you been? I been trying to reach you ever since dinner. You know what's happened?' he says. 'Kuttner's pulled it off.' Rob starts to swear a blue streak. Lita wants to know who's Kuttner and what's he done. Me too. I was right there with my ear glued to the door. Robby tells her this guy is a chemist that's doped out some kind of ersatz gasoline. Lita wants to know what's wrong with that. I was wonderin' the same thing. Sounded like a swell idear to me."

Beulah grinned. "Ole Charley, though, he says, real mad, 'Just the stuff's made outa soybeans or somethin', and it's so darned cheap nobody'll ever pay the price for real gasoline. All the oil companies'll go broke,' he says. 'Tough on you, Robby. Even if your wells come in, they won't be worth a dime. Nobody'll buy the stuff.' Robby tried to laugh that off. Said it'd be years till they could start makin' enough to do any harm, and he would of cleaned up by that time. 'Years hell,' Charley says. He says, 'Nick's goin' to Washington in the morning. Bighearted Nick! He's gonna let the gov'ment have it for free, so's to get quick action. It's my guess,' he says, 'they'll be putting the stuff out in another couple months. That's unless we stop it.' Rob wants to know how they could stop it. 'With a match,' Charley says, 'A match an' a can of kerosene.' "

Beulah reached for another cigarette. Stuart sat like a figure carved out of

ice, and Nicholas was equally rigid and cold. They waited through an intolerable minute of silence.

On the floor something moved. A small black shape scuttled across the
beige carpet. Beulah's leg shot out. She planted her foot on the creature,
squashing it. "Damn these cockroaches! You'd think the rent I pay for this
dump, they could anyway keep it halfway clean."

Nicholas said through clenched teeth, "Well, go on. Did Rob agree?"

"Not him. He up an' told Charley where to go, and what he could do when
he got there."

Nicholas slumped back against the cushions. This abrupt release from agony
was almost more than he could bear.

"Took a load off Beulah's mind," the woman continued. "I don't like mix-
ing in other folks' business, an' I don't like cops. But if Robby said yes, hell,
I'd of had to do somethin'. We got those damn Japs to lick. The way it was,
I went home to bed. This was just a few minutes before closin' time, y'see.
The three of 'em went off together. That's the last I heard, till next day when
I seen the papers." She added, with genuine regret, "I wish to God I'd told
the cops. But I figgered if Charley tried any monkey business, Rob'd stop
him. I guess, at that, he done the best he could."

Nicholas stood up. A reddish mist seemed to hang like a curtain before his
eyes. "I let him get away," he said in a choking whisper.

Stuart grabbed his arm. "Nick, wait a minute. Where you going?"

"I had him," Nicholas raged, still in that harsh whisper. "I had him, and I
let him get away."

## 4

Joanne met them at the door. She was wearing a short white fur cape over her
black dinner gown. Her dark hair fell straight and smooth to her shoulders,
where it rippled into silky curls. She had never looked more beautiful, yet
Nicholas was appalled at the sight of her.

She said softly, "I thought I'd better come out, instead of phoning, just to
make sure you wouldn't find a reception committee waiting for you." She
caught on fast, he thought. He hadn't intended to make his suspicions quite
so clear. She added, "Anyhow, I wanted to see Stuart." She gave him a look
that made even Nicholas' old heart beat faster, and probably made Stuart feel
as if someone had tossed an armful of stars into his lap. "Hero's in the library," said Joanne. Her dark brows lifted slightly. Nicholas understood. There
was no telephone extension in the library.

"How long have you been here?"

"Just a few minutes."

"Good. You did fine, Joanne, but it's all right now. The job's finished."

"You found it?" she whispered.

"Yes, I found it."

"Is that what . . .?"

"Yes. I left instructions for you. Stuart'll help."

"But, Nicky, won't you——"

"I'll be going back to Crestview," he said. "It's about time. I don't feel so good." He caught Stuart's eye. He glanced down at Joanne, then jerked his head toward the door. Stuart nodded.

Before he could make a move, heels clicked on the bare library floor. Hero strolled up to the open door. "What's all the whispering about?" Like Joanne, she was dressed in black, a long slim tube of a gown that made her look taller than she really was and incredibly fair. Nicholas realized that the ladies of his family were in mourning for Robin. Well, so was he, only he wore his black raiment inside where it didn't show.

"So you've come back, Nicky." Her clear eyes moved past him. "And Stuart! Well!" She stopped in the doorway. The light from the library fire drew a rosy halo around her blonde head. Her manner was composed, yet Nicholas understood that she was very angry. "Charley told me what happened. There's no possible excuse for that sort of thing."

Stuart said, "Oh, I don't know. Did he tell you why Nick lost his temper? Charley's been falsifying the company's books to cut down on the income tax."

Hero's lips curled. "What nonsense."

Nicholas said, "He told us himself, Hero. Boasted about it, in fact."

"I'm sure you misunderstood him. But suppose it was true? Did you have to knock him down?" She said this with a kind of violent distaste, as if he had committed some unimaginable indecency.

"I wish I'd killed him," Nicholas said in a savage voice.

Hero drew back a step. "You did your best, judging from the state your rooms are in."

Stuart gave an abrupt laugh, like a dog's bark. "It was the other way around. Charley was taking pot shots at Nick through the window."

"I don't believe that," said Hero promptly. At the same time she shivered. You could see the tremor pass down her smooth throat, over her shoulders, along her straight back. "Why do we stand here in the cold? It's much more comfortable in the library." She did not, however, move from her position near the door. "Oh, Nicky, you really should have stayed at Crestview, where you were safe."

He tossed his coat over the back of a chair. "I'm safe enough. He missed me. Beulah, too. Charley may be hot stuff with a target, but he's not so good at shooting people, especially when the light's bad. Anyhow, he won't try again. No point in it. Beulah's already spilled the beans. And Stuart was there. Charley can't save his skin now, unless he kills all three of us."

Hero's mouth twisted into a scornful smile. "Beulah! Who in the world is Beulah?" She stamped her foot. "And why do you blame everything that happens on Charley? Because you dislike him? Is that it?"

Joanne said, "Where is Charley?" She had been so quiet that they all turned to look at her. "Is he hiding here in the house?" Her eyes moved toward the curving staircase, toward the shadows that hung like a dark curtain in front of the upper hallway.

Hero said, "Don't be ridiculous, Joanne." She clasped her hands and held them tight against the black bodice of her gown, as if to quiet a sudden stab of pain. "But where can he be?" she murmured. "I looked all over the house. His car wasn't in the drive. Nicky! You didn't go to the police with this absurd notion of yours? If you've had my father arrested . . . Oh, Nicky!"

He said, "I haven't. Not yet. I wanted to hear what he had to say first."

"Indeed! How very generous!"

"I think he's here," said Joanne in her mild, relentless way. "Hero is probably lying. Just as she lied about Stuart."

Hero set her back against the doorframe, as if it were a wall. "My dear child! What can you mean?"

"I've been wondering why you did it," said Joanne softly. "You wanted to keep me quiet, didn't you? If nobody talked, if nobody told the police anything, you thought they'd drop the investigation. And you were right. The police never did find out."

Stuart put his hands on her shoulders and swung her around, facing him. "Joanne! . . . My God!"

"Yes, I know. I can't think why I believed her. If she had come right out with it, I probably would have laughed, but she was too clever. Hero's terribly clever, Stuart. She did it so subtly that I thought it was my own idea. 'We can't help Robin,' she said, 'by letting other people get hurt . . . people we're fond of.' I thought she was being kind to me. I'd forgotten that Hero would do anything to protect her father. She'd lie, or steal, or kill."

Joanne's voice had fallen, so that it was hardly more than a whisper. Although she seemed so quiet, Nicholas realized that she was very close to hysteria. He gave Stuart an urgent look, over the top of her sleek dark head, and gestured toward the front door.

"All right." Stuart slipped his arm around Joanne. "Darling, I'm going to take you home, and then I'm going to tell the police all about it. They'll get Charley before he can do any more harm."

Joanne hung back. "We can't leave Nicky here alone."

Nicholas said, "Don't worry about me. You go along with Stuart, my dear. Everything will work out all right."

Hero moved away from the library door and advanced toward them. She was smiling, not very pleasantly. "Yes, everything's just fine, isn't it? You've got it all nicely settled, between you. Put all the blame on my father. That's most convenient, since none of you ever liked him anyway. Call me a liar and Charley a murderer . . . get him sent to the gas chamber, and everything works out just dandy!"

Her eyes flicked from one rigid face to another. In the strong light from the crystal chandelier those clear eyes of hers seemed to shine with a green flame. "Too bad to spoil the setup, but unfortunately, you're quite wrong. I happen to know that Charley didn't murder Robin." Hero walked straight up to Joanne and stopped close to the girl, facing her. "It's true I wanted to keep you quiet. It's perfectly true that I was trying to protect someone I love, but not Charley."

Joanne whispered, "You never cared for anyone else."

"Oh yes. There's just one other person I care about. You and Stuart are supposed to be fond of him too." She turned her head and looked directly at Nicholas' face.

He was aware of a purely physical shock. Hero's words were deflected from his mind, like stones tossed against a wall, but where her glance rested his skin was tingling.

She said, "If you people are at all fond of Nicky, you'll think twice before running off to the police."

Joanne started to laugh, the shaky, breathless laughter of hysteria.

Stuart said in a mild, conversational tone, "What a bitch you are, Hero."

Nicholas had a sense of pressure under his skull, a low roaring in his ears, felt rather than heard, like the vibration that remains to trouble the senses after a plane has passed beyond earshot.

Joanne cried, "You told me Stuart murdered Robin. That was a lie. Now you're accusing Nicky. And when that's proved to be another lie, I suppose you'll accuse me." She was choking with laughter. "Or Bunny. Perhaps Bunny murdered his father! Why not? It doesn't matter, so long as Charley is safe."

Her words came to Nicholas muffled by the noise of a plane's motor, the crack of pistol shots, the screaming of a siren. He remembered jumping back, away from the brick wall. A figure brushed past him, running. In the first faint light of dawn he could barely distinguish the man's form, yet some trick of movement, some familiar outline, brought a flash of recognition. The fellow ran as Nicholas did, head forward, long legs working with precision, like pistons. He ran as Robin did. Behind him, in the still air, lingered the raw, telltale odor of kerosene.

Robin was young and fit. He should have been able to outdistance an old man, a tired old man who had worked the whole night through, but Nicholas was lashed on by a fury that was not quite sane. This was his son, this saboteur; a traitor to his own flesh and blood, as well as to his country.

Nicholas pursued him with a cold and murderous rage. He got his hands on a loose fold of cloth; he gripped one of the swinging arms. Then the world exploded all around him into noise and flame. The ground heaved under his feet. He was flung down upon the hard earth. Something struck his head. A blinding flare of light was followed by darkness.

Even in the spinning dark, rage convulsed his fingers. Death itself could not have broken his grip on Robin's arm. The boy's struggles roused him at last. He heard the sound of labored breathing, a voice that panted, "Let go. . . . Damn you, let go." He opened his eyes. Robin was crouching over him. In the glare from the burning laboratory his face and the deep V of his shirt front stood out like a red silhouette against the blackness behind him. His frantic struggles ceased. He looked down at Nicholas, as a trapped animal might look at the wicked steel claws holding him captive.

"Let go!" he shouted suddenly, above the roar of the flames. "Do you want to get me hanged?" He lunged backward, throwing his whole weight against the hand clamped around his right wrist.

Nicholas held on. He had no conscious purpose. He was too dazed for thought. He hung on as a child does when danger threatens, through a blind instinct to clutch at something. Instinct saved him when Robin made a fresh move, groping over the uneven ground with his left hand until he found a rock. Nicholas saw the arm swing up. He saw the rock start down toward his head. With a mighty heave he threw himself forward. His shoulder smashed into Robin's chest, drove the breath out of him, and sent him sprawling. They rolled over and over on the hard-packed earth, clinging together in a deadly embrace.

Nicholas felt his strength going. He managed to free his arms. His hands found Robin's throat. His thumbs dug deep into soft, throbbing flesh. He didn't let go until the flaying heat of the fire forced him to his feet and sent him stumbling away half blind, less than half alive, into a great gray waste.

## 5

Hero came to him in the wasteland. She said, "Don't take this so hard, Nicky. You had to do it. When they found him, he was still holding on to that big rock, and there was blood on it. You had to defend yourself."

She said, "There are worse ways to die. He didn't suffer at all, Nicky. The doctor said he must have lost consciousness in a few seconds. Something about the blood supply being shut off from the brain. Are you listening, dear? Can you understand me? The doctor said all that thrashing around was reflex action, just the way people struggle going under ether, though they don't know it and can't feel anything."

Nicholas made no response at all. If he kept perfectly still, perhaps she'd go away and stop bothering him. He had attained a dismal sort of peace, a kind of nirvana. He didn't care whether Robin suffered or not. He didn't care about anything except getting nicoline into the proper hands. That mattered so much that other considerations shrank to insignificance. The laboratory had gone up in smoke. Emil was dead, and Nicholas felt that he himself was dying. All that remained of their splendid accomplishment was a stack of papers in his office safe, and they were useless without the strange words and equations which existed only in his brain.

His one fear was that he might forget. If they'd go away, leave him alone for a few minutes, if he could get hold of a pencil and write it all down, then he could give up and rest. He could die, if need be, secure in the knowledge that his work was done. In the meantime all his faculties were narrowed to the size of a strip of paper covered with equations. He must remember every word, every numeral. The life that went on around him was nothing but an interruption. He tried to shut out of his mind the footsteps, the sound of the front door closing, the murmur of voices in the hall.

The sounds drew nearer. He couldn't keep them out altogether.

"What's the matter with him?"

"He had a shock."

"Is he dead?"

"No, no. Just unconscious. I telephoned the hospital. They're sending an ambulance for him."

"Well, thank heaven! It's about time."

Hero said, "This seems unnecessarily cruel."

"To send him back? Don't be sentimental, Hero. You know it's the only thing to do."

"Oh, that. Yes. I was thinking about myself. I've never cared a scrap for anyone but you and Nicky. I've built my life around you two, and yet I can't help one of you without hurting the other. It's most unfair."

Charley said, "I don't understand. What happened?"

"I had to tell him about Robin. They found out something, he and Stuart. They talked to a person named Beulah and came away thoroughly convinced that you strangled Rob. Stuart and Joanne wanted to rush off to the police. I had to stop them, didn't I?" Her voice broke. "Nicky's been like this ever since."

"Stuart and Joanne? My God, are they here too?"

"No, she had hysterics. He took her home. They've been gone at least fifteen minutes."

"Fifteen minutes!" Charley yelled. "Hero, have you gone crazy? Why didn't you tell me before? How do you know you stopped them? The police may be on the way out here right now. It's all very well to say Nicky choked him, but you can't prove it without admitting I was there. Don't you see what you've done? I'm getting out."

"Wait, Charley. You'll only make matters worse by running away."

He said, "I'll go down to Mexico. I can be over the border in two or three hours. Let's see, I'll need money. Have to get a check cashed at the hotel . . . you can send some more later on, when——"

Hero said, "No, Charley. I won't send you any money."

"My dear girl, do you want to see me convicted of murder?"

"Certainly not, but if you run away the police will take it as a confession that you're guilty. I want you to sit tight and say nothing. After all, they have no proof."

Charley changed his tactics. He said in an aggrieved tone, "I see. You're going to throw me to the wolves in order to save Nick. I suppose that's why you told Stuart I was at the field that night."

"I didn't tell him. Beulah did."

"Hero, I'm surprised that you'd lie to your father at a time like this. All Beulah knew was that I made a suggestion. We didn't talk much at the club. It was nearly closing time, so we went on to Carmelita's apartment. She was really the one who talked Rob into helping, she and two quarts of scotch."

"Then why were you so anxious to stop her mouth?"

"My dear girl, she knew about Rob's affair with Lita and his wildcatting. Certainly I tried to stop her mouth. I tried again tonight, but they had a head start on me."

"You go to such extremes, Charley. If this Beulah person knows so little, why didn't you just leave things alone?"

Charley forgot his pose of the injured father. "Oh, for God's sake, use your head," he snapped. "What's going to happen when the police get suspicious and make a real investigation, start sifting ashes and so on? They'll find bones and teeth and identify them. Moving the car down to the bus station was all right so long as they fell for it. But the minute they have reason to think Kuttner met with foul play, they'll dig up the whole story."

"You needn't shout. I have excellent hearing."

Charley said in a lower tone, "Are you sure Nick's passed out?"

Their words came to Nicholas all mixed up with figures on a sheet of paper. By no effort of will could he shut his mind to them. The insistent voices began to drive more important matters out of his head. A bright light flashed over his face. He didn't move.

"Yes, I guess he's out, all right. Anyway, they'll be coming to get him soon. I don't suppose he can do much harm when he's back in the loony bin."

Hero said coldly, "You might have thought of that before you tried to shoot him this afternoon. I'm very fond of you, Charley, but if you'd succeeded, I would have turned you over to the police myself."

"You'd have turned me in? Your own father?"

"I warned you not to let anything happen to Nicky."

"Hero, don't be angry with me," he wheedled. "Of course I never intended to hit him. I was just trying to scare him off."

"Scare Nicky?" She laughed. "You must be mad."

He didn't answer for a moment. When he did his voice was sticky with pathos. "Perhaps I am. Stir happy. It wouldn't be surprising. I had twenty years to reflect on the penalties attached to having bad luck." He spoke with the voice of innocence condemned. He was the tragic victim of man's injustice; he was a child punished for some fault it cannot understand. "Am I mad," he said with plaintive dignity, "if I try to force the luck my way?"

"Oh, darling! Yes, I know. I've been trying to make it up to you, but . . . if you'd just stop and think before you do these things!" Exasperation mingled with the tenderness in her voice. "However, we're wasting time."

"Exactly what I was thinking, my dear." He sniffed pathetically. "The police will be here soon to take me away. Unless, of course, you'll help me get across the border."

"I won't do that. I've told you why. We'll fight it out here, though I must say you've made things difficult. Talking where people could overhear! Letting that dancer in on it! I'm surprised she hasn't been around wanting hush money." Charley was silent. "Oh, so she has? Really, darling! You should have had better sense than to get mixed up with Robin. What possessed you to go to him?"

Charley said, "That damn place was as hard to crack as a bank vault. Rob was an officer of the company and he had a key to the gate. Kuttner wouldn't have opened the door for me, but Rob's voice was enough like Nicky's to fool him. And somebody had to drive Kuttner's car to the station. I couldn't do the job alone."

Hero said slowly, "I think you'd better tell me exactly what happened."

"You said you didn't want to know."

"I don't want to. I hate violence, but I can't decide what's best to do unless I know the truth." He said nothing. After a moment she asked, "Did you kill him? Or did Robin?"

"I don't know. That's God's truth, Hero. Rob had a blackjack. The idea was that when Kuttner opened the door Rob would give him a tap on the head and we'd get him out to my car. I was going to drive him down to the desert. Rob was to stay and set fire to the lab, and then take Kuttner's car to the bus station, so everyone would think he'd skipped. Well, it went sour. He opened the door, all right, but the minute he saw Rob he pulled a gun. Naturally Rob slugged him, hard enough to crack his skull, too. But you see, I was covering for him and I fired at the same time. Honestly, I don't know which of us did for him. We hadn't any time to waste. Someone might have heard the shots, you see. Rob got the kerosene and stuff, and I went back to cover the gate and make sure he wouldn't be interrupted."

Hero said, "Nicky told me someone tried to shoot him."

"My dear girl, I wasn't trying to shoot him. I nearly had fits when he came in the gate. It was dark as a pocket. Seemed to me I'd been waiting there for an hour. Any minute the lab was likely to blow sky-high. I had to keep Nick away from the place, didn't I? I fired over his head, naturally. I'm not a murderer."

Nicholas opened his eyes. This curious statement shattered even his determined abstraction. He saw that he was in the library, lying propped up with cushions on the big davenport. Hero stood at the fireplace, one black-sleeved arm reposing on the mantel. The light of the flames outlined the beautiful curve of her cheek in rose color. For a lady who disliked hearing of violence, she appeared admirably cool and self-contained. Charley was leaning on the high back of an armchair. His shaggy white head looked pink where the firelight touched it, dull green where it curved into shadow.

Hero said, "I told you not to take a gun."

Nicholas almost cried out. He hadn't been listening carefully. He hadn't, in fact, been listening at all, but surely he would have noticed any suggestion that Hero was in on the plot. Surely that would have pulled him out of his comfortable dream state, or the world of memory, or wherever he was. He closed his eyes and tried to get back to that place where he felt at peace, but it was gone. He had lost it.

When he opened his eyes again, Hero was bending over the fire, jabbing at the red coals with a heavy bronze poker. She said, "I told you not to hurt him, just get him down to the ranch and keep him there until I had a chance to talk to Nicky."

"Talk to Nicky! Have you ever known Nicky to let himself be talked out of anything? He would have laughed at you."

"No," she said, "I don't think so. We had a very clear understanding. I could have arranged matters if I'd had more time, if that strike business hadn't come up." She jabbed at the fire. An angry shower of sparks came spitting out against the copper screen. "I had the most abominable luck. This whole affair has been unlucky from start to finish."

Charley said, "Are you telling me? It's quite likely to land me in the death house."

"Darling, they can't prove anything."

"No? When Beulah tells her story, and Carmelita tells hers? When they sift the ashes and find what's left of Kuttner, along with a bullet that matches my gun?" His head jerked around. "Is that a car coming? No, I guess not."

"Charley! Didn't you get rid of the gun?"

"Why should I? I thought I was safe enough. And I'm particularly fond of that gun. You don't come across——"

"Charley, you must dispose of it at once. Where is it?"

"At the moment, in my coat pocket." He patted his hip. "You don't suppose I'd leave the damn thing around at the hotel, do you?"

"Give it to me. I'll hide it until I can find some way——"

"Oh no," said Charley with a grin. "I might have occasion to use a gun where I'm going. I guess you realize, now, why I'm so anxious to hop down to Mexico. . . . Or, wait a minute. Maybe you're right. Yes," he said in a low voice, as if he were talking to himself. "Yes, I'll dispose of it. I'll stick around. Why the devil didn't I think of that sooner?" Nicholas, watching through half-shut eyes, saw him turn and glance toward the couch.

Hero followed the glance. She frowned, evidently not understanding.

"This gun," said Charley with his jovial smile, "happens to be a present from Nick. Christmas, three years ago, if you remember. They wouldn't have a bit of trouble tracing it to him. When the hospital people find it on him, naturally they'll think——"

"No," said Hero sharply, "I won't stand for that."

"Why not? He's going to be shut up anyhow. What's the difference?"

She squared her shoulders, lifted her head so that the strong, stubborn line of her jaw stood out angular and hard against the firelight. "Plant evidence of a murder on a man who's lying unconscious? No, Charley. I think not."

The contempt in her voice whipped the grin from Charley's face. For a time the room was silent. Then he said, "How do you propose to stop me, Hero?" He turned abruptly and started toward the couch.

Hero laughed. "I shan't try to stop you. But later on I'll tell the truth. Don't imagine I'll hesitate because I'm fond of you. I'm quite as fond of Nicky, you see."

Charley swore. "Tell the truth! Don't be a fool. You don't dare tell the truth. You're an accessory."

"Yes?" She laughed again, scornfully. "Can you prove that?"

Charley stopped, halfway to the davenport. He drew the gun out of his pocket. He turned to face Hero. "I see. I've often wondered what you'd do in a pinch. Now I know. If you have to make a choice, you'll save Nick and throw me to the wolves."

"No, no." Her teeth clamped down on her lower lip. "I'll give you the money," she said. "I'll help you get away."

It was Charley's turn to laugh. "You're a bit late. I've thought of a better scheme. Nick's going to commit suicide with the murder weapon. And you're not going to do any talking later on, my dear daughter. Stuart and Joanne can testify that you were here, and I'll have half a dozen witnesses to prove I was somewhere else."

Nicholas swung his legs off the couch. Careful to make no sound, he slipped to his feet.

Hero gave him away. In spite of her self-possession, her eyes widened, her lips parted.

Charley turned with a jerk. He swore softly. "You've been listening! Oh well, it doesn't matter." He advanced toward Nicholas, lifting his right arm.

Hero screamed. "Charley! Don't!"

He came on. "This time I won't miss."

Nicholas waited, half crouching, ready to leap. Not just yet, though. For the scheme to work, there would have to be powder burns. When Charley got close enough . . .

He was so intent that he didn't see Hero move. He didn't, actually, see her at all. Out of the corners of his eyes he caught a swift glimpse of metal gleaming in the firelight, moving in a great arc. Just before the poker struck, Charley turned his head, warned perhaps by some faint sound or the sense of movement behind him. The blow caught him square on the temple, with such force that Nicholas could hear the bone splinter and crack.

Charley fell forward. There was another crack as his head slammed down on the hardwood floor. The gun slid out of his hand. The proud plume of hair fanned out upon the dark floor, white on one side, red on the other, where it lay steeped in the widening pool of Charley's blood.

## 6

Hero was on her knees beside Charley, her hand inside of his coat, over his heart. She drew the hand away and sat up on her heels. "He's dead!" She scrambled to her feet, awkwardly, because of the long tight skirt dragging at her knees. "I killed him." She took a step backward. "I killed my father."

Her voice was outraged, indignant, as if she were accusing someone else of an atrocious crime. She looked down at her hands, white and fragile against the sooty black of her gown. "How could I? How did it happen? I didn't mean to hit him so hard. I loved my father. I loved him more than anything in the world."

She backed away another step. "Why do you stare so, Nicky? Does it show on my face? Do I look like a murderess?" Her heel touched the leg of a chair. She whirled around, as if someone had tried to lay hold upon her. For

a moment she stood poised. Only her eyes moved, exploring the room, probing the shadows. Then she placed her hands on the chair back and leaned
against them. "The ambulance," she said. "The men from the hospital. They'll
be here soon. They may be coming up the drive now. Any minute the door-
bell might ring."

She raised her head, breathless, listening, but there was no sound. The
house was completely still. "Nicky, what are we to do?" She didn't wait for
an answer. "There's no time to do anything. For all I know, the police may be
on the way too." She beat her hand slowly against the chair back. "I didn't
mean to kill him. Is that murder? He moved his head. He turned his head
right around. I was only trying to keep him from hurting you. What will they
do to me, Nicky? . . . What's the matter? Why do you stand there staring at
me? Why don't you say something?"

Nicholas stepped across a thin, meandering rivulet of blood. He walked
around the body and stooped to pick up the poker which lay on the floor near
Charley's feet. He went on to the fireplace, stood the poker in its rack among
the other fire irons. He leaned on the mantelpiece. "I don't care what happens to you," he said.

Hero took a full breath. Under the shirred black bodice of her gown he
could see her breast lift and swell as the air went deep into her lungs. "I did
it for you," she said. "I saved your life."

Nicholas felt a shiver pass along his spine. He bent to take a log from the
wood basket and place it across the andirons, above a heap of red embers.
"My life's over," he said.

He watched the log begin to smoke. Steam hissed out at one end, where
the heat reached a bit of sap left in the wood. Abruptly the smoke stopped. A
pure yellow flame raced up the chimney. "My children are dead. My wife's
dead and gone. My work's finished."

Hero said, "What do you mean? I'm your wife." He smiled faintly. "Do
you mean that I no longer exist for you?"

"I mean you're not a wife. You're a kept woman."

She stood stiff and silent. A red flush crept up her throat and stained her
cheeks. Her eyes looked dead.

"We didn't get married," he went on; "we made a deal. You wanted money;
I wanted companionship. Seemed like a fair exchange at the time. I should
have known that loyalty isn't for sale." Hero said nothing. Her stillness had
an unnatural quality. It was as if a waterfall abruptly stopped flowing and
hung motionless in midair. He said, "You put on a good show. You had me
fooled. But when it came to a choice between me and the money, you didn't
hesitate to stab me in the back." He waited. Her silence was a trifle discon-
certing. "Isn't that true?"

Hero let go of the chair. She walked around it and came to a stop beside the chimney piece. "No. No, that isn't true." The color had drained out of her skin, leaving it white and cold. "I loved you. I can't imagine why. How very silly of me. What a fatal mistake, to allow oneself to care for people." Her voice had become as cold and colorless as her face. "Well, never mind. That's over, thank God! Or maybe I should thank you, Nicky, for letting me go in time. I was in a dreadful quandary. Now, of course, I know just what to do."

Nicholas gave her a blank look. "Do? About what?"

"My father's body," she said. "Has it slipped your mind that I murdered him? I wish I'd let him kill you, but then I didn't know the exact nature of your feeling for me, or lack of feeling. But perhaps it's better this way. They would have caught him. Charley wouldn't have liked dying in California's humane gas chamber. I have a marked repugnance for that sort of death myself." She smiled. "Not that I have any intention of dying, or even enduring the unpleasantness of a murder trial. There's no need to, since you were kind enough to handle the weapon and get your fingerprints all over it."

"What do you—— Good God, Hero!"

"Well, why not? Of course a wife wouldn't dream of doing such a thing, but I'm not a wife. I'm a kept woman, a mercenary creature, who cares nothing for you aside from your money. Why should I hesitate to save myself at your expense?"

She was still smiling. Against her pale face the curling red mouth looked like a daub of crayon on white paper, scrawled by an inept hand. "You say your life's over anyway. I don't suppose it matters much whether you spend the rest of it moping in an armchair here at home or in an equally comfortable one at Crestview. You see, Nicky, you are in a curious situation. They can't do a thing to you." She laughed softly. "You're legally insane, and therefore not responsible. Neat, isn't it? You won't even have to stand trial. How fortunate that you like Crestview, because I'm afraid, once they take you back, you're going to be there a good long while."

Nicholas looked at her thoughtfully. Her eyes met his, narrowed to level, sea-green slashes in her white face. "Yes," he said, "it's neat. An escaped maniac . . . a brutal, senseless murder . . . fingerprints on the bloody weapon . . . a perfect setup."

Hero stopped smiling. "I suppose you think you can squirm out of it?"

"No. I won't even try. I know when I'm licked." He bent over to put another log on the fire. When that was done, he sat down in an easy chair, resting his head against the cushioned back, stretching out his legs toward the fender. "Might as well be comfortable," he said, "while we wait for the men to come and get me. Why don't you mix up a drink, Hero?"

She leaned against the mantel. Slowly her eyes widened, like flowers unfolding. "Nicky! I don't believe you care one way or the other!"

"To tell the truth, I don't. Something's happened to me. I feel dead inside."

He yawned. "It'll be nice to get back to Crestview. I'll sit in the sun, and drink orange juice, and talk to the professor about the age of reptiles or the weather conditions on Mars. I'll read all the books I've never had time for. I might even get to be a famous sculptor. There's quite a vogue for the artistic output of the insane."

He watched the yellow flames leap and dance against the velvety black bricks of the chimney. "I was happy there," he said. "I would have been quite contented, only I had unfinished business to attend to. Now that's settled, I don't mind going back."

Hero straightened up. "What do you mean? What's settled?" She took a step toward him. "You've remembered! Is that it? You've got the rest of the formula." She clasped her hands, twisting the fingers together. "What have you done with it?"

Nicholas grinned. "Just a few hours ago I might have told you. That was before I found the trick bottle of ink in your safe, before I knew that you engineered the whole plot."

She took another step forward. "What have you done with it?"

He said, "Did you come into my bedroom that afternoon when I was talking to Stuart? Is that how you found out? I thought I saw something move in there, but I figured it was the wind blowing the curtains."

She untangled her hands, flexing the fingers as if they had become stiff from holding on to something too long, too avidly. "Yes, I was there. I heard you."

She said, "We made a bargain seven years ago, you and I. You wanted a combined housekeeper, mistress, and business partner. In return I was to have all the money I could spend, for the rest of my life. That was easy. You had so much that it cost you nothing. I don't think you got the worst of the deal. I was everything you asked for, and you had my love besides. That was a free gift. I didn't expect any return. I could have done with a little more affection, Nicky, but never mind. That wasn't in the bargain. I kept my part of it, didn't I?" She waited. "Well, didn't I?"

"As long as it suited you," he murmured.

"That's not true. I kept our bargain until you broke it. You intended to throw all the money away, let the business go to smash. You didn't even bother to tell me what you meant to do. I found it out by accident." She lifted her hands and pushed the fair hair away from her temples. "Speaking of stabs in the back," she said.

Nicholas leaned forward in his chair. Hero had found a way to reach him, to whip into uneasy life the part of him he thought was dead. "Is that how it looked to you? Good Lord, how do you suppose I got to be a rich man in the first place? If the oil business had gone under, I'd have built up something else."

"No," she said. "It's going to be different after this war. We'll be a hundred years paying for it. I think large fortunes are a thing of the past. And if I'd let you have your way, I'm sure we would have ended up paupers."

Nicholas said, "If we don't win this war, everyone will end up a pauper, and a slave as well."

Hero shrugged the war aside. "We can win it without ruining ourselves, but that's not the point. I relied on your promise, and you broke it. I think I was perfectly justified in using any means at hand to stop you and keep what was mine." She corrected herself. "Ours, rather. You see, I understood. You were carried away with patriotism. One of the phoniest of emotions, all gingered up by oratory and flag waving and fake atrocity stories. I don't know why people fall for it, but they do. You did. Believe me, Nicky, if you'd stayed at Crestview until after the war was over, you would have thanked me. You'd have been very glad that I saved Seaboard and kept nicoline from being handed over to our competitors."

"On the contrary, I would have felt like killing you." Nicholas yawned again. "However, it's an academic question. I didn't stay there. I got out, and what's more, I got the formula into the proper hands."

Hero drew in her breath, so sharply that he could hear the whistle of it. "You couldn't. You haven't had time." She set her teeth down on her lower lip. Her eyes narrowed again to green slits. "Oh, I see. You gave it to Stuart. . . . But fortunately Seaboard has the rest of the formula, and I'm Seaboard. I'll never give it up."

"Yes, you will, when you get a court order to that effect."

She thought this over. "I suppose you gave him written instructions? Predated to seem legal? My dear man, that won't help. I have excellent lawyers. They'll question your document. They'll appeal and make delays. Before the thing is settled, the war will have been over for ten years."

Nicholas sank back against the cushions. She was right. He knew only too well how the lawyers managed things. "Hero, listen to me." He stopped. She was thoroughly armored by her obsession. How could he reach her? "Hero, I'm taking this murder rap for you. Won't you do something for me in return? Keep the lawyers out of it. Let the government have this synthetic. Think of the lives you'll save, the misery, the destruction. Nicoline might cut the length of this war in half. It might even——"

He stopped again. She was laughing at him. Her laughter was without mirth, clear and cool like running water, uncaring as the voice of a mountain stream.

"What?" she cried. "Give up all that money?" She continued to laugh, yet tears gleamed in her eyes. Through the veil of tears she sent a twisting glance toward the dark figure sprawled on the floor. "There's nothing else left." She jerked her head, trying to shake the tears away. In a low, harsh voice she said, "It's all I've got. I'll never give it up."

An echoing silence put a period to her words. Hero meant exactly what she said. Nicholas was sure of that. Nothing he could do would move her. She was like one possessed. Her face was that of a poet lost in his dream, a martyr walking to the stake with a song on his lips. She had never looked more beautiful to him, or more strange. He wondered if he had ever really known her. *Who is she that looketh forth as the morning, fair as the moon, clear as the sun, and terrible as an army with banners?*

She was fair indeed; there were no muddy shadows in her character. She was an upright woman, a virtuous woman, yet she was terrible in the strength of her ambition.

To his great surprise, he felt a shock of pride in her. It was no mean achievement to have fought Nicholas Matheny and beaten him, for he was beaten. She had done it alone, too. Poor Robin was involved by accident. . . . Charley was no more than a weapon in her hands.

Hero lifted her head. She turned toward the windows that faced the drive. Nicholas heard it too, the sound of a car's motor whining in second gear as it labored up the steep hill.

He looked at the lovely curving line of Hero's white throat. In his mind he saw it lengthen; he saw it twist and coil like a snake, beautiful and deadly, right in the middle of the path he had to take, all that held him back from his goal.

Nicholas stood up. When you started a job you had to finish it, and Hero herself had pointed out the way. He said, "I suppose that's the ambulance coming for me. Hero, we've said a lot of hard things tonight. I didn't mean a quarter of them, and I hope you didn't either. God knows when we'll see each other again. We shouldn't have spent the time quarreling."

He said, "I don't want to go like this, with anger between us. I want to take something with me. I'll admit I haven't been a very good husband, but I think I've loved you more than either of us realized." Strangely enough, that was true. He had never been so close to loving her as he was at this moment. He hated what he had to do, but that couldn't alter his purpose. Nicoline was more important than any one man, any one woman. He said, "Won't you kiss me good-by?"

Her face softened. The color came back into her white cheeks; her eyes lived again. "Oh, Nicky! Oh, my poor darling!" She came to him swiftly, without a tremor of fear.

That was how he wanted it to be. He wouldn't have hurt or frightened her for the world. He held her close in his arms. He kissed her tenderly. His hands, gentle and kind, slipped up over her arms, along her slim shoulders. They went round her throat softly, like the hands of love, like a fond caress.

THE END

# About the Rue Morgue Press

Since 1997, the Rue Morgue Press has reprinted scores of traditional mysteries, the kind of books that were the hallmark of the Golden Age of detective fiction. Authors reprinted or to be reprinted by the Rue Morgue include Catherine Aird, Delano Ames, H. C. Bailey, Morris Bishop, Nicholas Blake, Dorothy Bowers, Pamela Branch, Joanna Cannan, John Dickson Carr, Glyn Carr, Torrey Chanslor, Clyde B. Clason, Joan Coggin, Manning Coles, Lucy Cores, Frances Crane, Norbert Davis, Elizabeth Dean, Carter Dickson, Eilis Dillon, Michael Gilbert, Constance & Gwenyth Little, Marlys Millhiser, Gladys Mitchell, Patricia Moyes, James Norman, Stuart Palmer, Craig Rice, Kelley Roos, Charlotte Murray Russell, Maureen Sarsfield, Margaret Scherf, Juanita Sheridan and Colin Watson..

To suggest titles or to receive a catalog of Rue Morgue Press books write 87 Lone Tree Lane, Lyons, CO 80540, telephone 800-699-6214, or check out our website, www.ruemorguepress.com, which lists complete descriptions of all of our titles, along with lengthy biographies of our writers. The following titles are in print as of Summer 2013, priced at $14.95 each. Include $2.50 shipping for first book, 50 cents for each additional title and mail to

**The Rue Morgue**
**87 Lone Tree Lane**
**Lyons CO 80540**

## Catherine Aird:
**A Late Phoenix**
**A Most Contagious Game**
**Henrietta Who?**
**His Burial Too**
**Parting Breath**
**The Religious Body**
**Slight Mourning**
**Some Die Eloquent**
**The Stately Home Murder**

## Delano Ames:
**Corpse Diplomatique**
**Murder Begins at Home**
**She Shall Have Murder**

## H.C. Bailey:
**Black Land, White Land**
**Shadow on the Wall**

## Morris Bishop:
**The Widening Stain**

## Nicholas Blake:
**A Question of Proof**
**Thou Shell of Death**

## Dorothy Bowers:
**The Bells of Old Bailey**
**Deed Without a Name**
**Fear and Miss Betony**
**Postscript to Poison**
**Shadows Before**

## Pamela Branch:
**Lion in the Cellar**
**Murder Every Monday**
**Murder's Little Sister**
**The Wooden Overcoat**

## Glyn Carr:
**Death Finds a Foothold**
**Death on Milestone Buttress**
**Death Under Snowdon**
**Murder on the Matterhorn**
**The Youth Hostel Murders**

## John Dickson Carr:
**The Case of the Constant Suicides**
**The Crooked Hinge**
**Hag's Nook**

## Torrey Chanslor:
**Our First Murder**
**Our Second Murder**

## Clyde B. Clason:
Blind Drifts
The Death Angel
Dragon's Cave
Green Shiver
Murder Gone Minoan
Poison Jasmine
The Purple Parrot

## Joan Coggin:
Dancing with Death
The Mystery at Orchard House
Penelope Passes, Or: Why Did She Die?
Who Killed the Curate?

## Manning Coles:
Among Those Absent
Brief Candles
Come and Go
Drink to Yesterday
The Far Traveller
The Fifth Man
Green Hazard
Happy Returns
Let the Tiger Die
They Tell No Tales
A Toast to Tomorrow
With Intent to Deceive
Without Lawful Authority

## Lucy Cores:
Corpse de Ballet
Painted for the Kill

## Frances Crane:
The Applegreen Cat
The Amethyst Spectacles
The Cinnamon Murder
The Golden Box
The Indigo Necklace
The Pink Umbrella
The Shocking Pink Hat

The Turquoise Shop
The Yellow Violet

**Norbert Davis:**
Oh, Murderer Mine
Sally's in the Alley

**Elizabeth Dean:**
Murder a Mile High
Murder is a Serious Business

**Carter Dickson:**
The Judas Window
The Peacock Feather Murders

**Eilís Dillon:**
Death at Crane's Court
Death in the Quadrangle
Sent to His Account

**Michael Gilbert:**
Close Quarters
The Danger Within
Smallbone Deceased

**Constance & Gwenyth Little:**
The Black Coat
Black Corridors
The Black Curl
The Black Dream
The Black Eye
The Black Goatee
The Black-Headed Pins
The Black Honeymoon
The Black House
The Black Iris
The Blackout
The Black Paw
The Black Piano
The Black Rustle
The Black Shrouds
The Black Smith

The Black Stocking
The Black Thumb

## John Mersereau:
Murder Loves Company

## Gladys Mitchell:
Come Away, Death
Dead Men's Morris
Death and the Maiden
Death at the Opera
A Hearse on May-Day
Laurels Are Poison
The Longer Bodies
Merlin's Furlong
The Mystery of a Butcher's Shop
Tom Brown's Body
When Last I Died

## Patricia Moyes:
Dead Men Don't Ski

## Stuart Palmer:
Miss Withers Regrets
Murder on the Blackboard
Murder on Wheels
Nipped in the Bud
The Penguin Pool Murder
The Puzzle of the Blue Banderilla
The Puzzle of the Pepper Tree
The Puzzle of the Silver Persian

## Sheila Pim:
A Brush with Death

## Craig Rice:
8 Faces at 3
The Corpse Steps Out
Home Sweet Homicide
The Wrong Murder

## Kelley Roos:
The Frightened Stiff
If the Shroud Fits
Made Up To Kill
Sailor, Take Warning!

## Charlotte Murray Russell:
The Message of the Mute Dog

## Maureen Sarsfield:
Murder at Shots Hall

## Margaret Scherf:
The Diplomat and the Gold Piano
Glass on the Stairs
The Green Plaid Pants
The Gun in Daniel Webster's Bust

## Juanita Sheridan:
The Chinese Chop
The Kahuna Killer
The Mamo Murders
The Waikiki Widow

## Colin Watson:
Bump in the Night
Coffin, Scarcely Used
Hopjoy Was Here